TWENTY HOUSES OF THE ZODIAC

Also edited by Maxim Jakubowski and available from New English Library:

TRAVELLING TOWARDS EPSILON

TWENTY HOUSES OF THE ZODIAC

An Anthology of International Science Fiction

Edited by Maxim Jakubowski

NEW ENGLISH LIBRARY/TIMES MIRROR

This one's for ADAM

A New English Library Original Publication, 1979
First NEL paperback edition July 1979

NEL Books are published by
New English Library Limited from
Barnard's Inn, Holborn,
London EC1N 2JR.
Made and printed in Great Britain by
William Collins Sons & Co Ltd, Glasgow

45004333 9

ACKNOWLEDGMENTS

"Oh, for a closer brush with God" by Brian W. Aldiss. Copyright 1979 by Brian W. Aldiss. By permission of the author and his agent, A. P. Watt Ltd.

"A kind of space" by Ion Hobana. Copyright 1974 by Ion Hobana. First published in *Viata Româneasca*. By permission of the author.

"Dealers in light and darkness" by Cherry Wilder. Copyright 1979 by Cherry Wilder. By permission of the author and her agent, Virginia Kidd.

"A hole in time" by Gerd Maximovic. Copyright 1979 by Gerd Maximovic. By permission of the author.

"High tide" by Elisabeth Vonarburg. Copyright 1978 by Elisabeth Vonarburg. First published in *Requiem*. By permission of the author.

"I can teleport myself to anywhere" by Robert Sheckley. Copyright 1979 by Robert Sheckley. By permission of the author and his agent, A. D. Peters & Co.

"Heavier than sleep" by Philippe Curval. Copyright 1979 by Philippe Curval. By permission of the author.

"An avocado pear for Dolorès" by Adam Barnett-Foster. Copyright 1979 by Adam Barnett-Foster. By permission of the author and his agent, Michael Bakewell and Associates.

"The gigantic fluctuation" by Arkady and Boris Strugatsky. Copyright 1973 by Arkady and Boris Strugatsky. First published in *Stazhery*. By permission of VAAP and Macmillan Publishing Co. Inc.

CONTENTS

Introduction

The field of science fiction is possibly the only area of publishing today where anthologies still flourish.

Unless they are specifically thematic (and there's a finite amount of basic themes science fiction encompasses), it is very easy for anthologies to lack genuine unity or cohesiveness if the editor's personality or idiosyncratic tastes do not impinge forcefully on the selection of the material or the authors he is commissioning. Writers with often diverging interests, techniques and ambitions meet uncomfortably within the pages of the anthologies where inner-space stories healthily rub shoulders with roaring space yarns while obsessed time-travellers paradoxically meet up with ghosts from the segregated lands of fantasy and other unusual incongruities occur.

But the anthologies keep on coming.

Because they are all things to all people and, in a sense, typify the very diversity which has become the essence of science fiction writing these days.

TWENTY HOUSES OF THE ZODIAC is a unique compendium of the craft of science fiction as practised in fifteen different countries, a demonstration of how international the field has become; some countries or even continents are not represented within the pages that follow, not for lack of quality material available, but merely due to sheer reasons of length. Apologies to all the overlooked who are hereby entitled to compile a counter anthology highlighting their SF talents and putting their countries on the map!

A natural consequence of this literary expedition into the science fiction of so many lands is that the panorama of alien vistas on view in this book is as varied as can be, demonstrating that if national borders are no obstacle for SF, they do however tend to stretch its definitions and territorial imperatives somewhat. Which is, I think, as should be expected: the major themes remain similar in most countries, but it's the way of treating them, the sensitivity of the approach, often at odds with the imagined national characteristics of the countries involved, which vary unpredictably.

The first and simultaneous publication of this anthology in several countries will coincide with *Seacon 79*, the 37th annual world science-fiction convention, which takes place in Brighton, England, in August 1979. This important event in the calendar of the SF world will also be one of its most international manifestations with participants (writers, readers, publishers, artists) from all over the world. I hope this book will be a small added reason for celebration for the SF community in emphasising the growing worldwide acceptance of the genre.

Do people really want to read anthology introductions? I'm not sure, so like the classic after-dinner guest-speaker I shall try and make this short and sweet.

Some writers on the menu are well known. Others are not.

BRIAN ALDISS, Guest of Honour at *Seacon 79*, needs, of course, no real introduction. His particularly "English" story of domestic life with a difference will, I am confident, surprise and delight.

The author of a clever variation on Wells' "The Time Machine", Romania's ION HOBANA is the Secretary of his country's writers' union and a veteran SF writer and specialist of UFOs and Jules Verne.

Worthy of the international tag of this anthology is Australian CHERRY WILDER who now resides in Germany and offers us an exotic other-world legend in the grand old tradition of C. L. Moore, Leigh Brackett and "The Thief of Baghdad".

GERD MAXIMOVIC's story, "A hole in time", mirrors some of the current political problems of West Germany with a fresh look at a classic theme of displacement.

ELISABETH VONARBURG, from Quebec, is a translator, folk-singer, writer and University lecturer from Chicoutimi.

Globe-trotter extraordinaire ROBERT SHECKLEY hails from the US of A but now lives in London with his wife, Abby, and their two small children, although he still enjoys migrating south to the Mallorcan sun for the winter.

Journalist PHILIPPE CURVAL, also an editor of the new magazine *Futurs*, is one of the leading SF writers in France. His novels and stories are about to become available in other countries, and not before time.

From the little-known island of San Serriffe, recently featured extensively in a series of articles in the London and Manchester *Guardian*, comes ADAM BARNETT-FOSTER, a pillar of the thriving local SF community, with a wry tale of musicians at large in a delightfully improbable future universe.

The STRUGATSKY brothers' fame has now reached well beyond their native USSR and their presence in this international gathering of SF writers was a necessity, as was Poland's prolific but controversial STANISLAW LEM.

A typical enigmatic inner-space story from that master (and inventor) of the form, J. G. BALLARD, sheds an oblique light on the modernisation of classic mythologies in his usual inimitable style.

Both Dutch writer HUGO RAES and Japanese SHIN' ICHI HOSHI are well known in their countries beyond the domain of SF, although their work in the genre is still frequent. Their stories are both short, respectively cryptic and tender, but quite 'different'.

BOB SHAW, Toastmaster at *Seacon 79* is also, at his best, one of the most humorous men in SF, although his writing is more often in a serious vein. "The cottage of eternity", his contribution to the anthology, is an hilarious exception.

Often described as the French Harlan Ellison, DANIEL WALTHER usually arouses reactions of admiration and hate amongst his readers. His lyrical, elliptical, intense story, inspired by the late Anna Kavan, should foster the controversy.

A far from unknown native son of Iowa, USA, JOHN SLADEK does his bit for our international angle by sporting a Czech name and now living in Hampstead, London!

TERESA INGLÉS' story was awarded the *Nueva Dimension* prize when it first appeared in Spain. A feminist journalist and ex-ballet dancer, Teresa Inglés lives in Barcelona.

"Hope you take advantage of editorial prerogative and include one of your stories in the anthology. No point in being an editor without having a little *fun* . . ." kindly writes Cherry Wilder. I suppose my pedigree is international: MAXIM JAKUBOWSKI, born in England of Russian/Polish extraction, educated in France, lived some time in Italy, married a Russian girl, spends six months a year travelling the world!

SAM LUNDWALL, from Sweden, in fact wrote his contribution in English, a sad but evocative fable that will stay in your mind. An active writer, publisher and editor, he is also Secretary of *World SF*, an organisation set up in 1978 at the Dublin SF Writers' Conference.

Closing the book is MICHAEL MOORCOCK, another author who requires no introduction and provides us with a fascinating alternate-world story which I admiringly rate as his best short story ever . . .

I must, finally, extend my gratitude to all the writers, agents and publishers who were instrumental in helping me put this book together at rather short notice. An individual vote of thanks goes to Monika Douglas, Penny Grant, Colin Lester, Peter Nicholls, Takumi Shibano, Daniel Walther and the Foundation for the Promotion of the Translation of Dutch Literary Works, who all helped this anthology along by providing information, locating translators and advising on stories in foreign languages.

MAXIM JAKUBOWSKI
London, October 1978

Oh, for a closer brush with God

BRIAN W. ALDISS

The house was modest. It was set in a side street, but the sound of traffic from the nearby main road into the metropolis could be heard as a steady roar in most of the rooms.

On these grey late autumn days, when mists carried the tang of pollutants into the ambushes of michaelmas daisies by the front door, the traffic started before the morning was light.

What roused Bill Carter was not the noise of the traffic, which he sometimes pretended he enjoyed, on the grounds that it reminded him of a distant ocean, but the buss of his daughter Judy's cassette-recorder, serving up the top twenty in thin tin slices. Sighing, he climbed out of bed, washed and shaved, and went downstairs to feed the dog and let it out for a run.

As he completed these chores, he heard his wife in the bathroom, also rising. He switched the kettle on and went into the dining-room to have a look at God.

God's tank was the standard size, just under two metres square on its base, and 1·4 metres high. Its top was open to the air. It contained nothing but air and God.

"Not much of a day," Carter said, indicating the smudgy twilight in the back garden beyond the window.

God was used to criticism and said nothing. He curled a flipper and made another circuit of the tank.

"I don't think Judy's 'flu is any better this morning," Carter said accusingly. "I can hear her sneezing in her room. Can't You do something about that? You know her exams are coming up."

"I have Judy's interests in mind," God said.

Carter sniffed. He edged nearer the tank. "You know I don't complain, O Lord, but I get worn down, worn down just by the days passing. Please let today be something special. Let something nice happen."

God's single eye was rather like a peony. Its petals opened; among the dense stamens and the kohl, something glittered, regarding the recesses of Carter's psyche. "All is well, Carter. Time does not really pass, you know. You live with me in an Eternal day."

Carter pressed a palm against the plate glass. It was warm from God's presence. "Christ, You always fob me off with words, Lord. This is Wednesday, don't kid me otherwise, and I've got another session with Batacharya coming up this evening. *Do* something for me, You bastard, I humbly beseech Thee."

"I'm only here as a witness to My presence in the universe. I really prefer not to work little local miracles, having found from experience that they're counter-productive."

"But You're omnipotent, *omnipotent*! You made the damned galaxies!" He was staring down at God now, fists clenched. "Don't give me that counter-productive nonsense."

"You will have to accept that even omnipotence has its limits."

"Oh, come on, will You, God? Look, You know the bloody mess my life is in. *You* got me into it. Help me, will You? I ask You every day – "

"And every day I do help you, Bill, in many ways . . ."

"You mealy-mouthed – You're as bad as Your parsons – You – " In sudden rage, Carter heaved himself into the big glass tank. God writhed away to the far side, but Carter grasped one of his trailing flippers and got in a swift kick at one of the three segments of his body. God let out a curious high-pitched cry. Throwing himself forward, Carter locked both hands round the smooth neck-like stalk connecting first and second segments. He found himself immediately twirled upside down, and his head banged against the glass, but he clung on grimly, tightening his grip.

When God manifested Himself to a troubled world in the closing years of the twentieth century, he chose to appear universally in a non-anthropomorphic form. Those people who were against racism applauded this substantial trans-substantiation; those people who were for it thought God was being silly – whilst acknowledging, of course, that He had His own logic.

"That hurts," God said, wincing.

"Serve you right." Carter managed to get the neck-thing gripped between his knees. He had God pinned down on one side of the tank, in a fairly undignified position. He grabbed one of the flipper-like appendages. It felt rubbery, soft inside, and rather disappointing, like Truth. He began to twist. God whimpered.

"You know I can't stand pain."

"You're as bad as Your Son. Almighty, my foot!"

"How else could We comprehend mankind's problems if We felt no pain? Have some sense, Carter. Owwwww . . ."

"I want a miracle out of You, then I'll let go. Quick."

"Have a bit of reverence. Ohhhhh . . . What do you want Me to do?"

"You can do anything, *anything*, and You ask me what I want? How about a bigger house, on a hill somewhere, beautiful views, with a stream – a trout stream, and a pretty wife. With a lake and power-boat on it. Two wives. Sisters, who get on well together. Good dress sense. Josie and Jean. No, Josie and Rebecca. Able to tell me jokes. And a good job. No, no work, just the estate to look after. I want to be a crack shot, really crack. A private armoury. Wild elephants in the grounds, really dangerous. Servants. Drink. Fame. Swimming pools – You know what I want. Make them materialise and I'll let You go."

"Yes, I do know what you want, Carter, and believe Me I sympathise, deeply. Owwwww, steady on . . . But you see all those things, those gross material things, would really be only a substitute for a state of spiritual – Owwwww, mercy!"

Carter never really expected that he could bully God into anything useful. Relaxing his hold, he said sulkily. "Well, see that Judy gets well enough for school again tomorrow, will you?"

"I'll try, but there are many factors to be considered of which you know not."

Giving a fin a sharp twist, Carter said, "You expect me to live in Faith. I can't. I've had enough. You always fob me off with promises. You're as bad as Batacharya, in Your way. Come on, one small miracle, right now, or I'm not leaving this tank."

"Don't be crass. You've got to go and see your old mother and you've got to go to work."

"One small miracle, come on, or I'm keeping You pinned down here all day, O Lord. How about a palm tree in the back garden?"

"The neighbours would complain. Ohhhhh, Jesus, Carter, you have a nasty streak in you . . ."

"Who put it there? Come on, a palm tree or I'll tear this flipper-thing right off."

Over the garden, emerging slowly from the soggy embrace of night, a flash of lightning played. By Laura's rockery, just beyond the tool-shed, a palm tree grew, its great straggling topknot of leaves blotting out sight of the chimney tops of the houses opposite.

Forgetting all about God, Carter rose and climbed out of the tank. He stood gaping through the window in astonishment. After a moment, he thought to hurry out of the back door and walk along the path under the palm.

Slight disappointment infiltrated his astonishment. He had anticipated a date palm, with huge heavy leaves like sabres. This was a coconut palm. The coconuts nestled about the untidy crown, green, bland, bigger than Carter's head. The enormous leaves of the palm, some of which hung down, some of which pointed out or upwards, resembled the rib-cages of fragile marine creatures. Carter rested his hand on the scarred trunk and stared upwards into the foliage, his mouth slightly open. He was still in that position when Laura called him in for breakfast.

Since he did not have to drive Judy to school this morning, Carter had twenty-five minutes to spare before he got to work. Kissing Laura goodbye, he drove to see his old mother, who was not settling happily into an old folks' home.

Standing in the foyer, he drew his gaunt frame to its full height, acclimatising to the smell of age and disinfectant.

"Good morning, Mr. Carter," said one of the nurses in the corridor. They were very polite and remembered his name, although his mother had been with them for only a few days.

Mrs. Carter was propped up in bed, hands resting on a magazine she was not reading. She was eighty-one, her skin blotched by liver-marks as if by a poisonous fungus. Her curtains had been drawn back; the tawdry daylight revealed rusty domestic oil storage tanks with pergolas beyond. God drifted in his glass tank in one corner of the room, behind the commode.

The old woman explained to Carter what a rotten night she had had, going into some detail and looking pointedly at God as she did so. She complained that the widow with whom she shared the room, Mrs. Walker, was very noisy during the night.

"He won't do anything to shut her up, however much I pray. I wish she was dead, I do really."

"Never mind, mother," Carter said. "At least I've got your vases safe and sound."

The vases had caused some distress. In her reluctance to leave her home, Mrs. Carter had left some possessions behind, although Rosemary, her daughter, Carter's sister, had come down from York to help her pack her things. Two old vases remained locked in a corner cupboard in the dining-room to which the key had been lost. Now there were lodgers occupying the house, and Mrs. Carter worried that they would get their hands on her property. She feared the lodgers because they were young and had long hair.

"I took some tools up last night after I left work," Carter said. "The lodgers were very friendly, and I had the hinges off the cupboard in no time. So the vases are safe."

"You've got the vases?" Mrs. Carter asked, pressing her mouth out of shape.

"They're under our stairs in a cardboard box."

Mrs. Carter's hands began to play with the bedclothes and to roll the sheet into a long sausage. Her eyes, and the dried skin round her eyes, became red. She darted unhappy glances at God, who did not move.

"What have you done with my vases?" she asked.

"They're safe under our stairs, in a cardboard box," Carter repeated.

Mrs. Carter looked hard at the faded wallpaper on the wall and clearly disliked what she saw there. With her gaze turned from her son, she said, "As if I haven't had enough traumas in my life without family unpleasantness. This really is too much. Have I got to remind you that those vases belong to your sister, not to you?"

Carter looked concerned. "Rosemary can have them the next time she comes to see you, mother. I don't want them. Laura and I don't want them. But Rosemary doesn't come to see you very often – she's so busy with her course in York."

"She comes whenever she can. You know how hard she has to work. It's a tragedy. In any case, all my personal possessions I've left to her in my will. You know that."

A yawn rose in Carter's throat and he could not stifle it. "Sorry, we had a bad night with Judy. She has the 'flu. We thought she was sickening for something yesterday morning."

"You're always yawning. Are you still seeing that psycho-analyst?"

"I've told you, mother, he's not a psycho-analyst, only a counsellor. It's a voluntary body, like the Samaritans. In any case, I didn't know you had left all your personal possessions to Rosemary; she didn't say anything about it when I told her on the phone I was going to rescue the vases. What she said was that they were worthless."

"A mother always leaves all her property to her daughter."

He looked at his watch. "I'm not arguing about that, mother, and I don't want the vases myself. Really, I don't – ask God. I'll bring them round here and you can keep them in your wardrobe if you're worried."

The old woman pouted. "Oh, I've offended you now. You always were sensitive, you were. Why I have to put up with this unpleasantness I don't know."

The door opened and old Mrs. Walker hobbled in; she pushed a wheeled contraption in front of her to stop her falling on her face. The contraption bumped against Mrs. Carter's bed. Mrs. Walker had paid a visit to the lavatory and was still muttering about the difficulty of pulling the chain. She took no notice of Carter, brushing against him as she made for her bed. Her God was in his tank on the other side of her bed; He did not move.

"She's stone deaf," said Mrs. Carter. "You should have heard her at two this morning. Disgraceful. Poor thing. No consideration. I'm trying to get them to move her out. God, *God*, why You don't help me I don't know! Nobody cares for a poor old woman any more."

"I care," God said. "That's why I'm here, suffering with

you. Be patient, my dear. All's well."

Carter had risen. He looked at his watch again. "I'd better be getting to work, mother. I'm not trying to pinch your vases, and I'll be getting them off my property soonest. I'll bring them round here next time I come to visit."

"You never stay long, do you?"

"You've got God to communicate with, bear that in mind."

"Oh, He's no company," she said dismissively.

"At least He loves us all."

"All this unpleasantness is getting too much for me," Mrs. Carter said, blinking rapidly.

He grinned at her, at God, and at Mrs. Walker, and nodded his way out of the room, allotting his mother a final big grin before disappearing. She waved back forlornly, her old face set in parodies of past disapproval.

After the usual traffic and parking problems, it was a relief to get in to work. The office building was well heated against the chill outside, and filled at this hour with noise and bustle, and an occasional snatch of song.

"How's the wife, Frank?" Carter called to one of his friends, as he hurried down the corridor.

Frank Heynes lowered his voice before replying. "They removed about a metre of her intestines at five-fifteen yesterday afternoon. She was still pretty groggy from the op when I visited her in the evening. Still, we mustn't let these things get us down. How about a glass of wine over lunch?"

"I must finish the bloody Zadar-World account, which means using Joe's NOVA 3 in the lunch-hour. I've got it booked. The processor was out of action all last week."

"Bit of a grey area, eh? See you in 'The Grapes' then, about eight, after hospital visiting hours?"

It was Carter's evening to visit Mr. Batacharya. That side of his life was a secret he kept from the office. Hesitating only momentarily, he said, "Make it half-past, and I'll be there."

"See you. *Ciao.*"

"*Ciao.*"

When he had installed himself before the computer in Joe's office at noon, Carter rang home to ask Laura how Judy was. He listened to his own phone ringing. The woman who answered was female but unfamiliar. He stared at her face, disconcerted.

"Laura? Is Laura there? Who are you?"

"Who are you, I'd like to know?" She stared at him poker-faced through the screen.

"I'm Carter, Bill Carter. Where's my wife? Who are you?"

It was a Mrs. Summerfield from some doors away. He could hear the living-room radio playing in the background as he stared at her image. She had come in to look after Judy while Laura was out shopping for an hour or two. Judy was lying in bed, reading. No, she didn't want anything to eat; she was playing her cassette-recorder and reading.

Carter thanked Mrs. Summerfield and put the phone down. He stood thinking for a moment, then he turned to the computer terminal.

"A bit of a grey area," he said to himself, using Frank's phrase, and smiling uneasily to himself. Then he got on with the work. It had to be done.

For once, the after-work traffic jams were not so bad that evening. He was stuck as usual in Church Street, but kept the car radio on, tuned to the local station. People were talking about the trouble they had with the servicing of microwave ovens. When the chance came, he swung across the traffic and drove up Mortgage Lane, where the jams were much lighter. He was home ust after half-past five.

He called out as he entered the hall. Sticking his head round the living-room door, he found Judy sitting over the electric fire in her dressing-gown, watching the television. Brightly coloured animals were tearing a policeman apart.

"Hello, my girl!"

She did not answer or look round, which was not unusual. Carter hesitated, then went into the room and put his arm round her thin shoulders. "How's my big girl?"

"All right, thanks." She kept her eye on the animals.

"How's the head?"

"All right."

"That's a speedy recovery."

She just went on staring at the television. The animals climbed up a tall radio mast and beamed themselves into police headquarters.

As Carter stood in the hall removing his coat, Laura came downstairs, smiling. She put her arms round him. He kissed her cheek.

"I thought I heard you," she said. "Sorry, I was upstairs, rooting in the airing cupboard. The tank is still leaking – we must do something about it."

"That's a nuisance. I'll have a look at it."

"Have some tea first. Come in the kitchen and talk to me."

Laura was in her mid-fifties and putting on weight. She wore her thick dyed hair coiled neatly at the back of her head. This afternoon she had on a sweater and shock-pink slacks. Carter tried to recall if she had been wearing them at breakfast.

They perched on stools at the bar facing one another as the kettle boiled. Laura lit a cigarette. Her God's tank was wedged in the space between oven and fridge.

"On the way home, they were playing Eydie Gormé's old number 'Blame It On The Bossa Nova'," he said. He hummed a few bars. "Do you remember that one, darling? Remember they played it the day we went to Leamington with the Hills, just before we were married?"

She exhibited signs of liveliness. "I associate it with 'Eso Beso'. It was about the same year, wasn't it? Who used to sing 'Eso Beso'?"

"I've forgotten – it's so long ago."

"Paul Anka," God said.

"Those sixties' songs had so much more zip than the stuff they pour out now. Somehow or other, the nineties are a bit of a flop, aren't they?"

"They haven't got much longer to run. Perhaps next century will be better." She spoke without much conviction, heaving herself off the stool to make the tea. "That's up to You, isn't it, O Lord Almighty?"

God said, patiently, "No, it's up to you and your husband and everyone else, my dear. I can only work through you, as you strive for a better world."

"That palm tree of Yours – it's wiped out my nice clumps of autumn crocus."

Carter yawned. "I wonder what happened to Eydie Gormé."

"I wonder what happened to the Hills."

As she was emptying chocolate biscuits from a packet, Carter said, "I phoned at midday, but you were out. I wanted to see how Judy was."

"Irene said."

"Who's Irene, for Christ's sake?"

"Mrs. Summerfield."

He decided not to approach closer to the danger area, and stifled another yawn with his hand. God was swimming idly about in the tank full of air, not looking at anything.

His wife eyed him through the smoke of her cigarette. "You do yawn an awful lot, Bill. Are you ill or something?"

"No, I'm fine. I'd better ring my dear sister Rosemary about those vases."

"You got a good night's sleep, didn't you?"

"I'm fine, really. I was just yawning."

"You ought to run round the park. Better than going to that man every Wednesday evening."

"I suppose so. Shall I go and have a look at the hot tank?"

As she stubbed her cigarette out, she said, looking at the ashtray, "I may take up French."

"What?"

"I said, I may take up French. If we are going to Paris for our holidays it would be useful. There's a refresher course advertised at the Poly. French Conversation. Wednesday evenings. Don't you think it's a good idea?"

He was unprepared. "We got on well enough last time we were there."

She came over and rested her head on his shoulder. "Darling, I wish you'd be enthusiastic about something."

"Oh, I think it's quite a good idea, really. Perhaps we could both take the course. I wouldn't mind learning to speak French."

"Mmm."

He went upstairs to look at the hot-water tank, smothering a yawn. Upon inspection, it did seem as if there might be a leak where a copper pipe was welded to the tank. He prayed to God to mend it for him but there was no response. He pottered between airing cupboard and tool-rack in the garage for a convincing length of time, eventually slapping a length of insulating tape round the joint. When he went downstairs to phone his sister, he felt obliged to explain to Laura about the trouble with the vases.

"That really is mean of your mother," Laura said. "She doesn't care for your feelings one bit. Besides, that box is only cluttering up our cupboard."

"It isn't as though we wanted the bloody vases. It's just the principle of the thing."

He stood in the hall and dialled York. As soon as his sister's face appeared on the screen, her voice started to crackle smartly at him.

"I hear you've been upsetting mother, Bill. I rang her just now and out it all came. You know she's nearly eighty-two and hasn't got long to go; God told me so Himself. Can't you be a bit more tactful?"

"Well, I suppose tact isn't exactly my strong point, Rosey, but she accused me of unpleasantness, and that certainly wasn't of my wishing. You see, I was only trying to help, and – "

"You're always only trying to help. It's your way of poking your nose in, isn't it?"

"Why don't *you* poke *your* nose in more often? Couldn't you get down to see her one weekend? You know it's you she loves, she'd love to see you for a few hours. I'm always going round there."

"I'm busy, aren't I? God knows, I just about run this bloody course single-handed. I said to the Principal this morning – "

"I know you're busy, Rosemary, we always hear how busy you are, but after all, I've got the family to look after, and – "

"It's no good sneering at me because I didn't marry, if that's what you're trying to do. I know what you think, right enough." He leaned against the coats, listening, staring at the hard lines of her face as she entered on a monologue of complaint. On the whole, he preferred palm trees to clumps of autumn crocus.

"Rosey, love, don't go on. I suppose you're upset about the vases, but honestly I don't want them, they're not worth quarrelling about, I'm only housing them here for mother. I'll be glad not to have them cluttering up the place. Tomorrow, I'll take them round to the home and give them to her."

The lines did not so much relent as change gear.

"Yes, look, I don't want to have to argue with you – I mean, it's demeaning to have to argue with one's brother – but mother left all her private possessions to me. Okay? You understand?"

"Yes. Yes, great. Well, as I say, I'll take them round there tomorrow. I'm sorry there's all this unpleasantness. I certainly don't want anything more to do with the vases.

Goodbye." His sister's face vanished as he switched off.

Laura had come into the hall to hear the argument. "You're so patient with her, Bill. Why didn't your mother leave you something in her will? Why don't you let go for once and say what you really feel? I would, for God's sake."

As she gave him a kiss on the cheek, he said, "Stupid fuss about nothing. As for those awful vases . . ."

"You've done everything you could for her. It's not your fault."

"Blame it on the bossa nova."

She gave him a cigarette.

"It's almost time for your session with your man. Have a sherry before you go."

Carter grabbed her round the waist. "I love you, Laura. You're so sexy."

"Not right now, you ape. I've got to get Judy some supper. Judy, fish fingers, okay?"

He was early at the clinic. He smoked in the car before climbing the dirty steps, then realised that he was arriving dead on six-thirty. The habit of punctuality was hard to shake, although Batacharya had once uttered a deadly insult and called him "anally-oriented".

As usual, Batacharya wore his peppery tweed trousers with matching waistcoat, a jacket that had once been cream, and an old-fashioned tie. He had a moustache and was bald. He kept God behind a fabric screen. He smoked and sucked a pipe throughout every session. His dark skin revealed a yellowish tinge. He panted and was too plump. As usual, Carter was glad to see him and yet hated the dependence that the man had built up in him.

"How have you been, Bill?"

"Teddy, I believe that my wife is continuing her affair with that bastard Gutteridge." It always took an effort to address the Indian as Teddy but, once that obstacle was past, words flowed as if from a broken dam.

Batacharya clutched the bowl of his pipe and listened with round brown eyes. He was a listener of the first order.

Carter poured out the details of the supposed shopping expedition and the proposed French lessons, and finally ran out of steam. Silence fell. The counsellor was staring at the floor as if puzzled by the entire concept of flooring. The clock on the wall ticked away the minutes. God scuffled like a gerbil behind His screen.

Carter felt bored and yawned. Not too long now before he was sinking a beer with Frank in "The Grapes". To break the deadlock, he said, laughing, "If I say I'm imagining Laura's guilt, you will say that I said it and you didn't."

"So do you instead invent this round-about way of telling me you imagined it all?"

"I don't know whether I'm imagining it or not. That's one of the things I expected you to tell me. What's imagination, what's reality. God's presence hasn't made the distinction between them easier to grasp."

"Both are aspects of my Eternal Being," God said from behind the screen. The men ignored Him.

"But it is a bit suspicious that Laura has refused to come and see you again. She regards all our problems as my problem." Carter paused, then laughed. "I'll tell you one thing, Teddy, I hate my imagination and reality about equally."

More silence. Batacharya puffed at his pipe and said, "Why do you think you laugh when what you say is not funny?"

"Oh, Christ, I don't know what I'm doing half the time. I beat up God this morning until He produced a palm tree – I suppose that's on my conscience."

"One measly palm tree," said Batacharya derisively.

"It was a *Cocos nucifera*," God said. "Twenty-two leaves. Intended to remind Carter of how much trees dump thousands of tons of fruit daily into the ungrateful laps of mankind."

"You're always preaching, O Lord," said Batacharya. "Take it from me, it's counter-productive."

"Laura *seems* perfectly nice and friendly to me again, after trying to sodding well castrate me for two years, but I suspect that may just be pretence. How can I know for sure?"

"Maybe you can't know. You must learn to trust."

"That's my line," God protested.

"That's nonsense, Teddy, honestly." Carter laughed again, checking himself quickly. "I mean, it only sounds like sense in this lousy faded room, where so many miserable secrets have been spilled. Outside, in the real world, people know for sure whether their wives love them or not."

"And in that real world, does Laura know if her Bill loves her?"

". . . I tell her often enough. Don't I, God?"

"Love lives in deeds as well as words. When I created the world, that was a deed of love, and you are all the children of it. You would save yourselves endless sorrow if you could remember that cardinal fact."

Batacharya replied with a measured sorrow almost rivalling God's. "Bill's trouble is that You created Gutteridge as well as Laura and himself."

More silence came between them, until Carter broke it with a laugh.

"I don't know what's real any more, what's true, what's false. If I'm Your creation, O Lord, why don't You help?"

"I help more than you know. You can't imagine what would befall, were I to desert you."

"Carter won't find *that* remark very reassuring."

At half-time, Batacharya made them tea in the ante-room, and Carter sucked on a cigarette.

As eight o'clock drew near, Carter said, "Look, Teddy, I do feel desperate at times. I know there's not much wrong with me. Despite the Lord's constant presence, I just feel isolated, not being able to understand Laura any more. Nobody expects to understand God – perhaps His motives in creating the universe were suspect too. Please simply give me a bit of sensible advice, man to man. Should I give up coming to you and shut up and get on with life, even if it has lost its savour? (Sorry, God, but it has . . .)"

Batacharya smiled and straightened his waistcoat. "You know I genuinely enjoy your visits, Bill. Let me just say this to you. Life is a series of changes. When you were first married, well, everything was very rosy, but that period has now been followed by a period that succeeds quite naturally when you grow older, when life is less pleasant for you. Don't be too possessive with everything, with people or with days. Try to enjoy more those things that can still appeal. Take a tip from God – He's content with nothing."

Carter shook his head. "I ought to feel sorry for you too, Teddy. All you've got is patience and a pack of old platitudes, isn't it?"

The Indian smiled sadly and spread his hands. "Maybe you expect too much from everyone, even from God. I mean, my gosh, that palm tree – pretty childish . . ."

As he put on his raincoat and went to the door, Carter said, in a flash of anger, "Why the hell do you think I laughed when it wasn't funny? I was trying to protect you from my pain. Couldn't you work that out for yourself, with a degree in psychiatry?"

"It is better that you understand for yourself. You know that." He placed a paternal hand on Carter's shoulder, and lowered his voice. "Don't be so preoccupied with love all the time, you understand. I know God goes on about it, but better to ignore Him. Frankly, I think this Second Coming business was a retrograde step on God's part. There are other valuable qualities which His presence has rather put in the shade."

"Such as what?" Carter asked eagerly.

"Rationality, for one. It's more durable than love. Settle for rationality and you will be content." He squeezed Carter's lean hand in his two plump brown ones. "Come and see me again next week."

In his car, Carter had a good stretch and a yawn. He laughed aloud to himself. Then he drove to "The Grapes".

"Prompt as usual, Bill," said Frank Heynes, grinning and ordering another pint from the barmaid. Both men drank deep and stood for a moment in friendly silence, contemplating the benefits of beer.

"We had a funny bloke in today from the Paris office," Frank said. "He was working with a Chinese firm in Singapore for a couple of years."

"I always wanted to get to Singapore."

"He was telling me about a Chinese detective he met, operating in Malaysia. This detective was called in by a local farmer, who thought that his neighbour was stealing his pigs by night. A pig would vanish one night, then another a few nights later, despite all the traps he set. So he hired the detective to spend the night in with the pigs, in the sty. Next morning, another pig had gone. Three nights later, another pig disappeared. So the farmer accused the detective of sleeping on the job."

Heynes took a deep swig from his glass.

"What happened?" Carter asked.

"The detective got the farmer to spend the night in the sty with him. They kept watch for two nights and, on the hird, they heard a scuffle. They switched the torch on and found a socking great twelve-foot python swallowing a piglet. Next morning they came back with crowbars and discovered a whole nest of pythons under the boards of the sty. The snakes were living there quite comfortably, feeding off the occasional leg of pork."

"Bit of a grey area down there," Carter said, and both men laughed. "I suppose they killed the pythons."

"No, that's the nice bit. The Chinese never miss a trick. In that part of the world, snake is regarded as a delicacy. It fetches more per kilo than pork. So they simply left the snakes where they were, eating an occasional piglet, and killed 'em off one by one when they reached full size, for considerable profit. Neat, eh."

"Rational, certainly," said Carter, nodding.

Over their second pint, Carter remembered to ask about Frank's wife.

"She was in amazingly good form, this evening, praise be to God. I took her a pineapple. The surgeon reckons she can come home at the end of the week."

"That's good news, Frank. Perhaps you and she'll come round for a meal with Laura and me, when she's really better."

"Yes, we'd love to."

Carter was silent. He remembered that he had issued such a general invitation before, and had never followed it up. Equally, Frank had never asked him home. He began to feel uncomfortable, despite the encouragement of the beer. He ordered two double whiskies.

"Frank, would you think I was rude if I went home after this round?"

"Course not. Anything wrong at home?"

"No. No, my daughter's a bit seedy. She should be back at school tomorrow."

They downed a third pint before Carter drove home. He sat in the garage listening to the local station on the car radio for some while; people were discussing the inadequacies of the educational system. At last he switched off and went through the side door into the house.

Laura was working at the table in the living-room, making a garment for Judy. The television was mouthing away to itself. She gave her husband a searching look.

"You're home early. Judy's only just gone to bed. What's

the matter? Not soused tonight, then?"

"Laura, I think that if you and everyone really knew me, you'd find that I was a very nice person underneath. You ask God."

"You have been hitting the bottle! Is that the effect that that man has on you?"

"I mean if you really knew me, if you bothered to know me . . ."

He turned away. He wandered into the hall, yawning. Opening the stair cupboard door, he reached in and pulled a cardboard box out from its recesses. The vases were unbroken.

After a moment's hesitation, Carter went into the dining-room to see God. Closing the door and leaning against it, he looked over at the Being who moved languidly in His tank.

"Well, Wednesday's almost over, and it didn't have much to offer. I'm sorry I hurt You this morning, by the way; that was a really disgusting performance."

"I'm touched by your penitence, but you should learn to control yourself."

"What about Judy? Is she going to be fit enough to go to school tomorrow?"

"I'm the Creator, Carter, not your family doctor."

He mooched over to the window and peered out, hands in pockets. The room lights, streaming into the garden, were enough to show him that the coconut palm had vanished; the patches of autumn crocus appeared undisturbed.

He looked down at God. "Surely You must be fed up in there, doing next to nothing, not getting through to humanity, just performing a minor conjuring trick now and again. Why don't You try a really major miracle for once? It might improve Your morale as well as everyone else's."

God opened that single, singular, floral eye at him, penetrating him with a cosmic glance heavy with fertility and transcendental pollens, "What do you suggest?"

"You see, You've no imagination." Carter shook his head. "I wish I had Your job!"

Lightning flashed. Next moment, he found himself dispersed among a myriad tanks, staring out at the whole of humanity. In the background, joy, trumpets, and the thrilling tintinnabulations of galaxies.

Countless representatives of humanity stared back at him, aware that something inexplicable had happened. For once, everyone's attention was centred on God.

Carter spake. "All is well," he said, "and all is eternally well."

What else could he have told them?

A kind of space

ION HOBANA

I usually read with the radio on. I don't really hear the music, or rather I'm not listening. What I need is some wall of sound to shield me from the sounds of the street, from my daily problems and my obsessions.

This was how I was reading "The Time Machine". I was reaching the end, where the Time Traveller, prior to leaving Richmond, admits to not having travelled to the future, that it was all his imagination. All of a sudden the commentator's voice, which had followed a musical interlude, faded and was soon no more than a whisper. Wanting to turn the knob and hear better, I got up from my armchair. I had only made one step towards the radio set when a sort of black and yellow whirlpool violently formed right in the centre of the room. A gust of air almost knocked me off my feet.

In the centre of the whirlpool, one could see a diffuse and transparent shape; behind it, the books on the shelves remained perfectly visible. The shape came into focus. Blurred objects slowly began to reflect the light from the fittings on the ceiling.

I closed my eyes one short moment and, when I opened them again, saw a strange contraption in front of me. Some parts of it were apparently made of nickel, others of ivory and others yet seemed to be carved out of rock-crystal. On a sort of saddle sat a man with a knapsack slung over his back and a small camera hanging over his chest. A newspaper emerged from the pocket of his tweed jacket, I couldn't help noticing the title: *The Pall Mall Gazette*.

There could be no doubt about it: it was the Time Traveller. I looked at him from head to toe, puzzled but unwilling to admit to myself that this might be an hallucination.

The Traveller had not seen me. Leaving his saddle, he walked over to the radio set which had since returned to normal. Keeping his hands in his pockets, he watched it from a distance. It looked almost as if he was making an effort to understand the commentator's words.

I was in an uncomfortable position: my right leg was benumbed. I stood up, propping myself against the back of a chair which grated under the pressure of my weight. Fast as lightning, the Traveller turned round, pulling out an old cylinder revolver from his pocket. Soon reassured by the fact my intentions were far from aggressive, he put his weapon away and, extending his hand, walked towards me:

"Hello."

I carefully shook his hand, muttering:

"You . . . you . . ."

He had lit his pipe, much too slowly for my liking and, with his head, indicated the shining contraption:

"It's a Time Machine."

"I know."

His grey eyes ignited.

"How do you know?"

Taking the book lying on the armchair's rest, I passed it over to him.

"Wells!" he cried out and his features went from grey to scarlet. "But I wrote to him, saying it was all my imagination, that . . ."

"The letter is reproduced in the book."

Displeased, he nodded his head and went on tapping the glass top of my desk with the end of his nails. I offered him some water, but he declined. I then took out an unopened bottle of "Black and White" which I usually kept for my guests. He drank a quarter of a glass with a wry look on his face. Probably wasn't his favourite brand.

It was very much like a commonplace meeting of acquaintances and this aspect of the situation was even stranger than his untimely appearance. I found myself saying:

"How did you get here, such a long way from Richmond? I was wondering."

Elbows propped on the desk, the Traveller was flexing his

hands over the glass and answered me above the slurping noise:

"Right from the beginning, I wanted to build a machine capable of moving through space and time at the will of its operator."

"However, on your first journey . . ."

"That particular night, when I was alone, I set up the mechanism that would enable me to move through space."

He stood up and walked towards the machine. I followed him and easily recognised the four dials indicating speed against time travelled: days, thousand days, million and billion days. Near these dials stood another, much larger and rectangular in shape: a map of Europe. At the intersection of the two moving surfaces one could read a word in microscopic type: Bucharest.

"It's all very simple," the Traveller continued. "At least, it looks that way. Say you want to go . . . By the way, where do you want to go?"

I shrugged my shoulders in answer to him.

"Let's see, past or future?" he insisted.

I had an idea.

"The past."

"Where and when?"

"In Sevenoaks."

"Sevenoaks?" he repeated, surprised.

"Yes. In 1894."

"OK, then."

It was only then I noticed the sixth dial, designed to encompass the time zone. Having adjusted the mobile surfaces, the Traveller turned towards me, a smug look over his face:

"All I now have to do is pull the left-hand lever."

Fascinated by its unpolished glare, I kept on watching the white lever for a few moments.

"By the way, tell me: why Sevenoaks?"

I had no time to answer. The telephone rang and the Traveller suddenly turned on his heels and knocked my right shoulder. I lost my balance and fell with bent knees on the machine's platform. My arms were still thrashing the air and I instinctively caught hold of the left-hand lever.

I did not experience any disagreeable feelings while

travelling through time. My thoughts remained clear and my eyes were not damaged by the twinkling succession of light and darkness. I just found myself all of a sudden by a country road, standing under a roof of branches. Coming from afar, I could hear dull, rhythmic sounds.

I thought, one moment, I should return immediately to the machine's owner. But it would have been foolish to waste such a unique opportunity. Remembering the Traveller's precautions, I unscrewed the white levers and slipped them into my pocket. I then left my shelter.

On my right, a hundred metres or so from where I stood, a few workmen were busy paving the narrow road. Walking unhurriedly towards them, I asked them where Mr. Wells lived. They interrupted their work, leaning on the wooden rammers.

"Just behind you," one of the men answered, putting his cap down on his shoulders. "But you're not likely to find him in now."

And they all began laughing, looking at something behind me. I turned round and saw a one-storey house in the centre of a small garden.

"I don't understand," I told them. "Is he in London?"

"No, he's training," they all laughed again.

I would have liked to ask them for further explanations, but the men had gone back to work, ignoring me in an ostentatiously suspicious manner. I soon was to find out why: a young man was approaching on the newly-paved road. I recognised him by the thick moustache covering his upper lip.

He stopped just by us, getting ready to climb over the embankment. I rushed towards him:

"Mr. Wells!"

"What do you want?"

His eyes were light and cold. My whole adventure suddenly appeared rather silly. What was I searching for in this time which was not mine? How was the Traveller going to react?

"You know . . . I intended to . . ." I stammered, looking all around me for some providential help.

Wells interpreted my hesitation differently.

"Inside, we can talk in confidence."

And he invited me to lead the way in walking towards the house now diagonally lit by the sun. I made a few steps in that direction while thinking of some excuse allowing for an honourable retreat.

"You have a strange appearance," he said, opening the door. "Your presence will only serve to reinforce my landlady's suspicions."

"I don't understand," I said, for the second time already that day. "I should anyway . . ."

"She does not think writing is a worthy profession," Wells went on. "And I am used to working at night . . ."

He had possibly guessed I was hoping to get away and was trying to reassure me. When I came to my senses again, I was sitting in a plush armchair. In front of me was a piano, lid open to reveal its keyboard, and on its music stand a sonata by Handel. Higher up, a rectangular window stained by the setting sun. There was a pervading smell of freshly-printed books and country flowers. The books were all on the small desk in front of which Wells had sat himself. I got up to look at them and Wells said, helpfully:

"New publications. I'm reviewing them for *The Pall Mall Gazette.*"

I distractedly began leafing through one of the volumes.

"So what do you want?"

I jumped.

"Me?"

"Well, I suppose you haven't come all this way just to meet a virtually unknown writer!"

"Unknown?!"

I then opened up and told him all: the apparition of the Traveller, the improvements he had made to the machine, the accident through which I had been thrown into the past . . .

Wells smiled:

"Are you trying to make me believe in my own lucubrations? Time is only a kind of space and all that . . ."

I went to the window. The workmen had gone. The road was empty.

"It's quite near," I said. "A hundred metres or so."

And I brought out the white levers from my pocket.

"Anyone can make two levers and then pretend . . ."

"You've devoted a lot of time to this little joke, haven't you?"

He shrugged his shoulders. I then grew increasingly serious:

"Have you completed 'The Time Machine'?"

"Yes. This very night. But who told you what I was working on? Have you spoken to Henley?"

"Henley?"

"The previous editor of *The National Observer*. He wants to publish a new magazine and offered me to . . ."

I interrupted him:

"Have you sent him the manuscript?"

"I've just told you, I only completed it last night . . . I have to revise it still."

"Perfect. Can I then remind you of the last words of the Traveller's letter. 'Take it as a lie – or a prophecy. Say I dreamed it in the workshop. Consider I have been speculating upon the destinies of our race until I have hatched this fiction. Treat my assertion of its truth as a mere stroke of art to enhance its interest.' "

"Enough," said Wells. "I don't know how you've managed to read the ending, but you've certainly stung my curiosity. At any rate, a walk before our meal will not harm us."

He was attempting to conceal his nervousness, but his lips were trembling and his movements were becoming feverish. A few moments later, we had reached the machine. Wells circled round it, without touching it. Under the roof of branches, darkness was delineating shadows full of the aromatic smell of grass.

"If only you knew in what conditions I had to write the story . . . Night after night in the hall, with only the light of a paraffin lamp . . ."

It was now getting cooler. I thought of the Traveller fuming in his time cage.

"Mr. Wells, we must absolutely . . ."

He didn't let me finish:

"Some people say that 'Life reflects art' . . ."

" 'and provides the dream of fiction with a true form'," I completed the quotation.

"So you've read Oscar Wilde!"

". . . which does not mean to say that the 'Intentions' are anything for me but a frame of paradoxes."

"Tell me, then, how you built the model of the machine."

"What about the story?" I answered back.

"I find it easier to believe you have a talent for reading things at a distance, like the late Madame Blavatsky."

Rushing towards the machine, I adjusted the mobile surfaces, fixed the levers and saddled up, saying:

"My disappearance will convince you."

"I hope you return," Wells answered with a thin smile.

"If only to bring you a copy of the 1962 Romanian edition of 'The Time Machine'."

"Romanian?" he said, with a look of surprise on his face.

I pulled the left-hand lever.

The Traveller stood half-twisted over the ringing telephone. I thought for one moment that my encounter with Wells had been an hallucination. I understood later that I had returned to the exact moment of my departure.

However, the Traveller's twisting movement did not stop there and his arms continued to move, this time away from the telephone. I saw his eyes and I shuddered under the impact of their lightning gaze. He now appeared quite different. He was tall and stronger, and the pallor of his features had been replaced by the even tan of someone who spent most of his time out in the open. With one hand, he picked me out of the saddle and set me down on the ground. Under the pressure of his stretched muscles, the buttons holding his jacket together were torn off and fell to the floor. It was then I saw his real clothing: some translucent material moulding an athletic body.

All of a sudden, with none of the phenomena which had accompanied its apparition, the machine disappeared. Absurdly hopeful, I rushed to the balcony. But only the lights of the city could be seen.

The coolness of the night helped me regain my composure. I understood it had all been staged. The Traveller had not come from the past, but from the future. He had assumed the appearance of Wells' hero to make contact easier with a world accustomed to seeing the anticipations in its books come true. No doubt he would have revealed his secret to me had my adventure not warned him that the past can become a labyrinth with no real issue.

Which, I agree, is a difficult explanation to accept. It would appear the "The Time Machine" has never had any ending bar the one we know. Sole trustee of memories concerning a lost version, I myself sometimes have doubts as to the reality of what happened. Then I open the drawer of my desk, I take my cash-box and pull out the three buttons. Many are the researchers from various Institutes who have tried to determine their composition. In vain. I examine them, turn them around between my fingers endlessly, then deposit them back in their cotton bed. I wish to keep them intact, as a gesture of goodwill, in preparation for my next encounter with the Future.

Translated by Maxim and Dolorès Jakubowski
Original title: . . . *Un Fel de Spatiu*

Dealers in light and darkness

CHERRY WILDER

There is a blind boy who takes his place every day at one of the gates to the city. He sits erect, all day long, listening; the farmers bring him presents. At a first glance this boy, Coll, is not much different from the other beggars of Rhomary who congregate at the gates on market days. Yet, under the dusty hood his face is striking. His hair is black; his face clear and unlined; his eyes are unblemished, pale blue in the dark face.

He has a friend, Gurl Hign, a beggar and the daughter of a beggar, a skinny, scabbed, dark-eyed wretch who collects his alms. The masters of the parmel caravans leave him fruit, wine, even meat; Gurl collects everything jealously. Perhaps she sells these goods down in the Warren, for they take more than enough for two persons.

At ten o'clock in the morning by the Sulvan Gate, there they sit. Coll's head is turned aside, he is listening to a long report an old woman is giving the gate-keeper: a miracle-worker on the Billsee has sweetened the wells. It is a typical cloudless day, the dust not yet risen. Gurl sits one brick below Coll on the rough work of the gate tower. She can look right to the Rhomary land, the patchwork of fields and irrigation canals, and left towards the city. Through the gate the road runs down, clotted with people, to the Warren, then the city rises in tiers to the walled gardens of the New Town. In the east Doctors' College gleams white and gold. The grey palace of the Envoys rises over the western wall like an undulant sea-beast.

A caravan comes in from the south; on the third parmel

is a double pannier of flowers and fruit. A girl in a striped smock sits on the beast's neck flicking at insects and urchins with a long whip. The blind boy turns his head, grips his staff a shade more firmly; Gurl Hign is all eyes and ears. The scent of the flowers and fruit engulfs them both at the same instant: Coll is transported, and his companion, shutting her eyes, is swept along with him.

. . . there is a garden; he sees, she sees with him. Damp grass underfoot and pottery urns full of flowers. Fruit . . . timbin, pechids, black plums . . . grow against a tiled wall or under conical hoods of lathe and straw. Two men and a woman are washing their hands at the well; they are uncommonly tall and pale. Their faces are more than beautiful, endowed with such a powerful radiance by the beholder, the boy, that it is impossible for Gurl Hign to see them otherwise . . .

The vision fades: back again at the Sulvan Gate with the caravan still passing. Gurl Hign leans her mop of hair against Coll's side, gazes at him with greedy admiration, with love.

One day is like another, sky cloudless, afternoons dusty and still. On the next afternoon or the next, two soldiers slouch up through the Warren to the Sulvan Gate. They have that touch of embarrassment which precedes an arrest: Coll gives no trouble. He reaches out to Gurl, touches her shoulder, to make sure she will not make a shouting match of it. The soldiers are taking him to the Dator's house; Coll walks ahead steadily, using his staff. Gurl Hign follows, lips compressed, dragging her dusty feet.

II

Urbain Bro, the Dator, lived in an ugly square box of a house on the lowest tier of the New Town. The word went that the place was as broad and deep below the ground as it was above, every inch of it packed with the records and the stored wisdom, such as it was, of the Rhomary lands. He sat at a huge desk in his private collating room, clacked tablets, rustled papers, nervously flicked at scrolls, wet a twisted corner of vellum and worked it between his fingers. He squeezed at his tired eyes and let the assistant bring in Coll. He was ill at ease in the company of blind persons because he feared for his own sight. He suffered from a miserable hypochondria and the pardonable delusion that nothing would get done unless he did it himself.

"What is your name then?" he began.

The boy had been placed before a chair; he settled into it.

"I am Coll."

"More than that!"

"My mother was Morag Dun Mor, a potter, from Pebble on the Billsee. I never knew my father . . . he was lost at sea in the flood-tides a few months before I was born."

Urbain examined his tablets and a brown folder.

"Yes," he said. "Now Coll, how long have you been . . . afflicted?"

"Five years."

"You have not been in Rhomary city so long."

"I spent three years home in Pebble."

"And before that you were a sighted person, attached to a villa here in Rhomary . . . a house known as The Pleasance?"

"I was hired by some visitors," smiled Coll.

"Visitors?"

"You know them," said Coll. "They came from Silver City, so they said."

"Their names?"

"You know that too, sir. Lural was the lady, and her brother Theo, and Ensor her husband. They were dealers in pottery and spices."

"You're very certain about what I know," grumbled the Dator.

"You sat at dinner with them more than once. I waited at table."

"Humph!" said Urbain, folding his hands behind his head and tilting his chair dangerously. "I don't remember every servant."

"You have seen me even before that," said Coll.

"I hardly think so. I was not in Pebble since the spring of 1051. Now tell me, how did you meet these visitors? What was the arrangement? Did your mother sell you to these people?"

"They came to our shop in Pebble," said the blind boy. "We sold them pottery. I came with them into Rhomary to work at the Pleasance. They were very kind; when my mother fell ill they sent for her. She died at my aunt's house, here in the Warren, when I had been in service half a year."

"What did they teach you, Coll?"

"All I know," said the boy coldly. "I could barely read when I came to the Pleasance. Before they left I had read all their books."

"There are not many books in private hands," said the Dator. "What books did you read?"

For the first time the boy's voice faltered; he sighed and blinked, and the Dator realised that he was fighting down tears.

"A manual of gardening," said Coll, "and a book of the stars and planets. These two were of a kind you read on a small screen."

"Cassette books!"

"Then I read a paged book of off-world fairy tales, full of wonders and dragons. Also the First Book of the Envoys . . ."

"They had *that*!"

"And a bible, also called a gideon. A Christian holy book."

"I know which book you mean," said the Dator.

Coll wiped his face awkwardly with one ragged sleeve.

"Sir," he asked, "why are there not more Christians in the Rhomary lands?"

"Desiccated if I know, boy," said the Dator dreamily. "They've come and gone like the Great Vail themselves. Still have a few Neo-Zionists operating in Silver City, and there's a little chapel called Bethel down here on the edge of the Warren. Our crisis of belief came with the Vail and their wisdom and the power of the Envoys. You were born what year?"

"Ten fifty-one."

"You look younger. The year before that was the most terrible year in our brief history on this planet. You do know, I take it, that our history is brief?"

"Yes," said Coll. "My friends at the villa used to be amused by it. When the inhabitants of Rhomary city numbered a thousand that was declared to be the year 1000."

"And that was in the year one fifty – one hundred and fifty years after landfall," sighed the Dator. "Damned foolishness to distort the record. At any rate we have been here . . . what . . . two hundred and twenty years? And in 1050 the drought had been going on for ten years and the Envoys had handled the food riots badly . . ."

"And the Vail . . ." prompted Coll Dun Mor.

"I was sent to the Western Sea when the first reports came in under heavy security. The Vail were our friends, no doubt of that. At least they believed in us a little . . . their minmers, their fairy-folk; they were patronising, I suppose, but the last book of the Envoys makes sad reading.

"I remember coming within a few miles of the narrows . . . the sky was brazen, hot, hot . . . you could imagine the waters of the Billsee draining away, And then the stink; it was like nothing I've experienced: it was death itself. The Western Sea was an oily grey, not a fin stirring; the heat seemed to darken the land. How many of the Vail had died down there we could not tell. As we were watching a crew-man pointed to the west . . . the headland overlooking that bay they called the Sea of Utner; one of the Vail came to land. I saw it through my glass; I saw it plainly . . . a mountain, a forest of great lizard trees, heaving itself on to the land and walking away. They go well over land but this one was tired . . ."

"Did any survive?"

"Who knows? The Envoys swear they will return."

"So I have heard," said the boy.

"It is four hundred kilometres to the Gann, the nearest river that empties into the Red Ocean. There are a few traders in the Red Ocean, they watch for the sight of them. Our Vail . . . our sea-wonders . . . The Envoys could never survive the loss. Oh yes, they consolidated the doctrine and came back into politics but the heart had gone from their teaching. I'll never forget that sight . . . heaving itself from the water . . . walking away. The water sank lower still during that year until we could see the pearl terraces where they met and the great whorls of their yellow bones."

Urbain sighed and chuckled at the way he had been side-tracked.

"All right, boy," he said. "Now you and your charlatans. What seditious nonsense did they teach you? And why? Have you fathomed that?"

"They were not charlatans!"

"How did they groom you, Coll Dun Mor? What's to be the next move? A miracle? Perhaps I should have a doctor look you over before you leave this house."

"Are you afraid of miracles?" asked the boy. "Perhaps this is the season for them. You have been watching me for a long time and now you start asking questions."

"Answer then! Did they make much of you? Lural was very beautiful, hair like a river of light. Or maybe the young men. What did you feel about these people?"

"What would I feel?" cried Coll passionately. "I was a poor boy. I loved, I worshipped them. They were beautiful, all three, and they knew more than there is . . . in this house. I do not believe I ever touched Lural's white hands; sometimes Theo would run races with me on the lawns. He always won. Ensor, now and then, laid a hand on my head as I read aloud. As a father, so I have heard, praises his child . . ."

Coll drew sobbing breath. The Dator was making notes on a glazed erasing tablet. As he fouled the pen and took up another his hand struck a bell in a pottery stand that rested beside his ink-well on the cluttered desk. Before the note had died away Coll was on his feet.

"The bell! You have it from the Pleasance!"

"You mean this?"

The Dator tapped the bell again and its rounded note seemed to spread in rings through the dim pool of the room. Coll walked forward hesitantly, then in a rush, until his fingertips touched the desk.

"I know its voice!" he said. "It is a round brass bell in a small archway of turquoise and white ceramic. There was a wooden hammer, a tiny thing, that rested on the stand. I am surprised that they didn't take this bell away with them."

"It was the only thing left behind," said the Dator, "hidden away behind a couch. The hammer was lost. Mind you, the search was delayed. So this was their bell . . ."

"Yes. The stand was a gift from my mother; almost the last thing she made."

"It is fine work."

Urbain thought he understood the boy's excitement but Coll was reaching out eagerly across the desk.

"But sir, I can bring them again, with the bell's dear sound."

Coll had found the bell and grasped the stand. With his right hand he reached out impatiently.

"Master Urbain," he said, pale eyes staring past the Dator, "take my hand . . ."

The Dator hardly knew why he obeyed but he gripped the boy's thin brown hand firmly. Coll shook the bell.

Urbain's esp rating was at least as high as that of Gurl Hign but he was unpractised. He felt as if he were being dragged across a dark threshold. He resisted for a few seconds, then shut his eyes. The dining-room at the Pleasance was all around him: fresh flowers, scented candles. The bell rang; there was music playing. Lural sat by the window in a white gown; the two men played Go with red and white pieces on a faience board. The music wound through the room: exquisite music played by many instruments . . . strings, woodwind, brass. An orchestra of a size and skill unknown in the Rhomary lands. The Dator was just able to direct his attention to the source of the music, a black container on a side table.

His hand was released. He came back with a jolt, like that thump of the heart which sometimes wakened him on the edge of sleep.

"Blast!" he sighed. "Where did you learn this, Coll Dun Mor? From our friends there?"

"It was born in me," said the boy.

He turned and walked carefully back to the chair, feeling about until he found it.

"Truly," he said, "they were taken aback when I showed them I was a Vesp. They would have preferred . . ."

"What?" the Dator prompted eagerly.

It came out with a rush.

"An empty vessel. A mind alert, surely, but mainly receptive, able to give back what they put in. A creature to speak, to remember what had never happened, to build within itself some great shining core of faith . . ."

"But why . . . ?"

The boy curled his lip.

"Don't you know yet, Master Urbain, what they would make of me?"

"Not entirely."

"You have all the evidence I had. The gideon and its New Testament. The legends . . . Osiris, Orpheus . . . Oh, I could take you to the day, the hour I saw the pattern. It was like my mother dreaming the shape of the finished vessel in a lump of clay. Or like my father . . . did I say that he was a fisherman . . . divining the run of the mekkle shoals. I saw the pattern and I was flattered. I had been chosen, me myself, from the hour of my birth. A birth that some said was miraculous."

The Dator had begun to fidget.

"Fifty-one? On the Billsee?"

"You begin to remember," said Coll. "The storms that broke the drought. The freak tides and the Tsunami. Where were you, Master Urbain, when that gigantic wave swept over the village?"

"In the lighthouse," said the Dator. "And the wave came, reaching almost to the platform where we stood. A wave more terrifying than a charge of Vail. Walls of water, crest upon crest . . . and in those crests . . ."

"A little boat," said Coll, "snatched from the flood by the few lucky officials who had commandeered the platform. In the boat was a poor woman, newly widowed. That night she gave birth."

"And you, you . . ."

"I was that child."

"Miraculous," whispered the Dator. "Do you suppose this was known to those three, the Visitants?"

"I suppose even more. Why were you invited to the Pleasance? Hell's dust, Master Urbain, they were keeping track of you too, for my sake. For the sake of their plan."

The Dator rubbed his eyes again until he saw stars and flashes of light.

"A miraculous birth," he said. "Yes, yes, I'm thick today but I begin to see it. What comes next? Miracles, as I suggested before? Political involvement? Healing, maybe, which will make trouble with Doctors' College. Had anyone the end of the story in mind as well as the beginning?"

"I never found out," said Coll, "never penetrated to the heart of the plan. Sometimes it seemed they acted from design, sometimes from mere whim, for the fun of it, for the experiment. They assured me, at the end, that they meant well. They believed the Rhomary land needed . . ."

"What would you call it?" asked the Dator harshly.

"A Redeemer," said Coll, "a God Son. The New Christ come to succour His lost children."

"So that is what you are!"

"No," said Coll Dun Mor. "No, I am not!"

The room was very still. The Dator could hear a flying gecko twittering and rustling outside under the eaves as it entered its nest.

"I could not do it," said the blind boy. "Once the pattern

was made plain I began to have doubts. I was not afraid, I had no sense of unworthiness . . . I expect, if there is godhead in us I have as much as the next person. If I had been blind to their design only a little longer they might have provided a revelation from which I could not escape. Their power over all minds was very strong. But my own revelation came too soon. My revelation of myself to myself. When anyone says 'You are, you will be a Messiah' then there's only one honest answer for me: 'No, I am not.' "

The Dator stared long and hard at the boy then deliberately put down his pen.

"How did they take it?"

"Very well," said Coll. "They were always kindness itself. Besides . . ."

"Besides they had another candidate."

"Several."

"Is that so? One has survived the tests."

"What is his name, I wonder?" asked Coll, lifting his head.

The Dator heaved across another file.

"Jenz Kindl. A good name. Born at the Lemn Oasis in the far north on the night of Jan 23rd 1049. I thought that date was familiar . . ."

He thumbed through the almanac.

"Yes, of course. The second night of the great meteor shower."

"He is in Billsee now, sweetening the wells," said Coll. "I wonder if he will be long in coming to the city of Rhomary."

"Do you want . . ." the Dator stumbled over the words "to see", "to meet this Miracle Worker?"

"I am curious as you are, Master Urbain."

"Suppose our Visitors are still in attendance? Are you still listening for their voices?"

"I did at first. Now I don't believe that I will ever meet them again."

Coll yawned and twisted in his chair.

"You are finished with me, Master Urbain. May I go now?"

"Soon," said the Dator. "A couple more points to be cleared up. Really, Coll Dun Mor, I am moved by your story but you must not play the innocent."

"How?"

"What was their nature?" snapped Urbain. "Lural, Theo, Ensor . . . names, fanciful names. They traded in names."

"I have no idea of their true nature," said Coll slowly, "but there was something in the names. I read in the First Book of the Envoys . . . do you have it here?"

"Yes, yes . . ."

The Dator scrabbled in a deep drawer then stopped as if his patience had run out. After all, the boy was blind.

"Go on," he said, "what passage?"

"The long preamble on the senses," said Coll. "I am not sure I have it right . . . The Recording Envoy lists or tries to list all the ten senses of the great beasts, the Vail. The Speaker, the Vail she attends, helps and prompts her. They speak of three of our human senses: *Ul*, *Thet*, and *Esoon*, sight, touch and hearing, roughly, in the language used by the Vail."

"They could use many languages," said the Dator. "We taught them three."

"The passage ends with a mystery," said Coll. "Do you remember? 'For these words are come from a race of strange capacity, less known, yet once more real to the Vail than ten thousand minmers or men. They are hardly to be seen unless they put on a shape to be beheld, but their minds are spacious.' "

"Yes!" said the Dator. "Yes!"

He jumped up from his chair as if pricked by a pin. He began to laugh.

"That passage has been heavily glossed, I can tell you."

"The Vail wouldn't explain?" asked Coll.

"Seldom," said Urbain.

He walked to a side table, poured two cups of water and carried one to the boy. He placed Coll's hands around the cup.

"A shape to be beheld . . ." he went on. "And beauty, we're told, *is* in the eye of the beholder."

His hand clamped down fiercely on the boy's shoulder.

"Coll Dun Mor," he demanded, "*how did you become blind*?"

The boy choked, recovered himself, and drained the cup.

"An accident . . ." his voice shook.

"Don't lie to me!"

The Dator shook him roughly then snatched up the boy's

staff from where it leant against the chair back.

"Shape-changers! Inhuman! Alien!" he cried.

"What could be more alien than the Vail?" Coll protested feebly.

Urbain thumped the staff upon the ground.

"This was your reward. This was the end of their kindness."

"No! It was my own doing."

"Liar!"

"Give me my staff again!"

Coll dropped the water cup and groped out from his chair. Urbain shrugged furiously and flung the staff back against the boy's legs. Coll began to speak in a low voice and the Dator turned back, surprised as always when his blustering worked.

"It was at night. They were leaving the Pleasance. I did not even ask to be taken along. We were all sad when the time came to say goodbye. They gave me presents and money and I set off for my aunt's house. But when it grew dark I stole back to the villa again. I'm not sure why I did this; I told myself it was from love, not to be parted . . . to stow away in their caravan if need be. But I did feel a deep curiosity.

"I climbed over the wall into the garden, then I saw that the villa was dark. I believed I was too late, somehow they had left. I remember sitting on the grass watching the stars come out; I felt empty and still, like the garden itself. I couldn't believe that everything was over, that I would never walk freely and happily in that place again.

"Presently I thought I saw a glimmer of light inside the dark house: it grew brighter and moved from room to room. I remained in the shadow, far away, under the trees . . . I thought this must be the landlady or her servants checking the place. Then it began, a disturbance of the air, a feeling of pressure in my ears. I thought it came from the furthest corner of the wall, where the shadow was very deep and reached up, like a tower, above the top of the wall. Then they came out of the house."

"What did you see?"

"Nothing at first. A thickening of the night. Two, three swirling pools of soft light on the ground. I knew, I felt very strongly that they were there. Then, as they moved through the garden, there were tubes, man-sized, larger, of green-black membrance like the skin of an oil-bubble. Inside the tubes there was a continuous pulsing and crawling, not good to watch. I know the Vail are terrible to behold, their whisper can knock a human being senseless, but their very size blunts our comprehension. This was more intimate. These were my friends and I could hardly bear to see them in this form. I do not know if it was their 'true' form.

"As they moved towards the tower of darkness by the far wall they became aware of me. I had heard their conversation all through the garden . . . odd bars of sound. I think there were high and low notes beyond my range of hearing. Now a voice rang out like a bell. 'Who?' There was an immediate change; they began to take on human shape again. If I had rushed forward then, called my name . . . but I could not, I could not movc. A broad beam of light struck the wall, rebounded, flashed again; it caught mc full in the face. It was light, strong light, nothing more . . . not a weapon or a death-ray or anything of that sort. I fell down on the grass; I dropped like a stone, unconscious. Next thing I knew, the garden was empty. I had lain there all night. I could feel the morning sun on my face and hear the birds and the cry of the water-seller in the next street. I was blind."

Urbain Bro instinctively shut his own tired eyes for a few seconds.

"Inconclusive," he said gently.

He bent back Coll's head and stared into his face.

"Medical opinion?" he asked.

"I felt my way back into the Warren, to my aunt's house. Later I was taken to Doctors' College with a tale about lightning. There had been thunder storms. The condition is what they call functional . . ."

"What?"

Coll Dun Mor smiled.

"The Doctors talked about shock. There is nothing wrong with my eyes. This is hysterical blindness. I will not always be blind."

Urbain strode up and down the room; he waved his arms and wanted to shout with exasperation.

"Boy, it has been five years! Shock? Trauma? This was done to you . . ."

"The condition usually passes off."

"In heaven's name," said Urbain, "what are you waiting for?"

"A miracle?" suggested Coll Dun Mor.

"For that you need faith. Could you believe in the healing powers of this candidate, this puppet . . . Jenz Kindl, our little Christ-child from the Oasis of Lemn?"

"I believe in his teachers," said Coll. "Who knows? Perhaps this will be part of the pattern too."

"I give up," said the Dator. "You're a fool. I might say a blind fool. If you see again, come back to my house, I'll make an archivist out of you."

"Thank you, sir, but when I see again I have my own plans."

"What? Aren't you satisfied yet? Are you still searching for these chimera, the shape-changers?"

"By no means," said Coll. "When I regain my sight I will go back to Pebble and buy a boat. I have a friend and some alms put by. We will sail into the Western Sea, then make a portage to the river Gann. I will sail in the Red Ocean and find the Vail again. There is much they have still to tell us."

"Go along . . ." said the Dator, "you're a fool and a dreamer."

"Perhaps you would care to contribute . . . ?"

"Get out!"

Urbain rang the brass bell three times for the attendant; after the boy had gone he sat in the darkened room. He began to sigh and then to chuckle and laugh; he detected signs of hysteria in himself. He walked to the window and looked out into the street. Coll Dun Mor stood on the footpath; a shadow detached itself from the deeper shadows at the mouth of an alley. Gurl Hign the beggar-girl came out, seized Coll's hand and began to run. He ran stumbling after her and they disappeared into the by-ways of Rhomary.

III

There is a blind boy who takes his place every day at one of the gates to the city. He comes in the early morning before the dust has risen and sits until evening, listening to all the traffic through the gates. One day is like another. Gurl Hign collects his alms and information of the sort that interests them both. They know every way-station that has been passed and the miracles that have been wrought there.

One market day the procession reaches the foot of the hill; Jenz Kindl is coming, among a great crowd of his followers. As they flow up the hill towards the Sulvan Gate the blind boy, Coll Dun Mor, rises slowly to his feet, waiting and listening. He draws Gurl Hign back to his side when she tries to elbow her way into the crowd: at the right moment he cries out in a loud voice. Jenz the Healer hears the cry and lifts his meek head; the crowd falls back to let the blind boy through.

A hole in time

GERD MAXIMOVIC

Herr Schmitz-Feller, managing director of Sebastian Manufacturing, contemplated the broad and vacant expanse of his desk. He had set aside his inevitable cigar in a large crystal ashtray, and held a telephone, his link with half the world, pressed close to his left ear. He had an important customer on the line. His face was slightly flushed, perhaps from the mental exertion of his conversation, but partly, too, from the high blood pressure from which he constantly suffered. His free hand held a sharply pointed pencil with which he had just jotted down some figures on an otherwise blank sheet of paper.

He made no further notes, because suddenly the line went dead. At the same time the lights went out, leaving the office in a dull grey half-light. Schmitz-Feller tried the telephone again, but without success. Angrily he slammed down the receiver and relit his dead cigar.

A few moments later, when the power showed no sign of being restored, he stumped impatiently to the door. Before he could open it, there was a knock, and it flew open. It was Fräulein Narr, and behind her was the production manager, Herr Schellenschmitt. Both were highly agitated, and a babble of excited voices could be heard in the passage behind them.

"What's going on?" demanded Schmitz-Feller.

Schellenschmitt stared past him at the window; the blinds were down. His eyes were wide and staring. "We don't know, sir. It's the same everywhere. The wiring is dead, there's no current, and outside the windows there's a jungle." He gestured ineffectually with his left hand. "And down in the works the machines have stopped."

Schmitz-Feller leant his head on one side and listened for

the throb of the factory, which was never out of earshot, even at the very top of the high-rise block which housed the offices. He listened in vain. He was never normally conscious of the sound, but it was so ingrained in him that he always knew at once when there was a strike.

"The window . . ." said Schellenschmitt.

The electric switch did not work, so Fräulein Narr had to pull the cords by hand. Schmitz-Feller started back in horror. Outside the window was a dark, twilit, green forest. Before him crowded a densely packed mass of scaly tree trunks; creepers snaked up them, moist blossoms opened their crimson flesh. The heat seeped in, and the window panes sweated in the steamy air. The managing director felt as if he were being struck in slow motion with a bludgeon made of compressed hothouse air.

The works council chairman, Orluff, put his head in through the door. "Morning, gentlemen, what's going on? Why have the machines stopped?"

Apparently this was the first time he had seen what lay outside the windows, and he froze. "Good God, where did the greenery spring from?"

Schmitz-Feller lit his cigar again. "Let's go," he said to Orluff and Schellenschmitt, "and see what's going on."

They went into the corridor and pushed their way past excitedly chattering office workers. All the doors were open, so they saw glimpses of forest through the windows of successive offices. The lift, stuck between the seventh and eighth floors, emitted frantic knockings. They made their way down the stairs. A crowd of office workers followed them, and more joined them on every floor.

In the works it was surprisingly dark and silent. The frosted windows prevented anyone from looking out, and the great machine-shop lay in twilight. The workers stood around talking; they had not yet grasped what had happened. Their unaccustomed visitors passed impressively but ineffectually through their ranks. The confusion on the workers' faces – and their pleasure at the interruption of work – were so patently genuine that no one mentioned the possibility of a strike or a conspiracy.

In the end, in the part of the building which connected the office block to the works, someone pushed open a frosted glass door which led into the open air. Where previously the cement floor of the courtyard had extended as far as the barred gate, the yard was now crossed by a towering wall of trees which obscured the sun. The yard had been cut off at the edge as if with a razor. The branches showed bare cut ends from which a sweet sap dripped heavily to the ground. It was as if bombs had unleashed a powerful vertical shock wave and cut a razor-sharp swathe through the primeval forest.

Out of the murk dropped bulky beetles, butterflies and moths. Even the most fleeting contact revealed their uncommon size and shape, which would have been surprising even in the Amazon jungle. A fat beetle struck Schmitz-Feller on the chest and rid him of the momentary suspicion that this might all be a dream. They shut the door, and Schmitz-Feller's cigar had gone out again.

"Keep the matches," said Orluff, "you may need them."

Opinions among the workforce were divided. Those who thought they would be sent home at half-past four, hooter or no hooter, were quickly disabused. The jungle crowded in all around, and in some mysterious way it had swallowed up the car park, the cars, the streets, the railway lines, the whole town. Little groups of men ventured into the forest, armed with sharp tools, and returned, amazed and perplexed at the mysterious thing that had happened to them, and which evidently had no spatial limit.

By about seven o'clock the forest had swallowed up the last green glow of the setting sun, and fear had settled in the hearts of the men and women in the factory. They did not know where they were or what was going to happen next; there was nothing to eat; and there was no light. No one had anything helpful to suggest. A deputation was sent up to the office block in the hope that the people there would know. But the outside telephone lines were dead, and the deputation returned with nothing but a directive that tools were not to be used without express authority.

Bergner, foreman of section five, had his wits about him. He turned out a waste bin, filled it with paper soaked in oil, and lit it with a match. That was the beginning of the first general meeting. In the flickering light they talked the problem through. How and why they had got into this mess was, for the time being, irrelevant. What mattered now – saving a miracle – was how to get through that night and the following day. A committee was elected, with Franz

Schaefer in the chair. The workers lay down between the machines, bellies rumbling, for a hard night's rest on the floor. The committee was in session until long after midnight.

The next morning the committee divided the workers into groups to gather food. Those tools that would be of use in the jungle were shared out.

Franz Schaefer asked to see the managing director who sat, flanked by three of his works security guards, looking unusually jovial.

"We're all in the same boat," he said, "and no one knows how long it will go on."

Schaefer nodded. "We badly need the guards' weapons," he said, "for hunting."

Schmitz-Feller smiled broadly. "That won't be possible."

"Brothers," said Franz Schaefer, without looking at the managing director, "I am in charge here now. I've been democratically elected. We don't know how long this will go on, or what is going to happen; all we know is that unless we stick together the forest is going to swallow us up."

After some hesitation, the men went with him.

All that day the sound of gunfire and the excited voices of the hunters could be heard. In the evening a big fire was lit in the factory yard. It was a good protection against the wild animals that lurked in the forest, and it was needed to cook the meat, as well as to clean wounds inflicted by the forest. As well as meat the hunters had brought back berries and other fruits, and it was not long before enthusiasts came forward who knew how to cook them. A share went even to those whose faces showed a tell-tale absence of jungle scratches.

A remarkable spirit of solidarity began to develop throughout the thousand-strong workforce. Now they found themselves in this tight corner, cut off from homes, partners and children, they drew close together, and envy, jealousy, dislike and fear receded like phantoms of a distant world. Here they were all equal, and everyone's value lay in what he did for the group. There were even sorry for their portly, cigar-smoking chief.

On the second evening they moved into the office block, which was not so draughty as the works and had a floor that was somewhat better than a hard block of concrete. Schaefer dispatched a party to reconnoitre the whole factory area for anything that might be useful. The food problem took absolute priority, so the electrical wiring was ripped out of the walls and used to make snares, which then served to catch a lot of meat. Every technological implement, every match, was deposited in a common store and used with great care and economy. It was immediately evident that they would have to invent some way of making fire.

Everything was done that could make their confinement at all bearable. The factory, with its half-completed steel goods, afforded little that was of use, and there was no current to drive the machines. Everyone contributed what knowledge he had. The production system, with its division of labour, had destroyed them as whole men and women; but it was astonishing how much hidden talent lay concealed in every one of them. Former hobbies were put to use for the good of the community. Everything helped, whether it was gardening, carpentry, angling or hunting, for with such a large workforce the span of available talents was wide.

The fight against the most pressing threat, the forest, was such a hard one that to begin with hardly anyone had a chance to try to think things out. But after a week in the jungle it was at any rate clear to all that their stay was of indefinite duration.

One extremely disagreeable fact soon became apparent: both works and office block were showing hairline cracks. It appeared that the forest soil was giving way under the unaccustomed load of the building and, above all, that of the machinery. It was only a matter of time before the whole concrete structure collapsed.

Schmitz-Feller and Schellenschmitt were the last to move out of the office block. Their particular talents had for some time been lying fallow. There was no one left to take orders from them; everyone worked both willingly and out of necessity, for his own sake and for that of the others. It was decided at this stage that generosity was an undue extravagance, and that from now on nobody would eat who did not go out to work.

In a month the village was built. The forest had been cleared near the factory, the trunks had been painfully felled and the creepers, which were already growing up against the windows, chopped up for firewood. There was even a sort of street: it was about two hundred metres long, and on rest days, for fun, they would hold a triumphal procession into the village with the forklift truck that had been parked in the back courtyard.

There was no room for satisfaction at the way things were going, but in the circumstances they were grateful for whatever could be done. Naturally they longed for another world which seemed a million years away, and for all the man-made amenities that civilisation had afforded. Nevertheless, the more perceptive among them were aware that in this world, in which the steamy jungle forced them to stick together, a new quality of life had been created.

Lansky, who was Schaefer's right-hand man, put it this way: "Here we're all equal, and inflated ideas of your own importance don't last long under pressure. Look at our managing director. Since he stopped being able to order anyone about, he's had to pitch in along with everyone else."

"But of course," Schaefer put in, "he still expects someone else to end up with callouses on his hands. He's not going to forget how good it was before."

"We must keep him hard at it," Lansky went on, "him and anyone else who thinks the same way. Everyone is equal; that's definite. We produce enough for everyone – food, clothes, living space and so on. But we aren't producing enough for anyone to cut himself an extra slice. And as long as this goes on there's no reason for anyone to set himself above anyone else. I'm not saying our production level is a good one. Of course it would be better if the work wasn't so tough and we had a bit to spare. We've got a long way to go before that, but we're putting everything we know into it."

Their thoughts went back to the comfortable standard of life they had enjoyed before. The torches flickered in their eyes, and they dreamed of a good bed, a snow-white bathtub, a television set, a car, and so many things, that they felt they had been plunged from paradise into hell.

Nevertheless, no one had had the idea of suicide; no one had complained of loneliness; no one drank to drown the frustrations of the day; their backs were straight, not bent – at least as far as self-respect was concerned.

One of them said it for everyone: "Our solidarity and the

old standard of living . . . why wasn't it like that in the old world?"

"This factory," said Schaefer. "It didn't belong to us."

And no one argued with him. In their world there was no police, no security men, no production surplus to make men greedy; and Schmitz-Feller *did* have callouses on his hands.

The factory had had more female workers than male; low-paid jobs set aside for women made for bigger profits. And so the question of morality arose in the jungle village. There was no problem for the few married couples present. But they and all the others were faced by an indefinite stay, and it seemed to stretch further into the future with every passing day. The one clear principle of life was the maintenance of the species. The old morality had come with them into the jungle; it could hardly have been otherwise. But it crumbled away of its own accord; not because the workers were immoral, but because the foundations of the old morality had disappeared.

Everyone was now equally rich and equally poor, so inheritance was meaningless. And the question of which man had begotten any given child also lost its meaning. But, as there were no means of contraception, and maternity was the only fact that could be established beyond doubt – and because it remained necessary to avoid inbreeding and the birth of imbecile children – there emerged the idea of a society, structured on matrilinear lines, which was divided into two halves, each of which expelled its own male children and took in the male children of the other group; the system underwent further refinements. The emancipation of women in accordance with their contribution to the work of the group, took place of its own accord. At first this new social structure was visible only in outline but everyone knew that the future lay in the children.

Olbrich, who had some scientific knowledge, had come up with the following explanation of their situation. The universe forms a closed space-time complex; a power inherent in the universe had opened up a crack somewhere, perhaps a shift in a gravitational field. Be that as it might, along the edge which was still visible, after six months, as a clean break between jungle and factory yard, the space-time structure had opened and let them slip through into another age or onto another planet. Both ideas had a certain plausibility, for they had not come across another human being.

Olbrich did not claim to be able to give an exact explanation, but one thing was clear to him: if the timeslip were visualised as a fold in a tablecloth – a tablecloth, his hearers thought, how far away that all seems! – then the possibility existed that one day someone or something, some latent pent-up force, would pull the cloth at both ends and smooth it out. It was not long before everyone was familiar with this hypothesis and, for want of a better one, it was accepted. In any case people were soon busy with the first jungle-born children.

Herr Schmitz-Feller had been through a highly disagreeable process of re-education. In formal terms he had lost his status; in concrete terms he had lost his power. In that other world he had been called a successful man, because he never let himself be dazzled by status but went straight to the hard facts. So the pain he now felt was the direct consequence of enforced abstinence from the activity of ordering other people about.

At the peak of his powers, full of the strength and vitality that gave him domination over other people, he had been plunged into a great, seemingly limitless, dark hole. No one any longer broke out into a cold sweat when he saw Schmitz-Feller. The opium provided by the social structure had evaporated in a single jungle night.

Whenever he lay awake for a few moments before succumbing to the exhaustion of a hard day's labour, his thoughts turned to the wealth that had receded so far away. He thought of his house in the most expensive part of town, his bungalow in Switzerland, his Mercedes, his BMW, his art gallery, his wife, his children, and everything else that belonged to him. As soon as he fell asleep he found himself tormented by a little hunchbacked man in blue overalls who came creeping round the side of his house and hoisted Schmitz-Feller's screaming wife, and the pictures, and the Mercedes, onto his broad back and plodded off with them as if wading through a swamp. The only object of value that Schmitz-Feller still possessed was hidden about his body: a precision watch, with a quartz regulator, which would still be accurate to a second in a hundred years.

Life had settled into a quiet routine by the time a year had passed. Of course no one forgot the anniversary; but as the timeslip had happened in the afternoon, and as no one cared much for formalities – especially as they needed to make the most of the daylight – Schaefer moved the celebration to the evening of the previous day. He made a speech in which he briefly referred to the achievements of the past year but soon passed on to outline a plan to provide the colony in the near future with electric power and an improved heating system. And so the first anniversary was treated not as a day of mourning but as a milestone on the path to a better future.

Schmitz-Feller listened to the speech, but left before the ensuing general discussion began. He went back, as he had not done for a long time, to sleep on the parquet floor of the office building. The next day he did not go to work, and the tension mounted within him as the afternoon drew on. In a hand that was damp with sweat he clutched the quartz watch; second by second, its motion seemed to promise him life. He was obsessed by wild imaginings.

If this is still the old earth, he thought, and we have simply landed in an earlier age, then it's possible that somewhere in the earth's orbit there has been an energy shift which has caused this timeslip, as if the earth had moved for a split second into a time shadow, or into the precise location of a window in time. And if the window is still there, what is there to stop the natural forces involved from producing another slip? If nothing has changed, the earth will pass through the same point exactly one year later.

He felt himself beginning to breathe heavily. His heart was pounding as he looked at his watch. The exact instant of the anniversary came. He sat silently for a moment, shivering, and suddenly it was light outside the windows, the green murk receded, and instantaneously, before his rational mind could grasp the full extent of the change, he was filled with a feeling of happiness which dispelled all the hate, resentment, envy and cunning, the ruthless manoeuvring, the deception, torture and barbarity, of his adult world, and carried him back for a second to his childhood.

He stumbled to his feet, trembling. It was still not clear which way the timeslip had gone this time, or what time he was now in. He looked down through the grimy window-panes, saw the glass-smooth edge, and beyond it the town, with its fields and streets, as if not a second had passed in the last year.

When he had gazed his fill, he cast a glance of weariness and contempt on the filth in which he had been confined for a year, and looked down at the old building and the primitive implements in the yard. He sniffed with some distaste the aroma of the stores piled in his office, and listened with delight to the rushing wind set up by the difference in pressure between the old and new atmospheres.

From one corner of the yard came the sound of pandemonium. A few men and women had been caught there by the timeslip. When they realised what had happened, they looked in vain for the jungle and their village, and fell into each other's arms with cries of joy. It was some time before they tired and fell silent, saddened by the thought that most of their companions were still living in the past.

The area was sealed off. An ambulance took Herr Schmitz-Feller and the other survivors of the catastrophe to hospital. Schmitz-Feller soon recovered, and it was he, as the person in authority, who was asked to give an account of what had happened. He embellished his tale with details for the press, who hung on his every word . . .

After four weeks in hospital and a lengthy convalescence in Switzerland, Schmitz-Feller was himself again. He sent for his wife and children, and made up for lost time; it was not long before all his old energy and spirit returned.

In the scientific world, the incident was the greatest sensation since the Siberian meteor. Experts crowded in from all parts of the globe, tapped on the glassy edge, measured the fields of force and the tensions involved, collected every relic of the distant past, living or dead, and subjected the survivors to tests and questionnaires to extract from them every last mite of information. An American team was soon fitting out an expedition in readiness for the next anniversary.

Shortly afterwards a court hearing was held to deal with the question of the property now lost in the past, and of the factory site, which had suffered such evident material damage. Schmitz-Feller gave evidence. He established beyond doubt what had happened to the equipment. He made it clear that the workers had not been in any doubt as to his title to act as representative of the lawful property interests involved. He testified to the powers exercised by the committee. Unfortunately, Schaefer, Lansky and the others were still in the past.

In their defence, counsel sought to establish the existence of an emergency to which normal rules of law were not applicable, but succeeded only in eliminating one charge, that of unlawful deprivation of liberty in respect of Schmitz-Feller, Schellenschmitt and the rest. Schaefer, Lansky and the other members of the committee, as the ringleaders, were convicted in their absence. The whole workforce was made collectively responsible for paying compensation to the owners.

On the second anniversary of the timeslip, not entirely unexpectedly, the rest of the workers returned (while the American expedition simultaneously went over into the past). When the workers were informed of the court's decisions there was a spontaneous demonstration of protest which was forcibly suppressed. Then there were paternity suits to assign responsibility for the maintenance of the illegitimate children that had been born. The factory was rebuilt on another site, and naturally very few of the former employees were re-engaged. Many of the workers who had returned from the past were put on political files as trouble-makers; they had difficulty in finding work.

Translated by David Britt
Original title: *Der Riss in der Zeit*

High tide

ELISABETH VONARBURG

They are trying to tell him something. They . . . it? Aärne is never quite certain what to call them. His dream ends and he calmly notices the multicoloured cloud of confetti hovering close to the window where the sun rises; as soon as he puts the light on, the olfits rush towards the bedside lamp.

On Mathi, that's how they call all the animals who change their colouring for protection. But the swarms don't change colour, they just arrange themselves into different patterns; and it's not for fear of anything. But the adults don't want to know that; they call them "olfits" and think it's sufficient. Even Tarinu, the Head Scientist, had shrugged his shoulders: "Communication by way of colours? With whom? Exchanges within swarms are not operated visually, olfits use ultra-sounds. Anyway, inside the swarm there is no need for it: the whole swarm *is* the 'olfit', a collective form of being." Aärne had wisely refrained from taking the matter any further; Kendu doesn't like him asking Tarinu questions.

And if ever Kendu saw this swarm . . . How did they get in, anyway? The thing is, they are here. Aärne sits up on his bed, switches the lamp off. The swarm hesitates; part of it stays close to the still-warm bulb, the other mass idly floats up towards the window pane gently suspended in the sun rays. Some linger a short moment over Aärne's hands and face, like tiny beaks pecking, imperceptible caress of minute ever-moving wings ("beaks", "wings"! no one even knows if they really are birds . . .). Then, the small coloured dots join up with the rest of the swarm vibrating by the window, motionless patterns of pleasure (blue volutes wandering among the red and yellow colours scattered throughout in regular blotches, green, black and purple all around, like a crown). They intercept the shafts of light from the sun and the room fills up with a marine glow, like an underwater treasure cave, an aquarium with magical reflections. Äärne sighs: maybe, if he had only managed to sleep longer . . . He had almost understood the message: some advice, a warning. But the sun had risen, the swarm had turned round towards the light and all form of contact ceased during the day. At night, Äärne becomes so deeply aware of the invisible presence, every time a swarm of olfits succeeds in penetrating the closely guarded houses, attracted by human warmth, like this past night.

"What the hell is THAT!" Mandura shrieks with disgust. Äärne rises, starts dressing without even glancing at his mother. She's bound to think he let them in . . .

"If only your father saw this!"

She feverishly wipes the window with an old rag: the peaceful pattern disappears one moment then resumes its original shape. Mandura makes disapproving sounds. "Go away, go away," frantically wishes Äärne, "before she gets the vibragun." But the swarm remains motionless, lost in ecstasy while facing the sun.

"You only have to open the window." Äärne has no real hope of being heard, but his mother just shrugs and does in fact do so. The multicoloured cloud slowly drifts out, orbits a while in the light then fades higher up, nearer to the nourishing warmth.

At the breakfast table. Kendu sits with a worried frown. Äärne wishes he could become invisible. His father's eyes are almost scarlet with anger. Could Mandura have told him? She never usually does. At any rate, Kendu seems in no mood to listen to anything; he mutters indistinctly that there are once more weeds in the tafa fields. Äärne sips his drink with an unhappy face: another rotten day by the looks of it, pulling harmless strands of grass out, just to provide those silly tafa stalks with more room to grow . . . As if there wasn't enough space for all of them! It's just like the olfits: they don't bother anyone, and they're so damn pretty. But when Mandura had woken up the other night to find a swarm over her face, she had screamed as if they were some form of venomous beast . . . You can't even feel them when you are sleeping: they're just harmless, endlessly searching for some sort of warmth. Adults are strange.

Aärne finishes his breakfast, slips out of his chair and walks out. He wrinkles his nose when he sees the large green and brown circle delineating the colony's territory: the smell of manure is very strong outside. Dark, leaning shapes are already busy among the tafa stalks – how can plants grow in the midst of such a stench? True, they have no nose and their roots are fond of manure, or so they say . . . Our own plants, it's understandable, they're used to those conditions, but what about the planet's own flora? They must also enjoy these circumstances: a thin yellow mist covers the ground between the tafa stalks. Yellow grass, how odd! All around the colony, all the way to the nearby ocean, the hills are sparkling, orangey yellow, a skin of grass constantly on the move around the small circular trees and the red boulders. The colony is just plain ugly, a nasty piece of work what with its tin-plate box-like buildings, its fields and rigorously geometrical prairies ending sharply at the Perimeter. Mathinë 20: "New-Mathi 20". How pretentious it was to have called this small expanse of ground "New-Mathi"! Kendu had pointed at the whole landscape, the ocean in front, the hills and the rocky plateau, and beyond it all the new planet, with its six seas and five continents:

"For your children, Aärne, this will become Mathinë, and so it will be for the children of your children!" he had said.

But, in his soul, Aärne only thinks of the colony in this manner; he just cannot bring himself to extend to the whole planet such an old and cherished name. Anyway, it's too difficult to picture it all, despite the big maps that hang in Tarinu's office. Should one be allowed to grant names in such a unilateral fashion? Maybe the planet doesn't approve and already has its own name! Or it might prefer the one its previous, unknown inhabitants had provided it with.

Morning passes slowly in the field where Aärne's family is working. Then the afternoon comes following meal time. It's heartbreaking, the little yellow shoots are everywhere, growing anew, happy to have found somewhere to nest amongst all this nice and nourishing soil.

"Do they harm the tafa?"

"Work, Aärne, and be quiet," says Mandura.

"But why do we have to pull them out if they do no harm?"

"We've told you countless times, Aärne," answers Mandura's patient voice, rising over Kendu's grumbling, "the grass eats away the tafa's food."

"Isn't there enough for all?"

"You can't allow weeds to grow," his older brother sententiously says, aping the adults. "You don't know where they'd stop."

"But, after all, they belong here!"

"WE belong here!" Kendu roars, eyes popping. "Do understand that, Aärne." He angrily pulls out another clump of grass and stuffs it into his bag. "And where we live, the only things to grow will be what we want to grow there: OUR plants!"

They do belong here, Aärne wilfully keeps on thinking. It's not because they've burned the soil, dug it up and sterilised it that this place automatically becomes "Mathinë". Native plants keep on growing and strange animals still roam about. Could there be a need for a real barrier, maybe?

"So they have no right to grow, then?"

Furious, Kendu straightens up.

"Mandura, your son!" He raises his arms to the sky. "You win, Aärne. Go home at once, I'll deal with you later."

Why does he get angry so easily? Maybe because of the yellow grass or because the unicorns trampled all over a teret field yesterday? Aärne slowly sets his bag down. Another good thrashing by the looks of it and double weeding duties tomorrow. And a sermon. He doesn't know what is worse: the beating and the work are not that bad, really. But Aärne dislikes it intensely when his father admonishes him on the subject of the Colony's Sacred Mission, the Mathaü ideal, the Oath of Remembrance to the Mother Planet . . . Aärne does not understand all these lofty words. Anyway, he can recognise when someone is just reading out some speech memorised by heart; at times like this, he really thinks his father doesn't himself fully understand what he's ranting on about. There are no answers to his questions: why grow plants brought over from Mathigovar, themselves transported over from Mathivar, and before that Mathi, when there are already plants on the new planet.

They're all plants, aren't they?

It's usually at this stage of the argument that Kendu loses his cool: "But they're not OUR plants or OUR animals! We are from Mathi, and Mathinë must resemble Mathi, and Mathivar, and Mathigovar!" Which is when Aärne keeps on asking "Why?" and Kendu slaps him. But it ain't logical: if we're from Mathi and Mathi is that important, we should have stayed there, not ventured out to Mathivar or Mathigovar or . . . what's its name, the planet of the ölfits, yellow grass and unicorns.

Tarinu provides other answers and always remains calm. But Aärne's curiosity is far from satisfied.

"On the other planets, at the outset of the Dispersion, whole colonies were destroyed because they allowed plants and alien animals to invade them. This is why an elaborate colonisation process has been established, which overlooks nothing. It's very important, Aärne. When the colonists arrive from Mathigovar, they will have no surprises, they will be able to eat, sleep and walk around with no danger to themselves. And if we return to Mathigovar, Mathivar or even Mathi, we shall also find them familiar. It is important that we Mathaü remain the same from one end of the galaxy to the other: that way we shall always understand each other. Would you want us to eat or live differently and forget that we are Mathaü? It once happened, right at the beginning, on the Lost Colony, and there was a war, many dead, a lot of unhappiness . . ."

But if Tarinu is so certain of his facts, he really is no more helpful than Kendu. Why not be different? Why always do the same things? It's not because there was a disaster once that there will necessarily be one again. And what would have happened here, if the original inhabitants had not died long ago?

Aärne reaches the house, hesitates one moment, then walks round it and reaches for the hills. After all, if he is to be punished, it might as well be for a good reason.

He crosses the quiet green meadows where the statutory animals are grazing and reaches the Perimeter's rim, a wide band of naked soil where nothing grows, the poisoned earth which functions as a barrier – not a very efficient one, in fact – against the rest of the planet. Aärne looks around him: no one, they are all working in the fields. He swiftly crosses the area of dead soil, anguish as usual forming knots in his stomach. What if the earth were suddenly to open and giant hands reach out to grab him? But once again nothing happens, and Aärne continues towards the hills, wading through the knee-high yellow grass. Clouds of insects and birds flutter on his passage, small animals furtively flee with their noses to the ground. All the invisible life surrounding the colony whistles, clicks, jumps, crawls and flies! Tarinu had one day said: "We're fighting a merciless war." With all the relentless swarming around him, Aärne now understands what the Head Scientist had meant. But was it not also a hopeless form of war? Could the Colony really win?

Still, the Colony was spreading steadily. The circle of black earth was wider than ever, new fields were beginning to encroach on the fire-cleansed, machine-beaten and poison-scoured areas. (How could poisons be "good"? "Good for our plants, bad for the others," Tarinu had answered; so even poisons have friends and enemies?)

"One day, all the circles will meet, and Mathinë will truly be Mathinë again," Tarinu had also said, his eyes damp with emotion.

It's true, there are other colonies, other alien circles across the planet. The map where Kendu charts the progress of the colonisation process is very much like that of an illness . . .

Aärne stops between the first two hills. He always stops here. The colony with all its noises and smells has now disappeared when the wind blows the right way, like today. There is only the yellow grass and the curving boulders shining like red glass: one might feel lost. It's forbidden to leave the Perimeter, but Aärne nevertheless does so: here, things are beautiful and clean. It is his own domain. Here are his paths, his landmarks, his rites (climbing the big armchair-like boulder, jumping three times and falling to the bottom, rolling down all the way, then crawling the distance between the armchair-boulder and the tractor-boulder, because one day the beast had been lurking there and ever since Aärne had been secretly hoping to surprise it again). Then he climbs the second hill and, on the third hill, there it is, high up: the town. Left in ruins, grass and trees almost covering it all, walls fallen down, maybe it had only been a village, but for Aärne, anything made of stone is a *town.* In the centre of the town, rallying-point of all his past escapades, stands the lampadary: sleek, round at the bottom, pointed at the top, with a luminous sphere set across the top. Äärne still remembers the day when the sphere had lit up. He was very small then, but the colony had hastily been evacuated and he had lost his gimmi in the ensuing panic. Later, they had all returned; the "Pylons", as the adults called them, were not dangerous. They were scattered all across the planet, and they had all began to glow at the same moment. When Äärne had later asked him something about them, Kendu had mumbled indistinctly and provided no satisfactory answer. The spheres had lit when the Mathaü had already been on the planet a long time and were settling in sufficient numbers. They were machines erected by the previous inhabitants . . . But from the way his questions were being answered, Äärne realised that very little indeed was known about the "Pylons". How, then, could they really know the things were not dangerous?

Äärne enjoys the town; it's his own. He has never brought anyone here, not even Tolithë, the neighbours' daughter. Even if they were to accept a bond of secrecy, the other children would not dare disobey their elders and follow Äärne beyond the Perimeter. They are scared. But it's so quiet in the town: water still streams out of the fountains near the lampadary, flowing sweetly down and, sometimes, when he remains quite still, animals come and drink; they are not afraid of him.

He sits, his back against the lampadary. It feels soft, vibrates imperceptibly. Looking upwards, he sees the sphere right above him, a miniature sun that doesn't shine. Probably doesn't even generate enough warmth, as the olfits never seem to settle on it, they just fly around. There's always a swarm or two in this town full of heartflowers. Which the olfits adore. Or the other way round, the relationship has never been very clear in Äärne's mind. He once saw olfits emerge alive from the open corollae; another time, he discovered several of the small birds lying inert and discoloured at the foot of the flowers. Later, new flowers had began growing on the very same spot.

A large cloud obscures the sun. The olfits are flying all around Äärne. He gazes at their changing patterns, feels their presence multiple and unique at the same time, like a tingling inside his skull, an indecipherable chirping . . . He recalls his dream of this morning, a form of tension . . . an appeal. They are trying to tell him something. Maybe, if he closed his eyes . . . Aärne tries to empty himself of thoughts, allows his body to go numb, the sounds of the birds and insects grow more distant. But the sun reappears and the olfits cannot resist its call. They move away towards its warmth. The chirping fades, disappears. He will have to wait for the night.

Towards the end of the afternoon, Aärne slips into the house. The adults are not yet back. Maybe Kendu will have forgotten his earlier anger. In fact, when he returns home, his mind seems to be on other things; Tolithë's father is with him.

"We shall require further men and machines, more weed-killer."

"Mathinë 4 will send us some. They've experienced similar problems. We should have listened to them earlier."

A new clearing of land?

Yes. The men from the colony are fed up, defending their plantations against the indigenous invaders. The ring of dead earth is to be extended further into the hills, so that the unwanted seeds no longer take advantage of the prevalent winds and reach the colony's fields. They will fall on poisoned ground and die. The animals, also, will have to die: an electric barrier is to be devised. If the dead earth doesn't stop them, then the high energy discharges will.

"Are you going to destroy the town?"

Surprised features turn towards Aärne, as do the cold eyes of Kendu.

"And what town is this?"

Aärne bites his lips. Kendu stands up beside him.

"Aärne, you've been out beyond the Perimeter."

It's not even a question and Aärne, resigned, looks down at the floor. He'd almost avoided the earlier punishment, but no chance of that now. A hard, calloused hand seizes his chin.

"Answer."

"Yes . . ." Aärne whispers. His father's eyes have almost gone scarlet; his hand rises.

"But nothing happened!" Aärne can't help himself shouting. Oddly enough, the expected slap doesn't come.

"Aärne," Kendu says, controlling his emotions, "it is FORBIDDEN to venture outside the Perimeter. Anything might happen to you, out there. Anything."

"But nothing did," Aärne keeps on saying, in a muted

voice, his head buried low between his shoulders. Still no slap.

"Children from Mathinë 12 went playing outside the Perimeter: they were trampled by wild animals. Men from Mathinë 27 were devoured by gerits," said Tolithë's father.

"But there are no gerits here; they are all in the mountains."

"There are dangerous animals, poison berries, snakes. And what about the town, think about what the natives might have left there, traps, snares, and god knows what else!"

"You're surely not about to reason with him, are you?" Kendu finally exploded. He grabbed Aärne by the arm: "Listen, if ever you go outside the Perimeter again, you will remember the beating for a hell of a long time, understood?"

The slap finally lands on his cheek, Aärne was no longer expecting it.

"And that's only for starters. Go to bed!"

His head still ringing, Aärne walks to his room. "And how will you ever know if I've been out there?" he thinks, full of anger. He throws himself onto his bed, trying not to cry. If he did cry, it would mean he's sorry and *that* he certainly isn't. He's convinced they're wrong. What good was it coming to this new planet just to remain inside a bloody circle, however large it may be? When would it become possible to walk about freely? When all the plants and the animals are dead? They've no right to do this, they've no right to destroy everything so that Mathinë might slavishly imitate Mathi.

Aärne watches the night fall and deliberately ignores how empty his stomach feels. Despite the pervading smell about, he opens the window to see things better: all the moons are in the sky, the big one full of holes and the three smaller ones; they're moving nearer to each other. For a short moment, Aärne complacently dreams of a cataclysm, but quickly banishes the dream. No, they're only going to pass in front of each other and that'll be it. Darkness will become complete when they all pass in the shadow of Mathinë.

It's such a weird light when all the moons are on parade, yellow, blue, pink, with multiple shadows . . . All of a sudden, one shadow moves faster than the others, the shifting colours whimsically transmute by the light of the moons, a swarm of olfits whirls past the window into the room. What do they want? The tenuous chirping becomes more insistent, the swarm eddies around the furniture, the patterns giddily merge into each other. It must be urgent. It's important. He must . . .

LEAVE THE COLONY, GO TO THE HILLS, CLIMB HIGH, TO THE HIGHEST POINT.

The message makes Aärne feel dizzy. Why climb? What danger where, when? The olfits keep on chirping their message away.

The door opens just as Aärne was about to reach the handle. Kendu stands on the threshold, his surprise immediately changing to anger when he sees the olfits rush through the opening and surge towards the light of the lamp in the common room.

"Father," Aärne says quickly, far from hopeful, "they've told me we have to leave, go into the hills . . ."

The large hand takes hold of him by the skin of his neck, pulling him into the next room.

"So, I should be kinder to him, hey? He brings olfits into our house!"

"They came in by the window," Aärne says in a strangled voice. He must tell them, but they just won't listen. They're going to punish him, or quarrel, but they just will not listen.

"Silence!" Kendu roars. He opens the cupboard, takes out the vibragun and aims it at the swarm now fluttering around the luminous globe transformed into a precious stone. The invisible waves destroy the olfits' delicate cohesion, the cloud of bird-like creatures shatters, the small coloured dots disperse around the room, aimless and lost, fading, becoming grey, drying up, falling like dead leaves towards the floor.

"We must go to the hills," Aärne says, in a final effort. "They've told me. We must leave this place and climb into the hills."

Kendu has put the vibragun away; he now turns towards Aärne, a whip in his hand. Aärne rushes to the door, opens it and disappears sobbing into the night.

He races with all his energy, rushes towards the hills. There are cries behind him, but he does not listen to them. He runs. Here are the meadows and the circle of black earth, blacker than ever in the deepening darkness. Aärne is no longer crying. He knows where he is going. Into the hills. He must get there while there is still enough light. In the town, he knows where to hide; they will not find him.

They are a bit all hesitant at the thought of leaving the Perimeter, they don't know their way around like Aärne. If he had sufficient time, it might be an amusing game to lose them in the boulder area. But the night moons, up there, are still moving towards each other, the big purple one is now only a half of its usual size. Soon, the eclipse. Soon, the night. Here, at last, is the town, the soft and pleasant light of the lampadary.

But a fog cloud of olfits rise from the heartflowers and comes whirling towards Aärne. He stops, dizzy, waves his arms about to frighten the swarm away and quieten the insistent chirping that fills his head. They want to talk, they're telling him something, but it's oh so loud, too loud! Aärne staggers, behind him the sound of steps approaching on the old paving stones, voices moving nearer, hands on his shoulders . . .

Soon, it's night. The shadow has rubbed out the second half of the moon. The olfits move away, brushed aside by the wind rising in the purple light. And, all over the horizon, out there from the ocean, something appears, a thin line, a pool, a tide, a blue tidal wave that shimmers while it surges towards the coastline, engulfs the lights of the colony and comes dying at the feet of the town, a quiet wave still quavering gently.

Translated by Maxim Jakubowski
Original title: *Marée Haute*

I can teleport myself to anywhere

ROBERT SHECKLEY

I can teleport myself to anywhere in the universe. This may seem an enviable ability to those who do not possess it, but I can assure you that it raises more difficulties than it solves. I found this out recently when I decided to make my first real journey as a teleporter. The latent ability had developed in me only a year before that, and I had used it at first rather timidly, and mainly in my own apartment, popping in and out of rooms and scaring my cat so badly that she took off and has never come back. (I was glad to see the last of her. She would never let me stroke her, but always tried to curl up on my face when I was sleeping.) So, one day when I was feeling stale and fed up, I decided I was ready for a big trip and made up my mind to teleport myself to Viridian V for a two weeks' vacation.

A teleporter can get from where he is to where he wants to go in just about zero time, which is considerably faster than the speed of light. It doesn't matter how far he's going, he still gets there as near to instantaneously as our current scientific instruments can measure. That's the speed at which teleportation works. You have no choice in the matter, no option to travel at fifty miles an hour sailing over the housetops like Mary Poppins with her umbrella open. There is a lot of conjecture about the nature of the medium through which teleporters move, but of course no one can slow up to examine it. When you teleport it's just hey, presto, and there you are at your destination.

Most people envy the few of us who have this teleporting ability. They just don't understand the difficulties involved.

All they see is, if a teleporter wants to go to Rome, he doesn't have to bother with an airline; if he wants to go to Mars, he doesn't have to spend six months getting there; if he wants to go to one of the newly discovered planets in the Wolff 32 star group, he doesn't have to be frozen first in order to get there during his lifetime. All the teleporter has to do is say, I want to go *there*, or some similar phraseology, and there he is.

People just don't examine the situation any further than this. They think that's all there is to it.

After I had decided to go to Viridian V, I went about doing the various odds and ends that you have to do when you're leaving town for two weeks, no matter what your means of transportation. But there was no urgency to my preparations. After all, I had no deadline, no spaceship schedule to consider. I could be wherever I wished within a second of when I decided I wanted to be there. So I continued living my usual life and the weeks went by while I continued slowly getting ready for my trip.

After two months of this procrastination I began to despise myself, to tell myself that at the rate I was moving I could have gotten to Viridian *faster* by conventional spaceship. I began to wonder if I really wanted to go at all, despite the fact that I knew that I *did* want to go.

There was a reason for my delaying tactics. I had a dim and unformed suspicion that matters were not going to be as simple and straightforward as I imagined. But I *had* decided to go, and so I set about making myself do it by nagging at myself, taunting myself, daring myself to set a deadline and stick to it. After a week or two of this I finally said, all right, I shall go to Viridian on this coming Friday at noon precisely and we need say no more about it.

Friday morning came, all too soon. I ate a light, nourishing breakfast, exactly as though I were going on a "real" journey, even though the actual travelling part is, for a teleporter, no more than a mental construct, a transition from place to place quicker than the blink of an eye. Nevertheless, I was tense, and this became worse as the time of departure drew near. At eleven-thirty I was pacing up and down the living-room floor, my suitcase in the middle of it (I can teleport anything that I am carrying), smoking too many cigarettes, fidgety as my digital watch flashed off the quick little tenths of seconds.

11:59. I took a deep breath and held it, just as if I were going under water. The final seconds flash by, my face is flushed, I know I'm making too much of the entire business, but now I can't help myself, I'm in the grip of it. Five, four, three, two, one, go!

Suitcase in hand, I teleport to Viridian V, to the resort town of Luu.

First I stand with my eyes tight shut and with my hands over them, as other teleporters have recommended, to accustom myself to the strange feel of the air and the sudden and alarming assault of odors different from those I have known at home. My body shudders with instinctive revulsion. My skin receptors, smell and hearing centers are all reporting to Central Intelligence (me) that something terribly upsetting and scary has happened, something which *they* were never warned about. In vain does Central Intelligence – poor shaking me with my hands over my eyes – try to soothe my startled senses. I have known for months that I was going to take this trip, but my body is oblivious to the past and future, intent always and exclusively on monitoring what is going on now.

After a while things begin to settle down a little. The skin and smell centers are easily satisfied with repeated stimuli, no matter how strange it may be at first. My hearing center needs a while longer, for it wants to make sense out of the alien cacophony that bombards it from all sides. That is the basic job of the hearing center, of course, and crucial for my survival. But in this case Central Intelligence must override that compulsion to separate signal from noise. This is an alien civilisation filled with alien beings speaking alien languages in an environment filled with other alien sounds. It would take years to make the slightest sense out of it, and I am here only for a two weeks' vacation. The hearing center is told sternly that it must regard *all* sounds it hears as mere meaningless noise unless it hears something spoken in English, Spanish, or Galactongue. It soon complies. It is a dreamy part of me, always willing to trance out and accept sound as music and to disregard the hard work of trying to make sense out of the clamorous world.

It is otherwise with my seeing center. My eyes are most truly the organs I rely upon to orient myself in the world, to make sense out of things, to find necessary order. They bring data to Central Intelligence marked vital, data which cannot be ignored.

Unfortunately, Central Intelligence cannot interpret or act upon this important data, because it cannot presently understand it. My eye beholds sights it was not prepared for. (It too is part of my body, concerned only with what falls under its gaze *now.*) Central Intelligence is swamped with important but unmanageable visual signals as I peek through my fingers with partially closed eyes.

It is a chaos of forms and colors out there, so I close them again. The visual center gets a stern lecture from Central Intelligence on exactly what is to be looked for in the environment. For the present, Central Intelligence demands that the eyes confine themselves exclusively to differentiating between moving and stationary objects. More demanding tasks will be asked of them after they accommodate to this one.

Slowly I open my eyes – my unruly eyes which, despite my orders to the contrary, keep on fixing their fascinated gaze on this sight or that, ignoring my basic survival needs in their childlike wonder. I am like a man wandering through a vision too exotic and varied to assimilate, in a state of dreamlike dissociation which refuses to lift.

And this condition never lifts entirely during my two weeks' stay on Viridian. Despite my best efforts, my entire time passes in a state equivalent to hallucination, a blown-out acid trip for all of the first week, easing only when the time to go home draws near.

At the end of the two weeks, cheerfully, gratefully, and without anxiety, I teleport myself back home.

Two shocks await me there.

The first is this: I am standing in my living-room with my suitcase in my hand and no sensory evidence that I have gone anywhere at all. The transition has been so abrupt that I could have dreamed the whole thing in my own bed in my own apartment.

But is it really my own apartment? This is the second shock: my senses refuse to accept this further outrage on their credulity and cry out for the bewildering but now familiar reality that they left behind on Viridian. My body refuses to accept the unreasonable. Even Central Intelligence (also a part of my body, despite its protestations to the contrary) cannot accept this unreasonable transition. It takes the position that *this* is hallucination, that there is no reality, that I am condemned to falling endlessly through a succession of stage settings that dissolve just as I begin to get used to them. This is an intolerable state of affairs for the awareness that directs Central Intelligence. My awareness points out that I cannot afford to be freaked out by appearances. Try to relax, it gently tells Central Intelligence cowering in its newly-found existential horror; we really must take a practical view of this matter and ignore the unthinkable if we ever expect to get some dinner tonight.

After a certain amount of internal haggling, awareness and Central Intelligence come to an agreement: I am to go on with my everyday life and label my experience on Viridian as "disorienting", and "forever inexplicable to one who was a participant in the event or pseudo-event", citing the Heisenberg principle of uncertainty to give myself an intellectual authority for this position.

Central Intelligence accepts that well enough. It is easily satisfied with a chunk of intellectual meat, and it doesn't much care what kind of animal or pseudo-animal it came from. Once the experience has been safely labelled, we file it away and agree not to pursue the subject any further.

Now I stay at home mostly, and when I take a trip I go by conventional means just like everyone else. Life is much better for me in that way, all things considered. I restrict my teleporting to occasional Sunday mornings when I am lying in a snug warm bed, too lazy and sleepy to walk my body all the way to the bathroom.

Heavier than sleep

PHILIPPE CURVAL

François staggered and ferociously held on to the cycle lamp of the night room.

"Good God! I've forgotten to take my tranycte again!"

His eyelids were heavy, oh so heavy, and he could feel his whole body fall backwards at an incredible speed, as if he were made of an infinity of tubes sliding into one another. He was twisting around, reaching an ultimate point where his consciousness had taken refuge, deep within his brain, to avoid dissolving inside the shadowy territory of sleep.

Dizzy, he fell to the ground. The impact awoke him. He forced himself to keep his eyes open and crawled on all fours towards the bathroom, sunk his head inside the bath-tub, hesitantly opened the shower's tap and allowed the stream of icy water to pour over his face.

For a few seconds, François thought his whole cranium was about to fall apart under the jet, like a sugar-loaf, and disappear through the bung-hole. He fought against this feeling of pleasure. React, he must react! The noctiles shimmered around him in the darkness. François could visualise them in his imagination; if he succumbed to sleep, they would impregnate him until a point of saturation where his personality would melt within the vast hypnotic body they formed, which already covered a large part of the planet.

The freshness of the water allowed him to sustain the fight. Soon, he was able to focus on the taps which no longer went on resembling large copper atoms whirling in the obscurity. He stood up, still feeling weak, opened the medicine chest, dropped two capsules of tranycte into his palm and swallowed them with one gulp. He then passed on into the kitchen, switched on the coffee machine and connected the toaster. A few minutes later, he was devouring his most hearty breakfast ever since the days of his childhood. Security. In his haste, he spread a large thickness of chutney by mistake onto the buttered slice of bread. The violent impact of the spices was a final factor in the total return of his lucidity. The tranycte then spread a holy form of euphoria all the way through to the furthest reaches of his body. This was living! Such a pity it was enhanced by a drug.

François put his hand to his chin, catching the bone between two fingers and pressing until it began to hurt. He had not yet reached the other side of the night.

By why in hell had he once again forgotten to take his protective tablets? This was the second, no, the third time such a misadventure had occurred, if not more. It wasn't even as if he didn't have time to think about it, all day long in fact, as he had now not slept for three years, ever since the noctiles had invaded Earth and the pharmaceutical laboratories had succeded in synthesising tranycte to combat their insidious action. Anyway, the product had a salutary effect: not only did it disconnect the sleep centre and stimulate the vigil lobe, but it also purged the organism of all toxins, acting like a true chimney-sweeper of the cells. François didn't understand. Or did not wish to understand. Not yet.

"Ten o'clock" sang the cycle lamp. Late! No need to hurry, then. François carefully put away all the items he had gathered on the bed to pass the long time of night, the books, the films, the sweets, the masturbator. He was an orderly bachelor.

A quarter of an hour later, he was at the office.

"Third warning, Dutourd. Next time, you've had it. Thirty per cent cut in salary," quietly said Charlier, his immediate superior.

"Yes sir, thank you sir," François answered, with a thin smile on his lips.

Oddly enough, he felt calm. He moved on, brushing close to the walls, under the disapproving eyes of Charlier.

"Hello Jeannine!" he shouted excitedly.

His secretary gave him a dull glance and asked him to close the door because of the draughts.

"So, you're in a bad mood today? Couldn't get here before, had a prior appointment with the Turbomeca people. Anybody ring?"

Jeannine made no comment, got up and dropped the list of phone calls on his desk. He could smell the discreet odour of the perfume his secretary used, and, sitting in his armchair, watched her: two superb breasts quivered above him inside the pink angora pullover. Jeannine had an ungrateful face, but her body was beyond reproach. Even if it remained on his mind longer than necessary.

Turbomeca had called. What bad luck! François clumsily dialled their number.

"Hello, Dutourd here, is Lundwall available?"

Switchboard noises, a few clicks and catches, a ring, François repeated his name.

"Oh, it's you, Dutourd, thanks ever so much for keeping me waiting! As far as the order for the six machines is concerned, it's all settled. I've asked your competitors to supply them."

"The Mining Centre?"

"Indeed," Lundwall laughed. "Good luck, old man."

And hung up. One more mistake like that and François would get the sack. The euphoria caused by the tranycte was sharply fading. He looked at the wall facing him: an ugly advertising poster for a fifty-ton press appeared to mock him. Shining beams seemed to be smiling away with all their teeth. He almost asked Jeannine to get rid of the poster. She was typing. Her sullen features discouraged him from asking. He had so many letters to dictate, all urgent answers.

"Jeannine?"

"Sir?"

"Is what you're typing urgent?"

She kept on banging on the keyboard while gazing up at him.

"Okay; we'll see about it this afternoon."

"No, not this afternoon, sir; can't you remember you signed the form for my housemother holiday."

Searching for an appropriate answer, François began rummaging in his drawer. Tired, he took out some writing paper so that he might draft the letters by hand.

The canteen's signal woke him from the contented torpor the letter writing had plunged him into. François rose. Jeannine was powdering her face; her figure was all warm, tempting, he couldn't resist, he approached her and gently caressed the downy shoulder-blade of his secretary.

"See you tomorrow, my dear. I know Louise and Jean Marie will be so happy to spend the day with their mother."

François would never know whether her dear offspring really appreciated the tea and the chocolate cakes. He was convinced however, that Jeannine truly thought of him as a dirty old man.

The food from the company's canteen was as dull as usual and the rest of the day continued as it had begun, under an unlucky sign. At six o'clock, it was over. Why all this? How was it possible to keep on living in such a shamefully traditional way when the noctiles were all around, slowly capturing more and more minds, nestling within the world of sleep and reproducing there?

The answer was obvious. François could read it in the eyes of his office colleagues travelling down with him in the lift, towards the therapeutic ward. Because they had not yet been deprived of their share of dreams.

Charlier was there, they were all there, even Jeannine who had returned from the walk with her kids. Although attendance in the therapeutic ward was not compulsory, it had become necessary in order to survive.

"So, Dutourd," Charlier joked, "going to kill me today?"

François gave him a cold stare. He would have liked to answer yes, but he could not. He steered the conversation on to a lighter subject.

"That's never been on my mind, sir, but tonight, however, I wouldn't mind shafting Jeannine; been thinking of it so long!"

Charlier smiled at him and showed him the way to the therapeutic ward, grinning like an accomplice.

The relaxation armchairs weren't as clean as they had been, three years before, when they had first been installed. However, they were still as comfortable. Sighing gently, François lay down. He was one of the first to settle in. Which gave him a good chance of a closer look at the others around him. They all seemed so unconcerned, these brainless colleagues of his who were now about to accomplish their most important social duty since the noctiles had invaded the planet, a ritual of exorcism like in the good old tribal days.

The managing director got up on the stage. He coughed quite deliberately as if he were about to improvise a speech, although they all knew exactly what he was about to say.

"Ladies, gentlemen, dear friends, the legal duration of the therapeutic session today will be of two hours and forty-six minutes. All I can say is: have enjoyable dreams."

He nodded and the light slowly dimmed, turning to blue. The dream stimulators moved into action. François barely had time to fasten his anti-sleepwalking belt on before he was taking off, senses still awake. Every time, he both feared and looked forward to this curious sensation of being overtaken by his subconscious, like an aerolite in full flight, being taken in tow by madness . . .

"Ah, Dutourd, late again," said Charlier, "come and lick my feet, Now, down, down!"

François unsheathed his knife and rushed towards the old bastard.

"Get off my fucking back, will you!"

But Charlier had disappeared long before he reached him. In his place stood a hippopotamus, clad in suit and tie, crying out loudly.

"That's not nice of you, Dutourd, you never get here on time. I was going to buy you a lollipop press."

Shit! It was all happening again, he was dreaming of the office! François looked around him: they all had their eyes closed. He knew they were not sleeping, tranycte prevented that. They were just concentrating hard and enjoying the full two hours and forty-six minutes of dream-like allocation the government bestowed upon them. It was not only legal, but vital, to preserve the mental health of the citizens. This was what mankind had devised in order to survive at all cost. But why dream together? Every time, the world of the office sucked François in, the way a dragon devours a chimera. He wanted to dream alone, in his own home, to pursue his domestic fantasies.

The arrival of Jeannine, completely naked, caught his attention. The dream stimulators were now functioning in top gear and the shock images drawn out by his own subconscious, still traumatised by a hard day's work, invaded his thought, as a cloud of ink spreads in water . . .

Her buttocks were remarkably curved. Jeannine, and her breasts were like the engines of a plane. Unfortunately, her nose had grown awfully and now resembled a penis. François' own member stiffened. He started running towards Jeannine; with every step, his penis flapped against his stomach. When he was just a few inches away from her, he stopped and gazed closely at her to see what sort of feelings he was arousing: neither desire nor repulsion, just indifference. He felt his backside blush, as if it were equipped with electrical sensors set into action by this close a contact. But, when he tried to touch his secretary, when his penis met her roundish belly, her nose began deflating, retracting, shrinking until it was once again a small cheeky appendage. At the same time, operated by remote control by this retractile phenomenon, François' penis reacted in a similar way and, reducing itself beyond the average size, ended up by disappearing completely, invaginating itself.

"You're really no good at anything, my poor Dutourd," said Jeannine, pitiless. "Come, get on your knees. I have a lot of letters to type."

François meekly complied. His secretary straddled him and began frenetically manipulating the keyboard she had implanted in his cranial box. All of a sudden, he became a faithful typewriter and copied the text he was being fed with:

"Further to your esteemed letter of 17th January last, I must regretfully advise you that the order you are referring to will not be delivered within the dates requested. The noctiles now control most of the Chilean territory and the copper mines are no longer accessible . . ."

François made a savage and concerted effort to escape the dream. The sight of the therapeutic ward was of great help to him: here they were, all his office colleagues, in voluntary hibernation, no longer capable of infiltrating his own dream-life. He watched Jeannine, now smiling blissfully, a few yards away from him. Maybe she had arranged it all, changed the course of his dream and made a nightmare of it. This was the sheer horror of these communal sessions, you couldn't follow your dreams to the very end, the others had the power to intervene when they felt concerned. Every time François wished to embark for Cythera, someone mucked around with his script. Never, since the beginnings of society, had there been such constraints upon its individual members! This interpenetration of dreams by all and sundry was an insult to liberty. But there was no way to avoid it. Even a millionaire could not afford an individual stimulator: manufacturing secrets were closely guarded by the State and the police took care to prevent any leaks.

The resistance of mankind to the noctiles had created a perfect form of dictatorship. No one could any longer refuse to acknowledge the pressures of society. Farewell to the private gardens of dreamland!

Although it was still possible, as François was now doing, to escape the great dream feast for a few moments, to side-step the collective unconscious, the influence of the stimulators was too strong for this to last. Anyway, it was dangerous, very dangerous in fact, because these rare moments of lucidity deprived him of part of his aggression-release quota. François soon faded into a particularly painful episode where ceaseless telephone calls were transformed into unending jets of ketchup sauce or mustard, reminding him of his business failures of the last few months. Fortunately, the session came to an end.

"Those who wish to attend the open forum can remain seated," said the managing director. "The therapeutic session is now ended. Good night. And do not forget to take your dose of tranycte before going to sleep!" he added, as if it was all a big joke which he repeated night after night.

Deliberately jostling Charlier, who was heading in his direction to discuss this morning's incident, François ran towards the exit. He needed some fresh air. In the street, he stopped and took a deep breath. Raindrops fell on his tongue. He looked at the clouds darkening the sky: a hell of a storm on the way! It was soon raining so hard he felt he was trapped inside a damp ball of cotton-wool. François decided to walk home. To have a wash!

Some months earlier, he would have stayed on for the open forum. Most of his colleagues did. Talking about their respective dreams, they had the impression of settling the day's scores. Now, François was no longer capable of accepting the mental strain.

He stopped, leaned against the clean wall of a plastic building, protected from the rain by a stainless-steel ledge. In front of him, the monotonous curtain of the rain, lit by the multicoloured letters of the signboards, obscured his vision of the street. The lighted windows of a tower-block were like the frames of a future hive where the bees had installed electricity. In the darkness separating two concrete buildings, the noctiles whirled about, minute micro-organisms, dust of the night. François had a sudden revelation: his fate was shared between two equally fearsome menaces. On one hand, a society in a state of war had claimed the right to control your dreams while pretending to defend you. On the other hand, the noctiles were looking out for any fleeting moment of weakness to take possession of your mind.

François felt himself somehow becoming a member of the Resistance; he was at last emerging from the air-conditioned nightmare. And he was aware of a solution: he must dream on his own. In which case, why not hide in a dark corner of the therapeutic ward after all the others had departed and set the stimulators himself? The idea was so obvious, so incredible, he couldn't help wondering why no one had thought of it before. Unless . . . The crowd was always too fond of being a crowd and marginal ideas had never been welcome!

The open forum was still going on. François slipped into the toilets, near the therapeutic ward. He had remembered a small overhung nook, thirty centimetres in depth, where the water and electricity pipes were lodged. He climbed up, knelt and waited for the session to end.

Some of his colleagues walked into the toilets.

"I think Charlier is a swell guy, his murder score is well on the way down. When I joined the outfit, two years ago, he was being killed off two or three times every session; now, it's just an occasional stabbing here and there every week."

"It's like rapes. I remember, every damn night. I would catch one or two broads in a corridor and fuck them to death. These days . . ."

The rest of the conversation faded out as they walked away.

François waited until he was certain of being alone and jumped off his roost. The security headlights bathed the therapeutic ward in a pink glow. He climbed down the short spiral staircase leading to the stimulation room. It was all so simple, unbelievably so, even the diagram describing how to set up the equipment was in thick easy-to-read letters. Basically, all you had to do was press down a solitary lever and the dream field would be switched on. François was, all of a sudden, scared. He didn't know why, but he was shivering. It lasted a few minutes, then his own private rebellion gained the upper hand. He set up the mechanism and went to sit down, alone, in the ward.

Still tense, he stretched out and closed his eyes to relax.

Soon, the dream assaulted him: he was at home, in his own night room.

Bliss! At last an original, individual dream stimulation, with no one around to interfere with his script. In fact, there wasn't even a script; he was content in his own flat and enjoyed being alone, for the first time in months. The cycle lamp called out the passing hours. He soon laid himself out on his rest bed, after gathering all the usual gadgets around him. The dream was soft, warm, smooth; François felt at ease within it, it was a dream of a past time, like before the arrival of the noctiles, a dream of fearless nights. Would he dare? He was after all under the influence of the stimulation and could interrupt it at any time. Yes, he could dream he was falling asleep, for the first time in three years. The most beautiful, forbidden dream he could ever experience.

François closed his eyes and sleep came, as fast as lightning. He tasted it with a happy kind of grief. A few seconds later, he was sleeping and no one, ever, would prove capable of awakening him.

Charlier switched the stimulators off and whispered: "Poor Dutourd, maybe it was the best thing, after all."

He approached closer and gazed at the waxen body of François, forever set in sleep. He was now part of another vast living body, that of the noctiles.

Today, more than ever, you had to choose which side you fought on, the society of humans or the society of dream.

Translated by Maxim Jakubowski
Original title: *Plus Lourd Que le Sommeil*

An avocado pear for Dolorès

ADAM BARNETT-FOSTER

The year I landed on Nova Polska, they were rebuilding the Emperor Maximilian's Palace of Bubonic Dreams. The famous tourist attraction had been pretty well destroyed a decade earlier by freak space-storms, shortly after Max's death in a star-skirmish with the massive Kerensky fleet.

It was a very bad year in the music business.

Coming straight from a two-year residency in the Asteroid Belt entertainment worlds, wandering into the dull streets of the grey cities of Nova Polska was almost like emerging from a time machine five or six years into your own past. Anonymous monuments littered the labyrinthine causeways and arteries of the stark metropolis, pinning the city down with a pervading atmosphere of gloom and rampaging desolation. Decrepit yellow and brown rusting tramways ambled through the streets in a most ramshackle manner, softly orbiting through the geometrical maze of the urban complex.

There was something quaint and delightfully old-fashioned about Nova Polska; men still deferentially kissed women's hands upon meeting them, wore carnations on their jacket lapels, and wolf-whistling was, here, a sign of delicacy and flattery. Some colony worlds just didn't grow up!

A very marked change after the jostling informality and coarse roughness of Barfos Centauri.

Walking out of the local spaceport after clearing customs and immigration with no undue complication, I hailed a hovercab and went to the cultural cartel where I had been given a good introduction by Ezra, my old tuning master from Aldebaran.

Coasting bumpily through the air currents and wide-swinging ramps of the dual-access freeway in the unmanned vehicle, I soon left the grey city behind me and reached the Pleasure Zone shortly before dark. The uneventful ride had taken barely an hour.

Here was the true centre of the city, as far as I was concerned. Where the arts are, my heart rejoices! The Pico Arcade stood proudly, with its central well of cast-iron balconies, titanium stair wells and open elevators, a shimmering relic of early colonial architecture that had no peers throughout the Galaxy. But, like so much else on Nova Polska, it towered as an unintegrated fragment in a confused scene that had slowly begun to disintegrate long ago. Most of the downtown areas were falling into a kind of desuetude and the local planetary authorities were only making the occasional token and irrelevant attempt to revitalise this once flowering area.

Being here was no choice of mine; I had barely managed to scrape the fare together to make my way to old Nova Polska and was now flat broke. Ten credits to my name, not even enough for a meagre souped-up dream pill. To journey further down the Great Ways, in search of another star, another note, a bit of hope, I had to find a job very soon. In other words, now. Space travel ain't cheap, whoever says that sure is a phony in my books.

I ventured into the debris-strewn grounds of the Arcade, walking through the faded simulacra portal, and closed my eyes for a moment.

Inside the curved dome, the spread-out internal landscape of the place was stupendous. I was an early arrival and the area was still almost empty. On Nova Polska, people rise late.

A gentle gush of subtly scented breeze from the conditioning system swept down over the brownish slopes of the circus, carrying a faint smell of cinnamon bark towards my nostrils. Down in the centre of the arena, two unfinished railway tracks met like opposing arrows, decorative, archaic, but useless.

Venturing deeper into the major Pleasure Zone, I soon came across the meandering zigzag patterns of the feeding roads connecting the perimeter with the internal hive where most activities took place. Multicoloured cans and eerie swinging pods hung from the revolving ceilings while timid tufts of grass (could it be genuine or just another megalomaniac attempt at counterfeiting reality?) edged their way through the concrete slabs of the arena's extreme reaches, patiently squeezing their way through the synthetic material like lizards, triumphantly emerging here and there through narrow crevices.

My left foot inadvertently kicked an empty metal box away, sending it rolling down towards the other side of the empty causeway. The Sanitation men hadn't yet cleared up the left-overs from the previous night's revellers. The can went hurtling up the corridor, the noise like a roll of thunder, vigorously echoing throughout the hollow chamber of the abandoned auditorium.

"Hello there," said a uniformed attendant, calmly appearing from behind one of the columns. "There's nobody on tonight. Just a small combo in one of the rehearsal rooms."

He showed me the way.

Versins, the music-maker, was slouched dejectedly in a far corner of the small studio, listening to the amateur band trying out their limited repertoire on him, hoping for an engagement. They weren't too bad, in fact. I introduced myself.

"Ezra said I could call on you."

"Nice to make your acquaintance, son."

"Same here, Versins," I replied. "Your name sure carries weight out on the Great Ways. They say you're the best manipulator there is this side of Betelgeuse."

"All lies, of course. But nice of you to say so. I am *the* best, with no spatio-geographical distinctions. What was your name again?"

"Rider Jackson."

"What do you play?" he asked, a wry smile over his face.

"Modified bass."

"Well," he said, chuckling merrily, "in that case, you now have a job."

"They said you were fast, but this sure is a surprise. Where?"

"Right here."

"Tell me more."

The musicians on the small stage were now quiet, watching us.

"See the paladin band over there," Versins pointed them out to me. "They just happen to have a vacancy for a modified bass. Don't you, kids? You walked into this room right on time. The reefs of space are real kind to you, Jackson, my boy."

I turned round and gave the motley crew a closer look. A bit ragged, maybe, but they didn't seem too bad a bunch as paladins go. Anyway, beggars can't be choosers, I said to myself, especially if you're stranded on old Nova Polska and don't quite feel like riding the Great Ways for a while. My joints were still aching from the prolonged holiday I'd had in the hibernation capsule; spaceship travel is no luxury, I assure you. The musicians kept on staring vacuously at me, as if Versins had put me on display.

"What's the name of the group?" I finally asked.

"The Newski Prospect," he answered. "Come, let me introduce you. They're a nice bunch of laddies, a lot of talent. You'll get on fine, I'm certain."

"Let's hope so. Most of my previous experience has been solo, but I've always wanted to play in a band."

"Fine, just fine," said Versins. "They used to be called the Consuls at Sunset, but I changed the name to Newski Prospect. More commercial appeal, don't you think so?"

"I suppose so," I tentatively agreed. Never say no to a manager, because he's got the credits. I went over to them, introduced myself more fully and met the various members of the band, my new band.

Flatt, from the remote Hodds peninsula, played the phosphoric zither. Corny Jherek, a large hulk of a man hailing from Melnibone, was main vocalist. Welsh blew the synthetised winds and dabbled with the Orion crystal chords, while Barbieri, a quiet blindman from nearby Procyon West, played lead balutherium.

As I was soon to find out for myself, the sound of the band was good, rough at the edges, though the musicians' unity was at times marred in my opinion by Flatt's tendency to indulge in free-forming cloud patterns during his obligatory set-piece solo spot for major stage performances. The Newski Prospect gave the impression of a ripsnortingly tight outfit. When performing to good, receptive audiences, not the usual space freaks in the downtown area bars or dream residences, they could be enormously exciting, running through all the good old Earth standards as well as their own original compositions with unflagging energy and with an overall sound that, for all the fast rippling instrumental tradeoffs, was always absolutely clear and pure. On most evenings, I was given a fair chance to demonstrate my skills on time-jump patterns with my modified bass and soon evolved a lengthy drawn-out duet piece with Big Corny.

Our band was hard, with so much metal in the range of melodics that we might often well have been some wild deep-space salvage team! We usually concluded our first set of the evening with a flowing number by Corny, adapted from a traditional tune of faraway Terra, the Pitiful Ballad of the Moscow Latrine. The first moments of the tune were quite devastating: Barbieri the blindman riding the first line of the tune and then lifting it all into place with one masterly motion, Big Corny's adenoidal singing sounding alternately terrified and full of charm, deformed by his subtle manipulations of the phaser unit, as the whole band combined in a brilliant show of force.

Versins, a shrewd operator if ever there was one, was booking agent and manager of our outfit and, very soon, after rehearsing together for some time at his summer residence on the Outer Archipelago to accustom ourselves to our diverse styles, the glorious Newski Prospect paladin band was out again trucking over the Great Ways of space, slipping and sliding, lining up our rhythms and bouncing along the space seas in search of that wonderful lost chord in the heavens.

We met Cyn, the lady of the horsemen, after a dubious show on Gamma Hexyl Aldone, where we had been forced to share the evening's bill with a horrifying combo from Altair, who specialised in incongruous sonic frequency improvisations. Not quite my type of music, but some space-dogs enjoy it. Cyn was in fact one of the few spectators to genuinely applaud us at the end of the set. A connoisseur of the arts, Cyn was. What with her strange brew of emotions, an uncanny mixture of guile and innocence, Cyn was soon adopted ipso facto as band mascotte and non-playing member of the group, joining us on our tedious journeys through the remote and disparate colony worlds of the Rigel Cloud.

Cyn always wore long fur coats reaching down to her ankles and harboured a crazy passion for astro-therapy. Travelling through normal space, riding the shock spiral waves, she would entertain us most regally, between gigs, offering herself unsparingly to every member of the band. A most compliant girl, soft, loving, affectionate, hailing from Bat-Yam, that most hedonistic of planets where pleasure is the ultimate high, a world I had always wanted to visit.

Star-trucking.

The polka-dotted curtain of velvet night all around us. Beyond the shimmering energy waves of the space seas and over the crests of the million and one myriad colony worlds, clusters of life towards which we were spinning madly, like flies in a cage.

In the back of the freighter cabin, bunched uncomfortably between our heavy distortion equipment, the other members of the paladin band were playing chance games. Cyn was dealing, a wry smile over her face. I asked Big Corny:

"How long have you been on the road, Corny?"

"Much too long, Jack. Started on Terra, as resident floor performer at the Euston Bypass Philharmonic. Holy qasars, those were the days!" he answered, sighing wearily.

"It's not a bad life, after all, is it?"

"No, I suppose not," he shrugged, glazed eyes and silly grin. "But nothing extraordinary ever happens . . ."

Back on Nova Polska, where the trees were getting all lean and hollow, wily Versins got the band a contract to tour the Haldeman Ore worlds the following month. In the meantime, the Nova Polska spring was here, glittering wildly all around us, the sunlit alleyways peering out shyly from the sun-drenched groundswells. The local guilds were out on strike, not an unusual occurrence, and we had nothing to do until take-off, thirty days away.

Barbieri, the blind balutherium-basher, suggested:

"Let's all take a holiday!"

"Where?"

"As far away as possible without flying the spacewinds."

"By the sea?"

"In the sun?"

"On the sand?"

A morning ferryboat left the grey city peninsula at the break of dawn and we barely all managed to get our rocks together on time to catch it; we even had to hire an old Nader transport van from Versins' fleet of secondhand wrecks. On board, small groups of local tourists cluttered eagerly around the imported symbiotic waterbeds, observing the ritual of crossing by throwing flowers into the passing waves.

Sitting in a hammock, not an easy thing to do, waiting for the night sun to emerge over the eastern horizon for Nova Polska, Cyn teetered, dressed in a bright new mauve outfit buttoned up at the front.

"We'll have a grand old time over there," she told us all. "I'm absolutely certain you'll just adore the pinky islands; they're so divine and, this time of year, the weather is fantastic. Before we left the metropolis, I sent my sister a message, asking her to come and join us there next week. The more, the merrier!"

"What's your sister like?" asked Flatt.

"We're twins. We worship the midnight sun."

So, the paladin band and I, we rambled out of port with a sparkle and a shine in our eyes, began trouping down through the old continent, sweeping past the antique cities of Nova Polska. Abandoned eerie ruins full of the yellow smell of aeons, incest, rape, plunder and untold violence, they had been here long before the arrival of the first human colonists. This was in fact where most of the normal tourists came, drifting in silence through the deserted streets, piously congregating around the bizarre monuments. The skyline of the major continent glowed brightly in all sundry shades of orange and yellow as we drove by; it looked as if the heavens were getting ready for some fiery carnival. None of us felt particularly at ease around here, and it was with undiluted relief that we raced on towards the pinky islands. Strange, depressing atmosphere, sort of reminding us that this was not our planet of birth and we were only tolerated here as long as we didn't offend the status quo of things.

Stopping for a rest, we stayed at a busy roadside tavern, where we had to sleep all together in a big room previously used as a chapel by migratory Inquisition monks. Awed by the occasion, we all crowded uncomfortably into the large bed, chaste but merry. The next morning, passing through the extreme outskirts of Borogoto, we noticed that the famous local fountains were all dry and empty. Both Cyn and Welsh who had been particularly looking forward to admiring the whispering fountains were very disappointed.

As a solemn gesture of protest against this untoward occurrence, we all got wildly drunk on cheap lingonberry wine and reached the border control hut in a somewhat frenzied state. Big Corny copiously insulted the bland attendants, while sneeky old Flatt succumbed to temptation and sodomised the station chief's wife, while we all watched with amusement on the sideline and cheered him along. I wasn't idle either: my hand wandered wildly under Cyn's tunic, occasionally encountering other busy fingers there belonging to some other member of the band.

In the multi-layered gardens of Jefferson Slick, leisurely prowlers, on a day outing, were playing complicated games; we ignored them and continued towards the balustrade of the sea, where the Mercator Ocean plumed itself in the wind like a lazy bird of prey. Finally, after a three-hour crossing of the Denny Isthmus, we set foot on dry land again: the pinky islands. Our holidays could begin!

The vacation began happy and carefree.

We hopped along the salty beaches in a high state of euphoria, relishing the local food and brews and enjoying the weather like kids in a bathtub. Through the heat-haze, we carefully watched the swaying movements of the nearby crazy pink marble hotels and laughed in close harmony. Cyn gave up wearing her fur coats and celebrated the event by ceremoniously burning all her heavy garments on the beach at midday as soon as we arrived. The band collectively composed a wealth of new numbers, enough to last us out a lifetime without senso-recordings, rehearsing most mornings on the elaborately decorated patio of our hotel, the soft flutter of the sea breeze nonchalantly absorbing the sheer weight of our thumping waves of cacophonic sound.

Sitting beside the mad hotel's baroque porch, feeling somewhat melancholy for a change, gazing at the private resident's beach, tracing geometrical patterns in the moist sand with my toes, I was joined by Cyn, who asked me:

"How are your own new melodies getting along?"

"They're not," I replied, sighing sadly.

"Why?"

"Dunno. Maybe it's not the right environment. The heat of the sun often does funny things to me, you know. Improvising with the band, like this morning, is all right, but on my own I seem to forget how to string along the chords, the harmonies."

"And with the band, it's different?"

"The improvisations just carry me along. No, I can't structure things any longer; I'm left with big unwieldy chunks of emotions. Lots of assorted random sound, illogical, alien, apocryphal, weird, affectionate, but no bloody tune."

"Well," said Cyn, putting her hands in mine. "It still sounds nice when you talk about it that way." She pulled back some long strands of dark hair falling over her eyes.

And smiled at me.

"Make love to me, Jack. Maybe it will make you feel better," she said.

"What? Here? Now?"

"Yes."

"What about the others? They might be coming back here any minute now."

"It doesn't matter. They won't mind."

"How do you know?"

"Oh . . . I know, don't you worry about that."

"You're a strange girl, Cyn."

We walked hand in hand up to my room in the hotel. Later, as she came, sweat on her brow, fire in my loins, I told her: "You know?"

"No, what?"

"Maybe it's that I haven't got anything to say, really."

There was only one other paying guest in the hotel, sharing most amenities with us. Rumours of an impending earthquake off the Denny Isthmus had scared away any other potential holiday-maker. We just didn't care. This odd man out among our little group of garrulous revellers was Anarchios Stavropoulos, Jr., the now-retired founding father of the Nova Polska Phosphorus Monopoly. A company so vast it owned over a dozen planets, feared by competitors and allies alike. However, Anarchios had now given it all up, although there was a rumour I'd heard on the Tri-D bulletins back in the grey city that he still held a majority of the voting shares. Anarchios Stavropoulos, Jr., was old and fat. He had also acquired the nasty habit since our arrival of pinching Cyn's backside whenever she innocently happened to brush past him. Dirty old man.

Then, one night, a coachload of off-world tourists arrived in the pinky islands. Amongst them, two young women dazed and confused by the sheer splendour of the mad marble hotel standing there at attention, among the pink sand and the pale shrunken moonlights, decided there and then to leave their organised planetary excursion and spend the rest of their holidays here.

The tired columns of the Hollow Man Hotel wavered and surged and, the following morning, the rest of the party unceremoniously departed without the two girls. Right now, on their home planet, it was the rain season, and my, oh my, how the sand here was fine and powdery, the sea so calm and warm and the breeze so eager to caress the body like sheer strands of silk!

I watched them from my room window joyfully gallivanting all day long through the low waves in flimsy attire, then falling exhausted but happy on the beach, basking in the sun until, finally, darkness came and the Nova Polska trio of moons teetered upwards, while all along the surging rhythms of our metal music machines bounced along in close harmony, the mellow sounds lingering insistently in the musky air.

A peeling tinkle of female laughter crossed the now empty beach coming in my direction. The two young women were moving their tent nearer to the Hollow Man Hotel to avoid the cool night breeze spreading along the shoreline. "I like it here, it's sort of funny around here," one of them said as she slowly undressed, the muted shadow of her body outlined against the fabric of the tent.

In the hotel, sitting on his balcony, trying to escape the stuffy, depressing atmosphere of his cluttered room, Anarchios lowered his heavy horn-rimmed spectacles and focused the sights. Out in the band's communal working-suite, Welsh and I were playing on the multi-dimensional pinball machines, and losing heavily.

Anarchios' hands were wet and trembling as he undid one by one the front buttons of his elegant mauve tunic, then poured himself a refreshing glass of Red Club cocktail and decided to take a short stroll on the beach, before settling down for the night.

"What's this tent doing *here*?" he wondered, stepping softly in the velvety darkness, surprised at seeing the girls' night-hut standing there in the middle of the beach.

When the young tourist maid from Gamma Hexyl Aldone hesitantly crept out of the tent to enquire, she saw this vast fat man gaping at her, rather old but quite jolly. He said nothing, watching her in silence ("why's he looking at me that way the old geezer good thing I slipped my nightie on before coming out") then finally muttered ("oh he still has all his teeth!"):

"God, I love you."

By now, it was almost dawn, night on Nova Polska can be very short in the spring, their journey across the flatlands on the way down to the pinky islands had been quite tiring, she still hadn't found out where her twin sister Cyn was staying, so, to avoid any possible argument, she answered him:

"Hello! My name's Dolorès. How do you do?"

And it came to pass that wealthy and old Anarchios Stavropoulos madly, illogically fell in love with beautiful, blond Dolorès, sister of Cyn, our lady of the horsemen.

In quick succession, in an attempt to woo her in the old-fashioned way, he offered her fantastic assortments of rare diamonds, necklaces made from wild pearls fished out of the depths of alien oceans, strings of delicate flowers and enormous, just enormous, quantities of money. To no avail. She would not accept anything. However, his passion did not decrease and he loved her even more.

Anarchios then proposed to set up an exclusive video deal for her, with total Galactic release and distribution outlets.

"A girl as beautiful as you should be in the videos!"

He proposed starring her in all the future video productions of the companies he controlled: Ariadne in a space-age version of *Theseus*, Patricia Primrose in Jakubowski's *Phosphorus War*, Catherine Tekakwitha in Cohen's *Beautiful Losers*, etc . . . but she would have nothing of it. She just didn't wish to get involved; all she wanted to do was simply enjoy her holidays here with her sister and the musicians of the Newski Prospect.

Anarchios despaired.

He even thought of creating a new rival organisation to compete with his original Phosphorus Monopoly, in an attempt to retrieve the vigour, enthusiasm and energy of his yesterdays, but Dolorès was not in the slightest bit interested in business or commercial ventures when he mentioned the idea to her, one evening.

"No thank you, sweet Anarchios," she gently told him.

Summer was approaching and none of us in the band felt like returning to the grey cities to undertake the proposed tour of the Haldeman Ore worlds. The last morning of the Nova Polska spring sported a bleak, sad sky, the sea was no longer so deep and blue, just a paler shade of grey. The pink sand itself had errant streaks of jaundice running through its thin but densely packed layers.

Big Corny hurriedly came knocking at the door of my room.

"Wake up! Wake up! The old man is dead!"

"Who?"

"Anarchios Stavropoulos Junior."

The broken-hearted old gentleman had passed away during the night.

"Poor man," said Cyn, a lone tear streaming down her right cheek, mingling with her still fresh early morning make-up.

"At least," I said, walking into the suite where the others had gathered, "he's now free of the tyranny of love."

"Well, the hotel staff are all having a day off. We'll have to bury him ourself," muttered Barbieri, practical as ever in the face of adversity. "With this sultry heat, there's a bit of a health problem. There's no one else on the island to do it."

"Us?" we all shouted back.

"Why not," said Welsh. "No harm being charitable for once."

Was it old age, illness or could the phosphorus tycoon really have succumbed because of the mad, impossible love-affair he had brought upon himself? Anyway, one way or the other, we sure provided him with a nice, decent burial. With music.

Lacking any precise guidelines, we elected to put the body to rest in the pink lazy sands. As good a place as any, with an eternal vision of the peppery shores of the sea, night and day, and the soft touch of the scented breeze to accompany him forever through the death zone.

Of course, we were all rather sad about it, but we did our best to put on happy, carefree summer faces for the occasion. Towering Corny Jherek sorted out his best voice as we unwrapped our various instruments and buried Anarchios to the sound of music. While we played, Cyn danced the ritual ballet of the ceremonies of the horsemen around the deserted beach, her agile, graceful movements punctuated by the pumping rhythm of my modified bass riffs.

We had chosen a pretty enough spot of deep, shifting pink sands some way from the main resort and all took turns at digging the hole, even Dolorès, who began crying when the paladin band echoed the Martian Fandango; she was a sentimental lass, after all!

On the way back to the hotel, the band improvised a makeshift dirge of sorts. The onlookers applauded the set, but it was somewhat ragged at the edges. I wasn't that much in form myself.

The following afternoon, the regular transit service to the grey cities complex stopped by and the two young spring tourists, Dolorès and her ever-silent companion, left without even saying goodbye to any of us. We were all still sleeping anyway. A couple of hours later, we were woken up by a strange chuckety-chunk noise coming from the sea. We rushed to the window and caught a glimpse of a splendid hydrofreighter rolling down over the waves, heading straight for the Hollow Man Hotel's private jetty. Cyn and I dressed hurriedly and slipped out to meet the embarkation. The others just moaned and slid back between the blankets.

Once the ship's awesome side-engines had been cut off, a hatchway opened and an inflatable raft was thrown out onto the sea. A group of austere, moustachioed, black-suited men crept out of the hydrofreighter's hull, carefully descended into the frail embarkation below and, with impeccable style, rowed the short way to the shore.

There were six of them, all proudly wearing the regulation Phosphorus Monopoly tie, cuff-links and badge. The leader of the small group of official executives could be recognised by the extra stripes on the lapels of his exquisitely tailored outfit. He introduced himself to us:

"I am the Right Honourable Guildsman Giuseppe Verdi. I am looking for Miss Dolorès of the Red Mountain. Are you her?" pointing to Cyn.

Holding my hand in a tight grip, she replied:

"No. I'm her sister, Cyn, the lady of the horsemen. Dolorès must have left just a few hours ago. I'm afraid you seem to have missed her."

"How distressing," said Guildsman Verdi.

Obviously surprised by this unexpected development, he wiped his sweating brow, scratched his forehead and appealed to us:

"But then what am I to do with the avocado?"

Pointing at the small parcel his team of Phosphorus acolytes were holding between them, a small oblong box with fancy wrapping.

"What in the name of the spacewinds is an avocado?" Cyn and I asked, bemused.

The dark suited bunch slowly set the small parcel down on the wet sand, and reverently proceeded to unrap it. There was wrapping and packing material galore, in fact most of the bulk of the package was taken up by it.

"It won't keep," Verdi kept saying, nervously. "But we couldn't get here faster."

And then I suddenly remembered reading about avocado pears in an old set of the "Encyclopedia Galactica", while lazing about in some spaceport lounge some years back, between freighters. I vaguely recalled it was a very rare fruit only to be found in certain areas on old Earth, depending on the seasons. It must have undoubtedly cost a small fortune to transport it here, from Sol system all the way to the pinky islands of Nova Polska . . .

The panting Guildsman soon explained: the late Anarchios had, at fantastic expense, purchased the avocado, the only one in existence in this part of the galaxy, in fact – it was being kept under strict climatic-control conditions in a museum on Barfos Centauri, for exhibition purpose only – and had it express-freighted here as a small gift he wished to present Dolorès with on the occasion of her birthday. But it was now too late, Anarchios was dead and Dolorès had left early.

We later put the matter to a vote and it was decided to plant the avocado over the old tycoon's grave out there amongst the sands. I was sure he would have liked it that way, the silly romantic bugger. The fruit's shining dark-green grainy skin blended agreeably with the pink surroundings, and the effect was most pretty and artistic!

Someone said:

"It's just like a jewel. Bit fancy for a grave, if you ask me . . ."

Big Corny remarked:

"Maybe, who knows, I could teach the avocado to sing?"

Guildsman Verdi, who also held important responsibilities on the Nova Polska council, also had a private 'gram for me. It came from Ezra, my tuning master. He had found a profitable solo performing gig for me in some new Pleasure Dome out on Terminus Epsilon 29. It was a most attractive proposal. Most of the musicians in the Newski Prospect had already decided to split the group and go their own way after this melancholy holiday. I was at loose ends and when I put the news to them, there were no objections to my departing before the farewell Haldeman Ore tour. I did the rounds, saying goodbye, shaking hands, kissing, hugging; when it came to Cyn, I tenderly brushed my lips against her freckled forehead, then asked her:

"What are you going to be doing now?"

"Don't really know. Bum around, I suppose. I don't quite feel like settling down yet and taking a nine-to-five job with the Monopoly."

"Come along with me. We might have a bit of fun."

She gave me a broad smile.

"It's a deal. You're on."

She didn't have much to pack, and minutes later we were boarding Verdi's hydrofreighter, ready for the short cruise back to the grey cities complex where we would find some transport to Terminus Epsilon 29.

As the ship majestically rose above the water, rapidly leaving the island behind until it was no more than a mere speck of dust in the flowing landscape, I looked round to watch Cyn. She was crying.

"What's the matter, pet?" I asked her.

"Dolly and Anarchios, it was a nice love story, wasn't it?" she sobbed.

"Love stories always have sad endings," I told her.

The slipstreams of space engulfed us. I had heard a lot of wild tales about Epsilon. Maybe now I would find out whether they were all true.

I was looking forward to that.

Translated by Sonia Florens
Original title: *Le pseudonyme fou vent de frapper*

The gigantic fluctuation

ARKADY and BORIS STRUGATSKY

I was only a boy at the time, and there was much I did not understand then and much I later forgot – perhaps the most interesting parts. It was night time, so I did not even see the man's face. And his voice was not at all exceptional, maybe a little sad and husky, and he coughed now and then as if from embarrassment. In a word, if we happened to meet again, on the street somewhere or, let us say, at a mutual friend's it is more than likely I would not recognise him.

We met on the beach. I had just been in for a swim, and was sitting on a rock. Then I heard the rattle of falling shale behind me – him coming down the embankment – there was a whiff of tobacco smoke, and he stopped beside me. As I have already said, this happened at night. The sky was overcast and a gale was rising out at sea. A strong, warm wind whipped along the beach. The stranger was smoking, and the wind cut long orange sparks from his cigarette, whisking them over the deserted sands till they vanished. It was pretty to see, I remember that well. I was only sixteen, and it never even occurred to me that he would speak. But he began to talk. And his opening words were rather strange.

"The world is full of marvellous things," he said.

I decided that he was merely thinking aloud, and kept silent. I turned to look at him, but could discern nothing. It was too dark.

"The world is full of marvellous things," he repeated, then took a drag, shedding a shower of sparks my way.

Again I did not answer: I was very shy then. He finished

his cigarette, lit another, and sat down on the rock beside me. From time to time he would mutter something, but the roar of the surf drowned the words and I heard only an indecipherable mumble.

Finally, he declared in a loud voice: "No, it's really too much. I must tell somebody about it."

And then he spoke to me directly, for the first time since his appearance.

"You won't refuse to hear me out, will you?"

Naturally, I didn't refuse.

"Only, I must work up to it, because if I tell you right off what it's all about, you won't understand, nor believe it either. And it's very important to me that you do believe it. Nobody believes me, and now it's gone so far . . ."

He fell silent, and then continued.

"It began when I was still a child. I was learning to play the violin, and I broke four glasses and a saucer."

"How was that?" I asked. A sort of funny story flashed through my mind about a lady who said to another: "Just imagine, yesterday the janitor threw us some wood, and broke the chandelier." There is such an old joke.

The stranger gave a sad laugh.

"Just picture it. This happened the very first month I started taking lessons. Even then my teacher said he had never seen anything like that in all his life."

I said nothing, but I also thought it must have looked quite odd. I imagined him waving the bow and occasionally sweeping it against the sideboard. That certainly could have led him too far.

"It's a well-known law of physics," he explained, unexpectedly. "The phenomenon of resonance." And in the same breath, he related the amusing example given in the school physics textbook, the one about a bridge collapsing when a column of soldiers marched across it all in step. Then he explained that glasses and saucers could also be broken by resonance, if you selected vibrations of the required frequency. I must admit that only from that moment did I really begin to realise that sound was also vibration.

The stranger told me that resonance in everyday life (in domestic economy, as he put it) was a very rare thing, and he took much delight in the fact that a certain ancient law-book included such a bare possibility by stipulating the punishment for the owner of a cock whose crowing broke a neighbour's pitcher.

I agreed that it really must be a rare thing. Personally, I had never heard of such a case.

"A very, very rare thing," he said. "And yet I broke four glasses and a saucer in one month, with my violin. But that was only the beginning."

He lit a cigarette, and added: "Very soon, my parents and friends observed that I was breaking the sandwich law."

Here I decided not to betray my ignorance, so I said: "A strange name, that."

"What name?" he asked. "Oh, the law? That's not a name. It's . . . how can I explain it? It's a sort of joke. You see, there is a whole group of old sayings, for example: 'Expect trouble, and you are sure to find it . . .' An open sandwich, or a slice of bread and butter, always falls butter-side down . . . the idea being that the bad happens oftener than the good. Or to put it scientifically: the probability of a desired event is always less than half."

"Half of what?" I asked, and immediately realised I had put my foot in it again. He was very surprised at my question.

"Don't you even know the theory of probability?" he asked.

I answered that we hadn't got to that yet at school.

"In that case, you won't understand a thing," he said, disappointed.

"Then you explain it," I said angrily, and he obediently complied. He told me that probability was the likelihood of one or another event coming to pass according to the ratio of the favourable cases to the whole number of cases possible.

"And where do the sandwiches come in?" I asked.

"A sandwich might fall butter-side down or butter-side up," he said. "And so, generally speaking, if you try dropping a sandwich at random, it will sometimes fall one way and sometimes another. In half the cases, it falls butter-side up, and the rest of the time butter-side down. D'you see?"

"Ye-es," I said, for some reason remembering I hadn't had supper yet.

"In such cases, they say that the probability of a desired

result is equal to half – to one-half."

He went on to say that if you dropped a sandwich one hundred times, for example, it might fall butter-side up fifty-five or merely twenty times, rather than fifty: that only by dropping it for a very long time, over and over, would it fall butter-side up in approximately half the number of cases. I pictured this miserable, open sandwich (maybe, even a caviare sandwich) after it had been thrown a thousand times on the floor, even if the latter wasn't too dirty. Then I asked, were there really people who did such stupid things. He set in to explain that, actually, sandwiches were not used for this aim, but money, like when you toss for something. And he explained how it was done, burying himself deeper in a labyrinth of examples, so that soon I stopped following him and sat looking at the gloomy sky, and thought it would probably rain. From this first lecture on the theory of probability, I can recall only the half-familiar term "mathematical expectation". The stranger used this term repeatedly, and every time I visualised a large hall, like a waiting-room with a tiled floor, where people sat with briefcases and blotting-pads, from time to time throwing money or sandwiches up to the ceiling, and awaiting something with fixed attention. Even now, I often see it in my dreams. And then the stranger almost deafened me with the ringing term: "the maximum theorem of Moivre and Laplace", adding that all this had nothing to do with the matter.

"You know, this isn't what I wanted to tell you, not at all," he said, his voice losing its former liveliness.

"Excuse me," I inquired, "I suppose you're a mathematician?"

"No," he answered dully. "How can I be a mathematician? I'm a fluctuation."

Out of respect, I said nothing.

"Well, so it seems I haven't yet told you my story," he recalled.

"You were talking about sandwiches," I said.

"You see, my uncle was the first to notice it," he continued. "I was very absent-minded, see, and often dropped sandwiches. And mine always fell butter-side up."

"Well, that was lucky," I said.

He sighed bitterly.

"It's lucky when it happens once in a while . . . But when

it always does! Just think . . . always!"

I did not understand what he meant, and told him so.

"My uncle knew a thing or two about mathematics, and was interested in the theory of probability. He advised me to try tossing money. We both tossed. Even then, I didn't realise that I was under a curse, but my uncle did. That's what he told me then: 'You're under a curse!' "

I was as much in the dark as before.

"First, I tossed a coin one hundred times, and so did my uncle. His fell heads up fifty-three times, but mine ninety-eight. You know, my uncle's eyes almost popped out of his head. And mine, too. Then I tossed the coin again: two hundred times. And imagine, it fell heads up one hundred and ninety-six times. I should have known then what would come of such things. I should have known that a night like this would come along, sometime." And at that, I think a sob burst from his throat. "But I was a bit too young then, d'you see, younger than you. I found it all terribly interesting I thought it was very funny to be the focus point of all the miracles in the world."

"The what?" I asked, amazed.

"Mm . . . the focus point of miracles. I can't find any other words to express it, though I've tried."

He relaxed a bit, and began to tell everything the way it had happened, chain-smoking and coughing. He told it at length, trying to describe all the details and invariably giving a scientific foundation to all the events he described. He astonished me, if not by the depths of his knowledge, then at least by its versatility. He showered me with terminology from physics, mathematics, thermodynamics and the kinetic theory of gases, so that later on, when I was grown up, I often wondered why this or that term seemed familiar to me. Frequently, he delved into philosophical questions, and at times seemed simply incapable of self-criticism. For instance, he repeatedly boasted of being a "phenomenon", a "miracle of nature", a "gigantic fluctuation". It was then I realised this wasn't a profession. He told me that miracles weren't miracles at all, that they were simply the most improbable events.

"In nature," he persisted, "the most probable events occur most frequently, the least probable much more rarely."

He had in mind the law of the non-diminution of entropy,

but it sounded terribly impressive to me then. After that, he attempted to explain a state of extreme probability, and fluctuation. My imagination boggled, then, at the well-known example of a room where all the air had been drawn into one half of it.

"In such a case," he said, "everybody sitting in the other half would die, and the rest would count it a miracle. But it would be far from a miracle: it would be a fully realistic fact, though an extremely unusual and unlikely one. It would be a gigantic fluctuation – a hardly probable declination from the most probable state of things."

According to him, he was just such a declination. He was surrounded by miracles. To see a multiple of twelve rainbows at once was nothing to him – he had seen this six or seven times.

"I am better than any amateur weather-forecaster," he boasted, but despondently. "I've seen the Northern Lights as far south as Alma-Ata, and the Spectre of the Brocken in the Caucasus; and twelve times I've observed the famous green ray or 'sword of hunger', as it is called. I went to Batumi and a drought began. Then I travelled to the Gobi Desert and was caught three times in tropical rains."

When he studied at school and the university, he always drew paper No. 5 at the exams. Once during a post-graduate exam, when everybody knew there would only be four papers from the number of students taking it, he still drew No. 5. An hour before the exam, the professor had suddenly decided to add one more paper.

His sandwiches continued to fall butter-side up. ("I am doomed to it, apparently, right to my grave," he said. "It will always remind me that I am not just an ordinary man, but a gigantic fluctuation.")

Twice he happened to be present at the formation of large air lenses (a macroscopic fluctuation of the density of air, he explained vaguely) and both times these lenses lit a match which he held in his hands.

All the miracles he had encountered, he divided into three groups – pleasant, unpleasant and neutral. Butter-side-up sandwiches, for instance, belonged to the first group. The inevitable cold he had, which began and ended regularly on the first day of each month, he assigned to the second group. In the last, he included various phenomena of nature which had the honour of taking place in his presence.

Once, for example, the second law of thermodynamics was violated: the water in a vase of flowers unexpectedly began to attract the warmth from the air around it until it reached boiling point, while the room was covered with frost. ("After that, I wandered around like a lost soul, and even now, d'you see, I test water with my finger-tip, for instance. before drinking it . . .") Ball lightning flew repeatedly into his hotel room – he travelled a lot – and hovered under the ceiling for hours. He had finally got used to them, using them as electric lamps for reading.

"Do you know what a meteorite is?" he suddenly asked. Youth is inclined to rough jokes, so I answered that meteorites were falling stars, which had nothing in common with stars that do not fall.

"A meteorite may fall on a house," he remarked, thoughtfully. "But that's a very rare thing. Only one case has been recorded where a meteorite fell on a man. The only case of its kind, d'you see . . ."

"Well, and what of it?" I asked.

He leaned over and whispered: "That man . . . was me!"

"You're joking," I said, with a shiver.

"Not at all," he answered, rather sadly.

It turned out that all this had happened up in the Urals. He was travelling on foot through the mountains, and stopped for a minute to tie his shoelace. There came a sharp hiss and he felt a jolt in his backside and pain from a burn.

"There was a hole in my trousers, that big," he said. "And a trickle of blood, just a little. Too bad it's so dark, or I could show you the scar."

He had picked up a few likely pebbles, and kept them in his desk – perhaps one of them was the meteorite.

Things happened to him that were absolutely inexplicable from a scientific point of view. So far, at least; at the present level of science. Once, for example, for no reason at all, he had become the source of a powerful magnetic field. This was manifest because all the iron objects in his room leapt up and whirled towards him along the lines of force. A steel pen pierced his cheek, something struck him painfully on his head, on his spine. Shaking with terror, he shielded himself with his arms, while knives, forks, spoons and scissors clung to him from head to foot – and suddenly, it was all over. It had lasted no more than ten seconds, and he hadn't the faintest idea how to explain it.

Another time, on receiving a letter from a friend, he discovered, to his surprise, after reading the first few lines, that he had got a perfect facsimile of the letter several years before. He even recalled that on the reverse side, beside the signature, there should be a large ink-blot. Turning the letter over, he actually saw the spot of ink.

"None of these things were ever repeated," he added sadly. "I consider them the most amazing occurrences in my collection. That is, I did . . . until this evening."

In general, he interrupted his discourse rather often to explain: "All this, d'you see, would be very fine, but what happened today . . . Believe me, that was the limit."

"And doesn't it seem to you," I asked, "that you would be of interest to science?"

"I thought about that," he replied. "I wrote. I made the offer, d'you see. Only nobody believes me. Not even my relatives. There was one who did – my uncle, but he's dead now. I simply can't imagine what they will think after today's occurrence." He sighed, and threw away his butt. "Perhaps it's best that nobody believes me. Suppose somebody did. They'd set up a commission, and would follow me everywhere, expecting miracles. And I'm not very sociable, by nature; and besides, my character's completely ruined from all this. Sometimes, I can't sleep nights . . . I'm afraid."

As far as the commission was concerned, I agreed with him. After all, you see, he could not bring miracles about, at will. He was only the focus of miracles, a point in space, as he put it, where very unlikely things occurred. They could not be settled without commissions or observations.

"I wrote to one scientist I knew of," he continued. "Mainly, though, about the meteorite and the water in the vase. But, d'you know, he took a very humorous attitude. He answered that the meteorite didn't fall on me at all, but on a certain driver, I believe he was Japanese. And he suggested, very sarcastically, that I get medical advice. I became very interested in the driver. I thought that he also might be a gigantic fluctuation – judge for yourself, it's quite possible. However, as it turned out, he died many years ago. And, you know . . ." He pondered for a moment, and went on. "But I went to a doctor, just the same. Apparently, I was not at all exceptional from a medical point of view. However, he found I had a slight nervous disorder and sent me here, to a health resort. And I came.

How could I know what would happen?"

He suddenly gripped my shoulder and whispered: "An hour ago, a lady acquaintance of mine flew away!"

I failed to understand.

"We were walking up there, in the park. I'm a man, after all – and I had the most honourable intentions. We got to know each other in the dining-room, went for a walk in the park, and she flew away."

"Where to?" I screamed.

"I don't know. We were walking, she suddenly cried out in alarm, was pulled right off the ground and rose in the air. I came to myself only in time to catch her by the foot; and here, look . . ."

He pushed some kind of hard object into my hand. It was a sandal, an ordinary bright-coloured sandal of average size.

"You understand, it's not utterly impossible," muttered the phenomenon. "Chaotic movement of the body's molecules, Brownian movement of particles of the living colloid became regular, and she was torn from the ground and carried away. I simply can't imagine where. It's very, very improbable . . . What do you think? Should I look on myself as a murderer?"

I was shocked, and could not say a word. For the first time, it occurred to me that probably he had imagined it all. But he spoke again, with a yearning painfulness.

"But even that, you see, isn't the point. After all, she may be caught on a tree somewhere. You see, I didn't start looking, because I was afraid I wouldn't find her. And now, d'you see . . . Until now all these miracles only concerned me. But now? What if these tricks begin happening to my acquaintances? . . . Today, a girl flies away; tomorrow, a colleague vanishes underground; and the day after . . . Take you, for example. Why, you aren't insured against it, right this minute."

I had realised this myself, and I became amazingly interested and terrified, too. That would be something, I thought. If I only could! Suddenly, it seemed to me that I was flying up, and I gripped the rock I was sitting on. The stranger suddenly stood up.

"You know, I'd better go," he remarked, plaintively. "I don't like senseless victims. You just sit there, and I'll get along. Why didn't I think of that before!"

He hurried away along the shore, tripping over stones, and then suddenly called back to me: "You'll forgive me, I hope, if anything happens to you! It doesn't depend on me, you know!"

He kept going further and further away, and soon turned into a small black figure against a background of almost phosphorescent surf. It seemed to me that he lifted his arm and threw something white into the waves. Probably, it was the sandal. So that's how we parted.

To my regret, I would not recognise him in a crowd. Unless a miracle happened! I never heard anything more of him, and nothing extraordinary happened at the seashore that summer, as far as I know. More than likely his girl did get caught on some branch or other, and later on they got married. You see, he had the most honourable intentions.

I know one thing, though. If I should ever shake hands with a new acquaintance and suddenly feel I've become the source of a powerful magnetic field, and notice, to boot, that this person smokes a lot and frequently coughs – a sort of hm-ahem – then that means it's him. You know, the phenomenon, the focus of miracles, the gigantic fluctuation.

Translated by Gladys Evans
Original title: *Rasskaz o gigantskoj fluctuacji*

Zodiac 2000

J. G. BALLARD

Author's note. *An updating, however modest, of the signs of the zodiac seems long overdue. The houses of our psychological sky are no longer tenanted by rams, goats and crabs but by helicopters, cruise missiles and intra-uterine coils, and by all the spectres of the psychiatric ward. A few correspondences are obvious – the clones and the hypodermic syringe conveniently take the place of the twins and the archer. But there remains the problem of all those farmyard animals so important to the Chaldeans. Perhaps our true counterparts of these workaday creatures are the machines which guard and shape our lives in so many ways – above all, the taurean computer, seeding its limitless possibilities. As for the ram, that tireless guardian of the domestic flock, his counterpart in our homes seems to be the Polaroid camera, shepherding our smallest memories and emotions, our most tender sexual acts. Here, anyway, is an s-f zodiac, which I assume the next real one will be . . .*

The Sign of the Polaroid

The skies were sliding. Already the first of the television crews had arrived in the hospital's car-park and were scanning the upper floors of the psychiatric wing through their binoculars. He lowered the plastic blind, exhausted by all this attention, the sense of a world both narrowing and expanding around him. He waited as Dr. Vanessa adjusted the lens of the cine-camera. Her untidy hair, still uncombed since she first collected him from the patients' refectory, fell across the view-finder. Was she placing the filter of her own tissues between herself and whatever threatening message the film might reveal? Since Professor Rotblat's arrival in the Home Office limousine she had done nothing but photograph him obsessively during a range of meaningless activities – studying the tedious Rorschach images, riding the bicycle in the physiology laboratory, squatting across the bidet in her apartment. Why had they suddenly picked him out, an unknown long-term patient whom everyone had ignored since his admission ten years earlier? Throughout his adolescence he had often stood on the roof of the dormitory block and taken the sky into himself, but not even Dr. Vanessa had noticed. Pushing back her blonde hair, she looked at him with unexpected concern. "One last reel, and then you must pack – the helicopter's coming for us." All night she had sat with him on her bed, projecting the films onto the wall of the apartment.

The Sign of the Computer

He sat at the metal desk beside the podium, staring at the hushed faces of the delegates as Professor Rotblat gestured with the print-outs. "A routine cytoplasmic scan was performed six months ago on the patients of this obscure mental institution, as part of the clinical trials of a new ante-natal tranquilliser. Thanks to Dr. Vanessa Carrington, the extraordinary and wholly anomalous cell chemistry of the subject was brought to my attention, above all the laevo-rotatory spiral of the DNA helix. The most exhaustive analyses conducted by M.I.T.'s ULTRAC 666, the world's most powerful computer, confirm that this unknown young man, an orphan of untraceable parentage, seems to have been born from a mirror universe, propelled into our own world by cosmic forces of unlimited power. They also indicate that in opting for its original right-hand bias our biological kingdom made the weaker of two choices. All the ULTRAC predictions suggest that the combinative possibilities of laevo-rotatory DNA exceed those of our own cell chemistry by a factor of 10^{27}. I may add that the ULTRAC programmers have constructed a total information model of this alternative universe, with implications that are both exalting and terrifying for us all . . ."

The Sign of the Clones

He steadied himself against the balcony rail, retching

onto the turquoise tiles. Twenty feet below his hotel room was the curvilinear roof of the conference centre, its white concrete back like an immense occluded lens. For all Professor Rotblat's talk of alternative universes, the delegates would see nothing through that eye-piece. They seemed to be more impressed by the potency of this over-productive computer than they were by his own. So far his life had been without any possibilities at all – volleyball with the paraplegics, his shins bruised by their wheel-chairs, boring hours pretending to paint like Van Gogh in the occupational therapy classes, then evenings spent with TV and largactil. But at least he could look up at the sky and listen to the time-music of the qasars. He waited for the nausea to pass, regretting that he had agreed to be flown here. The lobbies of the hotel were filled with suspiciously deferential officials. Where was Dr. Vanessa? Already he missed her reassuring hands, her scent around the projection theatre. He looked up from the vomit on the balcony. Below him the television director was standing on the roof of the conference centre, waving to him in a friendly but cryptic way. There was something uncannily familiar about his face and stance, like a too-perfect reflection in a mirror. At times the man seemed to be mimicking him, trying to signal the codes of an escape combination. Or was he some kind of sinister twin, a right-hand replica of himself being groomed to take his place? Wiping his mouth, he noticed the green pill in the vomit between his feet. So the police orderly had tried to sedate him. Without thinking, he decided to escape, and picked up the manual which the Home Office horoscopist had pushed into his hands after lunch.

The Sign of the IUD

He could smell her vulva on his hands. He lay on his side in the darkened bedroom, waiting until she returned from the bathroom. Through the glass door he could see her blurred thighs and breasts, as if distorted by some computer permutating all the possibilities of an alternative anatomy. This likeable but strange young woman, with her anonymous apartment and random conversation filled with sudden references to qasars, the overthrow of capitalism, nucleic acids and horoscopy – had she any idea what would soon happen to her? Clearly she had been waiting for him in the hotel's car-park, all too ready to hide him in the jump seat of her sports car. Was she the courier of a rival consortium, sent to him by the unseen powers who presided over the qasars? On the bedside table was the intra-uterine coil, with the draw-string he had felt at the neck of her womb. On some confused impulse she had decided to remove it, as if determined to preserve at least one set of his wild genes within the safekeeping of her placental vault. He swung the coil by its draw-string, this technological cipher that seemed to contain in its double swastika an anagram of all the zodiacal emblems in the horoscopy manual. Was it a clue left for him, a modulus to be multiplied by everything in this right-handed world – the contours of this young woman's breasts, the laws of chemical kinetics, the migration song of swallows? After the camera, the computer and the clones, the coil was the fourth house of that zodiac he had already entered, the twelve-chambered mansion through which he must move with the guile of a master-burglar. He looked up as Renata gently pushed him back onto the pillow. "Rest for an hour." She seemed to be forwarding instructions from another sky. "Then we'll leave for Jodrell Bank."

The Sign of the Radar Bowl

As they waited in the stationary traffic on the crowded deck of the flyover Renata fiddled impatiently with the radio, unable to penetrate the static from the cars around them. Smiling at her, he turned off the sound and pointed to the sky over her head. "Ignore the horizon. Beyond the Pole Star you can hear the island universes." He sat back, trying to ignore the thousand satellite transmissions, a barbarous chatter below the great music of the qasars. Even now, through the afternoon sunlight over this provincial city, he could read the comsat relays and the radar beams of Fylingdales and the Norad line in northern Canada, and hear the answering over-the-horizon probes of the Russian sites near Murmansk, distant lions roaring their fear at each other, marking their claims to impossible territories. An incoming missile would be fixed in the cat's cradle of his mind like a fly trapped in the sound-space of a Beethoven symphony. Startled, he saw a pair of scarred hands seize the rim of the windshield. A thick-set man with a hard beard had leapt between the airline buses and was staring at him, his left eye inflamed by some unpleasant virus. To Renata he snapped: "Get into the back – we've only a week to the First Secretary's visit."

The Sign of the Stripper

As the music stopped they took their seats in the front row of the strip club. Only three feet from him, on a miniature stage decorated like a boudoir, the naked couple were reaching the climax of their sex act. The bored audience hushed behind them, and he was aware of Heller watching him with an almost obsessive intensity. For days he had been numbed by the galvanic energy of this psychotic man, this terrorist with his doomsday dreams of World War III. During the past few days they had followed a deranged itinerary – airport cargo bays, the approach roads to missile silos, secret apartments packed with computer terminals and guarded by a gang of arrogant killers, hoodlum physicists trained at some deviant university. And above all, the strip clubs – he and Heller had visited dozens of these lurid cabins, watching Renata and the women members of the gang run the gamut of every conceivable sexual variation, perversions so abstract that they had become the elements in a complex calculus. Later, in their apartments, these aggressive women would sidle around him like caricatures from an erotic dream. Already he knew that Heller was trying to recruit him into his conspiracy. But were they unconsciously giving him the keys to the sixth house? He stared up at the young woman who was now leaving the stage to scattered applause, showing off the semen on her thigh. He remembered Heller's frightening violence as he grappled with the young whores in the back of the sports car, assaults as stylised as ballet movements. In the codes of Renata's body, in the junctions of nipple and finger, in the sulcus of her buttocks, waited the possibilities of a benevolent psychopathology.

The Sign of the Psychiatrist

Professor Rotblat paused as Vanessa Carrington returned from the window and stood behind the young man's chair, her hands protectively on his shoulders. His face seemed to embody the geometry of totally alien obsessions. "The role of psychiatry today is no longer to cure the patient, but to reconcile him to his strengths and weaknesses, to balance the dark side of the sun against the light – a task, incidentally, made no easier for us by an unaccommodating nature. Theoretical physics reminds us of the inherent right-hand bias of all matter. The spin of the electron, the rotation of both the solar system and the smallest sub-atomic particles, the great tides that turn the cosmos itself, all embody this fundamental constant, reflected not only in the deep-rooted popular unease with left-handedness, but in the dextrorotatory helix of DNA. Given the high energies involved, whether in galaxies or biological systems, any attempt at a contrary direction would have catastrophic results, of a type familiar to us in the case of black holes. A single such individual might become the psychological equivalent of a doomsday weapon . . ." He waited for the young man to reply. Had he returned to the hospital to remind them that he had transcended the role of patient and was moving into a sinistral realm where the ULTRAC predictions should be read from right to left?

The Sign of the Psychopath

He stood by the stolen Mercedes as the women loaded the ambassador's body into the trunk. Heller was watching from the elevator doors, the heavy machine-pistol held in both hands. The terrorist's swarthy face had closed in on itself, exposing the loosening sutures around his temples. During the hours of violence in the apartment he had gripped his pistol as if masturbating himself to a continuous orgasm. The torment inflicted upon this elderly diplomat had clearly served a purpose known only to Renata and her companions. They had watched the murder with an almost dreamlike calm, as if Heller's deranged cruelty revealed the secret formulae of a new logic, a conceptualised violence that would transform the air disaster and the car crash into events of loving gentleness. Already they planned an ever-more psychotic series of spectacular adventures – the assassination of the visiting party leader, hijacking of the plutonium convoy, the reprogramming of ULTRAC to destroy the entire commercial and banking system of the West. These women dreamed of

World War III like young mothers crooning over their first pregnancies.

The Sign of the Hypodermic

He watched Dr. Vanessa's reflection in the window of the control room as she adjusted the electrodes on his scalp. Her uncertain hands, with their tremor of guilt and affection, summed up all the uncertainties of this dangerous experiment conducted in the converted television studios. Despite Professor Rotblat's disapproval, she had become a willing conspirator, perhaps out of some confused hope that he would make his escape, embark from the causeways of his own spinal column and fly away across some interior sky. The television director's face swam through the heavy glass of the control room. During the previous days, as they set up the experiment in the studio laboratory, Tarrant had begun to hide behind these transparent mirrors, as if uncertain of his own reality. Yet he seemed to sympathise with the need to come to terms with this nightmare world of terrorists and cruise missiles, objects seen in a deformed mirror that might one day be reunited in a more meaningful sequence. Multiplied by the ULTRAC computer, the wave-functions of his hallucinating brain would be transmitted on the nationwide channels and provide a new set of operating formulae for their passage through consciousness. He touched Dr. Vanessa's knee reassuringly as she held the hypodermic to the light.

The Sign of the Vibrator

He listened to the monotonous, insect-like buzz of the elegant machine in Renata's hand. She lay on her back, muttering some complex masturbatory fantasy to herself, for once unaware of his presence. Was she really convinced by these shudders and gasps of her own sexual fulfilment? Since his return to her apartment he had often reflected that sex offered to any would-be tyrant the easiest and most effective means of political take-over. However, he had made his own choice elsewhere. Within a few days the terrorist groups would attempt to start World War III, and the psychological year would move to its climax. Already the subliminal films were ready to be transmitted through the emergency news bulletins. Relaxed now, he looked down at Renata's straining thighs and pelvis. By the time the television transmission of this exhausting sex act had reached the nearest stars any curious observers there would assume that she was giving birth to this unpleasant machine, offspring of her marriage with the ULTRAC print-outs.

The Sign of the Cruise Missile

He knelt in front of the television set, waiting for the overdue emergency bulletins. By now the skies over central London should have been filled with helicopters, the streets deafened by the treads of armoured troop carriers, the whole panoply of nuclear alert. Waiting patiently, confident that the logic of the new zodiac would be fulfilled, he stared at the silent screen as Renata lay asleep on the bed. Deep in his mind he dreamed of cruise missiles, launched from the surfacing submarines and heading out across the lonely tundra, following the contours of remote arctic fjords. Soon he would be leaving, glad to abandon this planet to its nightmare games. He had played only a small part in this reductive drama. The true zodiac of these people, the constellations of their mental skies, constituted nothing more than a huge self-destructive machine. Leaving the set, he looked down at the young woman. As he placed his hands around her neck, ready to satisfy the faultless logic of the psychological round, he was thinking only of the cruise missiles.

The Sign of the Astronaut

Through the glass window of the isolation ward he watched Dr. Vanessa speaking quietly to Professor Rotblat. Her nervous anxiety when the police returned him to the hospital had given way to no more than a neutral and professional concern. He pressed his elbows against the restraining sheet, thinking of Renata's bloodied body, with its strangely resistant anatomy that he had tried to arrange into a happier and more meaningful geometry. He knew now that he had been tricked by them all, that there had been no nuclear crisis, and that the subliminal messages had been intended only for himself. Had it all been no more than a fantasy, and was the search for the zodiac imposed upon him unintentionally by his too-sudden release from the hospital? However, Renata's body remained more than a small clinical embarrassment. One day the murder of this intellectual woman gangster might really seed their society's destruction. He had been trapped by the zodiac they had urged him to construct, but he had escaped through the side door of this young woman's death. The great round had come full circle, raised him on its shoulder and returned him to the institution. However, they had made no allowance for a wholly unexpected contingency – his recovery of his sanity, a treasure abducted from the twelve mansions. Now he would leave them, and take the left-handed staircase to the roof above his mind, and fly away across the free skies of his inner space.

A sunrise

HUGO RAES

Then the sun set and it became evening. It was no longer so warm now. So he seized her tits and raised them lightly. She cooed, a laugh, and he thought, now her light will go on.

I am unscrupulous, conscienceless, corrupt, he thought, but it is her business if she likes it. He pulled her toot. She blinked and he felt her trembling in irregular spasms. She was tensed like a spring about to be released. He felt the tingling in his joins himself. He felt carefully between her folds for her joins, which were firmly set together. It was a big one. Shall we play stretcher? And he grabbed her, not relaxing his sharp gaze, and stretched. Gurgling in a somewhat provocative way she laughed. You like this game, don't you, she said. He stretched and suddenly let go, then grasped again and went on repeating this.

After half an hour he heard her sighing, then rustling like a soft breeze, at high speed. He deftly titillated her tapper (oh, mine is not so deep) making it disappear more and more, and a large pink patch became visible, expanded and grew brighter in colour. A glassy sheen came over it and the brightness became watery. He played gently with her breast-paws and waved all his projections rhythmically, which affected and delighted her greatly. How you stir me up inside, Krisnamari, I never felt my inside so moved, so much in action as now, she sighed, and the hair on her back lay flat on her carapace. He went on like this for almost an hour.

Deliberately he touched the unpetrified external vertebra and received the shock. The first one hurt, but the second was less charged, and gradually decreasing in power to a constant level they affected him more and more pleasantly. Perhaps her charge was not decreasing but he was getting more used to it. After forty minutes the closed circuit was accomplished, he noticed, looking at his chronometer. She is definitely quick, he reflected. The symmetrical waves streamed through him and his organism sent them back to her. Normally this would go on for three hours, but she was quicker than the others and he knew her tower would certainly rise considerably sooner, so he must prepare for more hurried capsuling. He pressed nickle against the shining pink patch and waited in readiness. Again he looked at his timing instruments. They would have about thirty minutes before entering on the next phase.

It was now completely dark. The sound of the planets had about reached night strength. Perhaps we had better have our night packet now, he suggested. She smiled and nodded and they took it, accurately in the required places, so as not to forget any. In the meantime she made jokes and teased him and pressed her shoulder-fingers against his temples and said: Here were your prehistoric ears, and that was your blob of a nose, but . . . what do I see? Yes, you've got a little lump, perhaps you will get one back again. He grinned and grabbed her by the repples and folded them over so that she complained and cried out: Ow, you're hurting. She pushed him straight in the middle opening, but he closed it smartly round her pale orange stickle and squeezed. Now I'm not going to let you, he said, and thought: I'll hold on to her till her tower comes up and while I am working on it. She was sensitive to it, he felt, and so he slackened his hold a little, squeezed less hard and saw that it gave her more satisfaction. I must not relax any more or perhaps she will pull it out when the tower comes up. His thoughts flashed quickly through the attention he was giving to the other parts. He pushed more firmly through her upper segments, so that she kept still and noiseless and seemed to be waiting, to have stopped breathing. The suspended tension lasted more than a quarter of an hour and when she began to get more lively he saw his trembler vibrating more violently than ever. Then he clamped himself fast with his side hooks to her white and mauve scales, one by one, so that she felt the process for a long time.

The night was now sultry and Saturn was clearer and neater to the world than ever before.

How long had they not discussed the night of love, prepared, described it? With some anxiety. It could so easily be a failure, it could easily be cruel. But as he felt her more securely and inflexibly joined to him, his hooks as though crystallised behind her scales, but one with her, joined as if grown together, his certainty became great.

Some time later he began to push her breast-paws down till they would go no further, entirely pushed in. In the meantime he stuck the thorn-shaped appendage for the first time against the curving, soft surface of her belly. She cried a little and water came out of her dark eyes, which were now less fiery. So that he stopped and instead pushed still deeper between her segments and joins and rubbed violently between a few of her rings.

Now the parallel vibrations of her closed circuit were gentle enough for him to stroke her lubber. The discharges pulsed constantly through him and her as if they were one. He worked on her lubber and stroked and stroked. She licked the shining skin of his skull and teased him by withdrawing her lubber for a time and making it disappear altogether.

He gave a short, rather nervous laugh and knew that this time it would not be a failure. Otherwise he would hardly be allowed to again. They die so soon if it is not a success and your identity is made public every time one dies. He had to laugh inwardly. But this one must not die. She did not know the ones before and arranged the night of love and waited for it so long, and after seeing her last week he had impressed on her that she must rest the whole time, so that she was as strong and powerful as possible, and that she must bathe a lot in the light of Saturn, so as to be charged. You do not get a sufficient charge in one night. Have you often done it, as you seem to know so much, she had asked. He did not go into that, so that she should not ask how many successes and failures there had been.

When her dark eyes, now burning more fiercely, saw his green belly with its irregularities, she felt violently stimulated. She suddenly realised that he was experienced. The uncertainty about the number of successes and failures made her rather anxious, so that the heat under her scales and her skin increased. Krisnamari felt it, gripped her firmly and more roughly between the rings. And he saw that snogs were coming through the upper nipples and that they were moving up and down and getting whiter. And he blew on them.

The sky grew lighter. Saturn was less sharply outlined. Dawn would soon break. It would happen in the next ten minutes, he calculated, after a glance at his timing instrument. Her folds were already becoming softer, her white lips wider and harder, and the smallest, transparent scales were sliding over each other. He could hear their strange sound. Then he made her big tummel go up and down, as it should, while he made little snips with the pincers, more and more, quicker and quicker, so that it seemed that she was being snipped on all sides, snipped into a thousand pieces, so quickly, more quickly, at last almost invisibly.

And then, just as the first ray of the sun probed the horizon, all her breast-paws stiffened. He clung closer to her scales, cutting involuntarily into her flesh, penetrated with the point of his hooks further into her inside, and then, softly and slowly, her tower began to rise, wet and shiny, higher and higher, inch by inch, red changing to pink, and whiter and whiter and the air stimulated it immensely, vulnerable, and the sun shone on it with more and more rays till it gave a golden tinge. It rose higher and higher. He pushed away a little with his main grabbers, and carefully watched the tower growing and approaching his own extremity. It went on and on. It seemed to take a quarter of an hour instead of the usual twelve minutes. It was shining unusually and it was whiter than he had ever seen one, and it went on rising, higher and higher, inch by inch, and he could feel her tits bouncing and her nipples snogging and saw her eyes staring at Saturn. Gently but at a great rate her toot tapped his thorn-shaped appendage, her tits wobbled in the motionless, hard breast scales and the radiating waves in the closed circuit tore through all his joins and hers. Her tower was now an almost perfect cone, and just before he began the decisive phase he turned on the electric metal poker that poked her in the place left free by nature, for which no corresponding male organ was provided. And just as the sun came right above the horizon he began capsuling. A shining, moist haze like mist spouted out of him, over her tower, billowing and forming a bright cloche, shutting it off and protecting it from the air. And while he was finishing it he noticed how quickly everything of his and hers was moving and making sound, and how brightly and gloriously the morning irradiated them.

Translated by R. B. Powell
Original title: *Een Zonsopgang*

Love keys

SHIN'ICHI HOSHI

Everyone has a secret word. A word he should neither forget nor tell others. Although it has no real meaning, the word is highly important to its holder for it functions as a key to their private locks. Undoubtedly a very modern sort of key. This is why in those days briefcases had no keyholes, nor did doors or windows anywhere. A small thing shaped like a human ear was provided instead. All the owner had to do was whisper his secret key-word into the "ear" and the lock automatically opened. One might mutter "A tulip blooms" while another says "Wake up, man!" A man of culture might even softly sing "King's ears are donkey's ears".

No more problems losing keys, and every thief had to seek a new job; this is because even if one of them uttered the right word or another at random, the possibility of hitting on exactly the right combination at the right moment was almost impossible. So, these modern keys appeared to be so much safer than all the old traditional ones. None but the owner could open the lock, unless he failed to keep his word a secret.

Occasionally, someone would forget it and would then have to call on a policeman to break open his own lock, but this seldom happened. More often than not, there would be instances of drunken men having trouble enunciating their words. But even then, there was no real reason to worry, all you had to do was invent a new key-word and insert it into the back of one's lock. And, if you were afraid of revealing your key-word by mistake, through a slip of the tongue, you could then conjure up absolutely meaningless words, like those produced by typing blindly at random on a sheet of paper; you then kept the word on you rather than having to learn it by heart. Thus, nobody ventured any longer to open the locks of others.

A girl lived in a room locked with such a key-word of her own. She was young and pretty. Her beauty was even improving constantly, for she was in love. And her affair was progressing well. She was seeing her handsome boyfriend a few times every week, at the cinema, at dances, out sailing and in other places.

But today, however, she was unhappy. She had quarrelled with her boyfriend over some insignificant trifle.

Really a trifle. Just because she had been late meeting him at the tea-room!

"It's quite unkind of you to keep me waiting so long," he had complained at first.

"I'm sorry, but you musn't let it aggravate you," she had answered.

"But you know very well I had to postpone an important business meeting to arrive here on time."

"And so have I. I was slightly late because I dressed up for you."

"That's no excuse. It's something you would have done anyway, isn't it?"

On previous occasions, it had been their unwritten rule that the one who kept his temper would soothe the other and thus avert a quarrel. This had always worked until now, but on this particular occasion it failed.

"I'm going home," she had shouted at last, turning on her heels. His hand moved towards her shoulder, to stop her, but he missed and instead brushed against one of her ear-rings which fell to the ground.

"So, if you want it that way, go home," was all he could say.

On her way home, she bitterly regretted what she had said and done. How stupid I have been! I might well lose him. I was late for our date and he was right to blame me. Why didn't I apologise nicely? Am I really such a selfish girl? I did not apologise, but it's still time to do so now, isn't it? Why don't I go back? Am I that selfish? Oh, I just can't. I'm not capable of apologising to anybody . . . even to him. So it now looks certain that from tomorrow I shall have to spend long boring days on my own.

As we all know, there's nothing harder for a teenager than having to apologise.

Feeling downright miserable and dragging her feet along, she reached her door. To encounter another form of embarrassment. She must whisper "What a pleasant day it has been" into the ear-lock, for this was her key-word. Most difficult words to say right now, but if she didn't she would not be able to enter the room. After a prolonged moment of hesitation, she forced herself to mutter the words, in a disinterested fashion, as if she were reading from a book.

As soon as she was inside and the door had closed again, she decided to change the key-word. She wondered what would be most suitable. She had no idea whatsoever. But she just had to change it, whatever happened. The girl was absent-mindedly playing around with words in her head when she noticed she had written down "Gomen'nasai" ("forgive me") a few times.

"How silly of me to write that now," she thought. "If only I could have said it only one hour ago . . . Well, it might be a good idea to have to say it again day after day from now on. I shall say it until I die. Just the sort of punishment my foolish heart deserves."

The next morning found her boyfriend standing uneasily in front of her door. He, too, was not much good at apologising. But his need to see the girl again had proved stronger. He had inwardly convinced himself that he had only walked back here to return the ear-ring, not to apologise.

He was about to ring the bell but suddenly drew his hand back. She must not think he had come here to apologise. He accused himself of narrowmindedness, but there just was no way he was going to apologise to her. He finally decided to fix the ear-ring on the ear-shaped lock and move away. He took the piece of jewellery out of his pocket and began fastening it onto the lock, lest it should fall down.

As he was fastening the ear-ring, he recalled all the pleasant moments he had spent together with her. He could mentally picture her sweet ear into which he had whispered gentle words of love while they had been sitting on a bench in the park. Now, it was all too late. He regretted once more that his own narrowminded character had failed him the previous day.

Once the ear-ring had been safely fixed to the lock, he unconsciously kissed the lock, whispering the word he had been harbouring within his heart:

"Gomen'nasai."

The door slowly opened. The girl, who had been sitting sadly inside the room, ran crying into his arms. She cried in silence, but inside she was furiously repeating her new key-word on and on.

The door was now fully open and the ear-ring swung lightly from the ear-shaped lock.

Translated by Noriyoshi Saito and Maxim Jakubowski
Original title: *Kegi*

The cottage of eternity

BOB SHAW

When a young man devotes a lot of time to a scheme – a scheme which culminates in his slipping a vital question to a young woman – he usually feels pleased when she says yes. With Barney Seacombe, however, things were different. On hearing the affirmative answer he had at first refused to believe his ears, then had come the numb conviction that his life was in ruins.

The question was one he had rehearsed many times, and he uttered it with a brash and breezy confidence. "Have you," he said, "a vacancy for a nuclear physicist?"

The young lady, a clerk in the employment exchange in the rural community of Daisyford (population: 8,324), glanced through the card index on her desk and said, "Yes."

"That's a good one." Barney chuckled to show his appreciation of the witticism, then returned to the serious business of the day. "Now, where do I sign on and how soon can I have some money?"

The young lady gave him a look of cool reproach. "There's no question of your drawing benefit while there is suitable employment on offer."

"Wait a minute," Barney protested. "I've got my old mother to look after – I can't go away off to Aldermaston or Windscale or somewhere like that." The part about his mother was a lie – she was being quite well looked after by her current boy friend – but he had thrown it in to win sympathy.

"The vacancy is in Gibley End," the young lady said, keeping her sympathy to herself.

Barney shook his head in disbelief. "But that's only three miles from here."

"I know."

"There aren't any nuclear establishments there."

The young lady's eyes flickered like those of a bad poker player. "Are you refusing to consider this offer of employment?"

"Give me the address," Barney said, acknowledging defeat. He left the employment exchange and stood for a moment in the sunshine of a glittering spring morning.

The main street of Daisyford was a scene from a tourist poster, painted in exuberant acrylics, but Barney was not in an appreciative mood. When entering university he had chosen to concentrate on nuclear physics for no other reason than that it was a field which offered zero employment opportunities in his home area. The plan was that, having prolonged his education for as long as was humanly possible, he would return to Daisyford and settle down to a state-financed life of fishing the numerous local streams and sipping real ale in the equally numerous local hostelries.

It had seemed a good plan, virtually foolproof, and the last thing Barney had expected was for it to go awry on the first day, especially on account of someone who styled himself:

Arthur Haggle, Squientist,
Gibley Castle,
Gibley End,
Herts.

He thought hard about the name and address which had been supplied to him and, as he rode his motorcycle through the lanes which tenuously connected Daisyford to Gibley End, his natural optimism began to return. Gibley Castle was too old and dilapidated to have been taken over by a research organisation looking for low-cost accommodation, so the whole business was either a mistake or a hoax which had been perpetrated on the humourless clerks of the employment bureau.

Squientist, indeed, he thought scornfully as his engine pulsed its note into vistas of quiet fields. *What a give-away! If the idiots in the dole office had any brains they would have realised immediately that there's no such word.*

By the time the compact grey mass of the castle came into view, hulking up incongruously from pastures and ploughed fields, Barney was rehearsing a jocular account of the expedition for his friends in the "Daisyford Arms". He was slightly taken aback, therefore, to find on drawing near the old building that a gleaming letterbox had been fitted into the gnarled timbers of the main entrance, and that above the letterbox was a brass plate engraved with the words: A. HAGGLE, SQUIENTIST.

Frowning a little, Barney took stock of the building's exterior and noted the renovated stonework and freshly painted window frames. Gibley Castle was a comparatively modest affair, more like a manor house with delusions of grandeur than a proper castle, but it appeared that someone with money had taken up residence in it. Perhaps, Barney speculated, he had been too quick to assume that no research company would have bought the place. Perhaps there really was a prospective employer lurking inside. Perhaps – Barney's spirits quailed at the thought – he was on the verge of obtaining work and would have to spend the forthcoming summer at a desk instead of lingering on the banks of murmurous streams. Numb with apprehension, he thumbed the new electric bellpush and waited to see what fate held in store for him.

After a minute's delay the door was opened by a thin, middle-aged man whose rusty black suit, walrus moustache and white-gleaming cranium made him look like a character from a Mack Sennett comedy. His gaze hunted suspiciously over Barney's face, and Barney – with a swift, sure instinct – knew that here was a man with whom he could never form a working relationship of any kind. He made an immediate decision, assuming he was looking at Haggle, to flunk the job interview in as spectacular a manner as possible.

"You must be Seacombe, the one they phoned me about," the man said in a fussy voice. "I must say you don't look like a nuclear physicist."

"Cyclotrons weigh thousands of tons," Barney explained. "That makes it difficult for me to wheel one up to people's front doors and ask them if they have any atoms they want smashed."

Disappointingly, Haggle appeared not to notice the sarcasm. "You'd better come down to my laboratory – we can talk better down there. Quickly, man!"

He closed the heavy wooden door and took Barney through an antechamber, a hall, and into a small elevator. The elevator was smooth in operation, but seemed to go an inordinate distance into the earth. When it stopped Haggle led the way into a tunnel-like corridor. The passageway was warm and dry, and was illuminated by modern electric-light fittings, but Barney began to feel cool fingers of unease caressing his spine. It was quite obvious that he had descended into the castle dungeons in the company of a complete stranger whose motives and intentions were shrouded in mystery. Barney tried to draw comfort from the fact that Haggle resembled a silent movie comedian, then recalled that as a child he had been terrified of silent movie comedians because, one and all, they looked like frightening maniacs.

"Mr. Haggle," he said brightly, "what exactly *is* a squientist?"

Haggle replied without looking back. "I presume you've heard of a squarson?"

"Can't say I have."

"What's the education system coming to? If you look squarson up in the dictionary you'll find it means a squire who also happens to be a parson. I'm a squire who happens to be a scientist."

"I see." Barney was still turning the explanation over in his mind when they reached the end of the passage and were faced with a massive steel door set flush with the surrounding stonework. Haggle straightened his tie, smoothed a fringe of hair down over his neck, rubbed the toe of each shoc against the back of his other leg, then took a remote control box from his pocket and pressed a button on it to operate the door. Barney's apprehension increased as the door swung open a short way with a muted electrical hum, giving him his first glimpse of a large, dimly-lit room of cavernous aspect. He followed Haggle through the narrow opening, glancing about him with some disquiet as the door quickly whispered shut at his heels, imprisoning him in an ambience of vaulted ceilings, floor slabs which were big enough to cover graves, and thick pillars behind which armies of shadows lay in ambush.

Remembering the way in which Haggle had preened himself before entering, Barney looked around him – half-expecting to see an occupant, possibly a woman – but the chamber was empty except for a scattering of benches, equipment cabinets and a large divan bed. For no reason he could explain, the sight of the bed in such an unlikely setting brought Barney's skin up in goose-pimples, strengthening his resolve to get out of Gibley Castle in a hurry and never come back.

"This is my laboratory," Haggle announced, "and it's where you'll be doing most of your work."

You want to bet? Barney thought. He said, "What kind of work are you engaged in?"

"Research into the fundamental nature of particles. I have only recently hypothesised an entirely new class of particle."

"Really?" Barney felt a faint stirring of professional interest. "What properties do your particles have?"

"Size."

"Size?" Barney considered the word, trying to place it in context with other scientific whimsicalities such as strangeness, colour and charm. "For a minute I thought you meant *big* particles."

"I do," Haggle's eyes glittered briefly. "My particles can be a metre and more in diameter, with corresponding volume."

"I see," Barney replied, meaning exactly what he said. It had finally become clear to him that Haggle not only looked crazy – the little man was a genuine lunatic. And, with the cunning of the true madman, he had successfully inveigled Barney into his underground lair . . .

"I can handle all the practical work, looking after the particle detectors and so on, but I need an assistant to deal with the theoretical side," Haggle said, giving Barney a penetrating stare. "How are you on theory?"

"Very sound," Barney said, realising the time had come to start disqualifying himself in no uncertain manner. "Of course, I've thrown out all that garbage about wave mechanics and distribution probabilities and so forth."

"You have?" Haggle looked suitably perturbed.

"It's totally unnecessary. Needless complication." Noting that Haggle was reacting in a satisfactory manner, Barney warmed to his subject. "What these modern eggheads don't seem to realise is that Nils Bohr's model of the atom was absolutely correct. Particles really are like little snooker balls – all different colours, all bumping into each other – and I can explain any interaction on that basis. It's quite simple, really."

Haggle took a step backwards, the stricken look on his

face making it obvious that he felt he was the one who was incarcerated with a lunatic. "Are you feeling all right, Mr. Seacombe?"

"I feel fine." Barney put on a broad smile. "I hardly ever get the headaches now."

"I'm glad to hear it," Haggle said, moving towards the door. "Thanks for coming to see me, Mr. Seacombe. You realise, of course, there are other applicants . . ." He broke off as a telephone began to ring somewhere in the shadowy reaches of the room. "Will you excuse me?"

Barney, now feeling he was in control of the situation, made a generous gesture of acquiescence. He watched Haggle disappear into a cell-like room adjacent to the main chamber and a few seconds later there came faint and fragmentary sounds of a telephone conversation. Humming a popular tune, his mind full of green visions of the afternoon's fishing, Barney sauntered around the nearby benches, examining the various items of equipment without much curiosity. He was pleased at having managed to think his way out of a tricky situation and he resolved that he would never again allow anybody or anything to spring surprises on him.

At that moment – as though to demonstrate the vanity of such thoughts – fate confronted Barney Seacombe with the two biggest surprises of his life.

Within the space of five seconds he saw a ghost and fell deeply, irrevocably in love.

The ghost was in the form of a slender young woman with an oval face, large eyes, long hair and a style of dress which – to Barney's startled and inexperienced eye – might have dated from the Restoration. She was partially transparent, glowed with a delicate violet radiance, and was beckoning for Barney to join her in the shadowy area behind one of the largest pillars.

His first and natural impulse was to take flight, perhaps emitting a scream or two for good measure, but that was counterbalanced by an emotion of an entirely different nature. Barney, although a presentable young man, had never had much success with the girls of his own generation, most of whom regarded him as being too dreamy. Undeterred, he had continued to cherish the belief that one day he would meet a genuine soul-mate, a girl predestined to be his and his alone, and when that happened both he and she, without a word being spoken, would experience a pang of recognition, ecstasy and fulfilment. Now, gazing silently at the girl, he knew that his faith had been vindicated.

In his daydreams the event had been scheduled to take place in a crowded room – the onlookers largely made up of insensitive females who had previously rejected him – but the meeting itself was all that mattered, and Barney was not going to be put off by a few peripheral drawbacks. Here, in the converted dungeons of Gibley Castle, he had found the light of his life, and it mattered little to him that some kind of slip-up in the celestial book-keeping had resulted in his being born a few centuries too late for true love to run its normal course.

Smiling a tremulous smile of hope and joy, he went towards the beckoning figure. He was rewarded with an answering smile, but it faded almost at once and was replaced by a look of haunting anxiety.

"Please do not leave," she said. "Please stay here. Please do not leave me here with . . . *him*."

Barney was not sure if he had really heard her voice or if the words had merely echoed in his mind, but the plea for help was unmistakable. "Do you mean Mr. Haggle?" he whispered.

"Yes, yes. I implore you to save me from him."

"But you're a ghost, aren't you?" Barney glanced down at the girl's figure to confirm his diagnosis and made the discovery that her semi-transparent state of being made it possible for him to see a variety of distracting curves beneath the insubstantial dress. "What can . . . ? What can . . . ?" He made a valiant effort to gather his thoughts. "What harm can he do you?"

"He is keeping me a prisoner in this terrible place," she said, her ethereal features registering distress.

"But . . . I thought a ghost could just flit through walls."

"If I could do that," the girl said, and it almost seemed to Barney that a note of impatience was creeping into her voice, "I would hardly be standing here now, would I?"

"You should nip out through the door next time he opens it. You could pass through him, couldn't you?"

"And mingle my body with his! Never! How can you suggest such a thing?"

"Sorry. I guess I wasn't thinking. You see, this is the first time I have ever . . ."

"There is no time to talk," the girl cut in. "Will you please help me?"

"Gladly. What do you want me to . . . ?" Barney stopped speaking as a faint *ting* from the telephone signalled that Haggle had just hung up, and in the same instant the girl disappeared. He turned away from the empty space she had occupied and, more than a little overwhelmed by what had happened, prepared himself to face the mysterious Mr. Haggle, squientist and abuser of pretty ghosts.

"Sorry about the interruption," Haggle said, walking towards the door.

"It's all right." Barney gave a hearty laugh to conceal his nervousness. "I really had you going a minute ago, didn't I? All that nutty stuff about particles looking like snooker balls! Sometimes I let my sense of humour run away with me."

Haggle's heavy moustache twitched several times. "You mean, that was a joke?"

"Of course!" Barney spoke quickly, anxious to gain the initiative. "Look, Mr. Haggle, I've been weighing up your new concept of large-volume particles and I think it's absolutely brilliant. In fact, I'm so impressed by it that I'm prepared to come and work for you without payment – the privilege of helping in your great work would be all the recompense I would need. What do you say?"

Haggle looked furtively gratified. "You wouldn't expect any salary at all?"

"Not a penny."

"And you'll bring your own lunch?"

Stingy swine, Barney thought. "I'll bring some for you, as well. My mother is a great cook."

"Well, in that case," Haggle said, in the manner of one who was yielding to a generous impulse, "I'm prepared to take you on for a trial period. You can start work immediately."

"Wonderful!" Barney found it quite easy to sound enthusiastic despite his aversion to work, especially of the unpaid variety. His intention was to remain on the premises only until he had rescued the translucent damsel, and with any luck that task might be completed in a matter of minutes. As a first step he would have to speak to the girl again and find out exactly why she was unable to pass through the stones of the castle walls like any other spirit. He looked around the shadowed recesses of the room, hoping to catch another glimpse of her, but all the corners and niches remained impenetrably dark.

". . . particles, which I have named maryons, can easily penetrate solid screens up to a tenth of a metre in thickness," Haggle was saying, "but the evidence seems to show that they can be trapped in a container whose walls are more than half-a-metre in thickness."

"Really?" Barney tried to bring his thoughts to bear on the other man's preposterous notions about particle physics.

"Yes. And according to my understanding of wave mechanics, that establishes them as objects whose associated wave functions decrease to 1/2.7 of their full amplitude at about 0.1 metres from their boundary. Do you agree?"

"Absolutely," Barney said, still covertly scanning his surroundings.

"Their wavelength must be of that order of magnitude – so what sort of rest mass would they have?"

"Huh?" Barney floundered for a moment and then, realising he would have to play along with Haggle until there was an opportunity to be alone, took a calculator from his pocket and fingered its buttons. "It looks like the rest mass would be less than an electron's by a factor of around 10^{16}. That's pretty small."

"So it wouldn't take much energy to accelerate a maryon to Earth escape velocity?"

Barney did more calculations, all the while wondering at what point Haggle would begin to appreciate the absurdity of his own theories. "Only 10^{-38} joules."

A gleam appeared in Haggle's slightly protuberant eyes. "Would pressure of the solar wind be enough?"

"More than enough."

"*Hah!*" Haggle began to pace the stone floor, his hands fluttering like white moths. "This confirms all my ideas."

"Does it?" Barney's wariness of the little man returned as a strange thought began to take shape at the back of his own consciousness. Haggle's large-volume particles were the product of an eccentric mind, but it was possible to suspend disbelief for a moment and predict that if they did exist they would be very rare on Earth because the solar wind would sweep them away into space. The only places where they might be found would be inside buildings with very thick walls – for example, in the dungeon of an old castle. It looked as though Haggle had come to the same conclusion and had designed his underground laboratory as a sort of bottle for capturing maryons.

Was it possible, Barney wondered with a growing sense of excitement, that Haggle's arrangement for trapping non-existent particles was also responsible for imprisoning the ghost? If so, all he had to do to set her free was to get Haggle out of the way and open the door. It was all quite simple and straightforward, and yet alarm bells had begun to clamour in Barney's subconscious, warning him that he had not taken his idea to its logical conclusion, that there were implications he had overlooked. The girl – whose name he had yet to discover – had given him the impression that Haggle was *deliberately* preventing her escape. And it was odd, very odd indeed, that the postulated physical characteristics of Haggle's strange particle should be exactly the same as . . .

"What's the matter with you, man?" Haggle moved closer to Barney, one of his eyes narrowing critically while the other grew correspondingly larger. "You look like you've seen a . . ."

"I haven't," Barney cut in. "I haven't seen anything."

"You weren't listening to a word I was saying."

"It's just that I'm rather tired," Barney said. "Haven't slept much lately. Worrying about not getting a job."

Haggle scowled his dissatisfaction. "I have to go upstairs for a while. Can I trust you to familiarise yourself with the equipment and not fall asleep as soon as I leave?"

"Of course," Barney said eagerly, pleased at the prospect of being alone with his ghost-girl. He hurried to one of the benches and stared fixedly and conscientiously at the instruments on it until Haggle left. As soon as the door had swung shut behind the little man Barney turned and walked towards the dark area where he had last seen the ghost. She appeared to him almost immediately and he felt an upsurge of tenderness and concern as he saw that she was more distraught than ever.

"You mustn't worry," he soothed. "I'll get you out of here in no time. You'll see."

She shook her head. "I can scarcely believe it. After being bricked up in a cell for almost three hundred years I have begun to feel that I shall never escape."

"Bricked up in a cell!" Barney was horrified. "Who did that to you?"

"My uncle – Lord Cyril."

"But what made him do such a terrible thing?"

The girl lowered her gaze. "I fancied myself in love with a stable-boy. My uncle said that if I could not find it within myself to behave like a lady it was incumbent on him to remove me from all worldly temptation by locking me in the castle dungeon."

Barney felt a twinge of jealousy towards the long-dead stablehand and was at once consumed by intense curiosity about how far the affair had progressed. Unable to think of a diplomatic way of obtaining the information, he asked the girl's name and was told that it was Mary Grey. Further questioning revealed that Mary had died of pneumonia soon after her incarceration and that her uncle, who probably had not intended things to go that far, had hidden his misdeed by having her cell bricked up. Mary's ghost had been imprisoned there for almost three centuries – until Haggle had knocked the wall down in the course of constructing his laboratory.

"In a surfeit of joy I made myself visible to him, wishing to express my gratitude," Mary said. "You can imagine how quickly my gratitude turned to fear and loathing when I discovered the kind of creature Mr. Haggle is. Not only has he continued to keep me prisoner here, but he has made me the object of his base and carnal lusts."

"I'll kill him," Barney gritted, quivering with rage. "I'll go up there now and tear him from limb to . . ." He paused in mid-vow as certain practical difficulties in what he had just heard presented themselves to his mind. "Um . . . if it's not too delicate a question . . . what exactly did he do to you?"

The violet radiance of Mary's face deepened to magenta. "He asked me to disrobe for his vile pleasure."

Barney gave a relieved sigh. "At least he isn't able to . . ."

"Not yet," Mary said in a tragic voice.

"Not yet?" Barney frowned at her in bafflement. "I'm sorry, but I don't see . . ."

"He is not a well man. His heart is not strong, and that is why he spends most of his time in this room. Some day, perhaps quite soon, he will die, then he and I will be locked in here for ever – and I will not be able to escape him."

Barney gave a low whistle, words failing him as one part of his mind took in the full extent of Haggle's nastiness, while another was swamped with speculations about the sexual proclivities of disembodied spirits. Mary had certainly retained all the externals of a nubile female, but Barney found it difficult to envisage, for example, the production of spectral hormones. A possibly vital clue lay in the fact that Mary, who had been a ghost for rather a long time, still thought like a woman and apparently was confident that Haggle's ghost would act like a predatory male. It was a subject to which Barney had never devoted any thought, and he found it intriguing.

"Mr. Seacombe!" Mary silently stamped her foot. "Are you going to help me, or are you content to stand there dreaming?"

"I'll help you, of course," Barney said fervently. "I'll get you out of here in no time – all I have to do is open the door."

"How will you do that?"

"Nothing to it! I'll just grab the handle and . . ." Barney's voice faltered as he noticed that the inner face of the door was a smooth sheet of metal, devoid of any manual controls.

Mary toyed with one of her tresses. "Mr. Haggle always opens it with a magic box."

"There's nothing magic about it," Barney explained. "It's a remote control device operating on radio or ultrasonic frequencies. Very common. Very simple."

"Have you got one?"

"Ah . . . no."

"Can you make one?"

"No, not in here."

"In that case," Mary said, "it cannot be as common or as simple as you appear to think."

"You don't understand," Barney replied, suddenly aware that seventeenth century girls could be as irritatingly illogical as their space age counterparts. He took out his nail-file, went to the door and – trying to look as though he knew what he was doing – inserted the sliver of metal into the hairline crack at the door's edge and wiggled it up and down. The door swung open immediately.

Barney's delight at this unexpected development was tempered, however, by the discovery that Haggle was framed in the narrow aperture, holding his remote controller in one hand and a mug of coffee in the other. He advanced quickly into the laboratory and the door swung shut behind him.

"I've brought you a drink," Haggle said, looking almost affable. "Something to pick you up a bit."

Barney checked discreetly to confirm that Mary had vanished, then accepted the mug. "This is most kind."

"Think nothing of it. Living alone has made my manners a bit rusty, but I do want you to be comfortable."

"Thanks a lot." Barney sipped the coffee and deduced from its flavour that it had been made from some rather inferior brand of powder, but at the same time he was intrigued by Haggle's desire to be hospitable. It appeared that the little man, in spite of some serious character defects, had a better side to his nature. *It just goes to show*, Barney mused, *nobody is all black*.

"How is your coffee?" Haggle said, watching Barney with a look of intense solicitude.

"It's very nice." Barney made an appreciative slurping sound. "Delicious."

Haggle looked pleased. "I'm glad to hear it – most poisons spoil the taste of a drink."

"I'm an anti-caffeine man myself," Barney riposted, "but I wouldn't go so far as to call it . . ." He stopped speaking as a curious tingling sensation spread through his limbs,making it difficult for him to move, and causing him to fix Haggle with a look of abject pleading. "You *are* talking about caffeine, aren't you?"

"Hardly." Haggle took the mug from Barney's numb fingers and put it aside. "Caffeine takes decades to kill a person, but the substance I put in your drink will do the trick in about fifteen minutes. You can consider yourself well and truly dead."

Barney had read somewhere that the imminence of death was a powerful aid to concentration, but he found himself unable to string two thoughts together as Haggle caught his toppling body and dragged him to the door of the laboratory. It obviously took most of the little man's strength to get both of them through the narrow opening during the brief period in which the door was ajar, and when it closed again Haggle leaned against a wall, panting and clutching his chest. As soon as his breathing steadied he bundled Barney into the elevator and thumbed the top button on the control panel.

"You're not going to get away with this," Barney said, aware that the near-final utterance sounded disappointingly like a line from an old B-movie.

Haggle appeared not to mind the lack of originality. "I'll get away with it, all right. After all – what motive could the police establish?"

"Motive? I'll tell you what motive." Barney paused for a moment, his brow wrinkling. "Why *did* you do it?"

"Bringing you here was part of an experiment," Haggle explained, smirking. "I did need some theoretical help, but I was also interested in finding out if Mary would be visible to other people. I guessed from the expression on your face that you had seen her when I was on the phone. That was why I went out and left you alone with her."

"I take it that the lab is wired for sound," Barney said, getting his first inkling of what had been going on.

Haggle nodded. "You take it correctly. I suspected Mary might try to be unfaithful to me – there's a touch of the wanton in that girl – and when I heard you begin plotting with her so readily I realised you would have to be put out of the way." Haggle's brows drew together. "It's a fine thing when you invite someone into your home and the first thing he does is try to steal your wife."

"Mary isn't your wife," Barney protested.

"She soon will be." A look of lascivious anticipation appeared on Haggle's face. "I don't think I'll have long to wait until I'm free of this mortal shell."

Barney felt a strong desire to take part in the little man's discorporation, but as his paralysis was now almost complete he concentrated instead on assuaging his curiosity. "Do you reckon that male and female ghosts are able to . . . you know . . . ?"

Before Haggle could reply, the elevator came to a halt and the door slid aside to admit strong sunlight from a conservatory which appeared to have been constructed on the roof of the castle. Haggle manhandled Barney out of the elevator and unceremoniously dropped his body onto the rush matting of the floor. The rough treatment caused Barney no pain, a reminder that he was close to death. He gazed up through the glass roof, into the clear blue vault of the sky, and made the astonishing discovery that he was unafraid. Previously, death had always been equated in his mind with total extinction, but he had learned a lot in the past hour. He had met Mary, had fallen in love with her, and passing from this world into the next merely meant that . . .

"There's something you seem to have forgotten," he said, experiencing a pang of mingled triumph and joy as the new thought was born in his mind. "You're doing this to keep Mary and me apart, but when it's all over I'll be a ghost – just as she is – and then we'll be together. What do you think of that?"

"I think you must be as moronic as you look," Haggle said contemptuously. "Have you learned nothing in the past hour? Why do you think I went to all the trouble of bringing you up to the roof? Answer me that."

"I . . ." Barney struggled unsuccessfully against a wave of mental confusion. "Can you give me a clue?"

"What name did I give my new particle?"

"Ah . . . the maryon."

"And what is the name of the young lady down in my laboratory?"

"Mary, of course, but I don't see . . ." Barney lapsed into silence, teetering on the edge of a philosophical chasm which abruptly yawned before him.

"I named the whole class of particle after her, you oaf." Haggle's eyes bulged with excitement as he glared down at his victim. "Human ghosts and my large-volume particles are one and the same thing! It may be that all the matter in the universe is made up of greatly condensed maryons – that concept could reconcile the religious and scientific views of creation, but it's outside the scope of my researches. It was enough for me to prove that a ghost is a particle with the properties we discussed earlier, because it explains so much about psychic phenomena.

"Maryons can pass through thin partitions, but not thick walls – that's why ghosts are most often found in very old buildings, although if the human body has chains or ropes around it at the time of death they can hold the ghost in place, too. A maryon has very little rest mass, but if it gets speeded up or agitated for some reason, perhaps because of anguish, its mass increases and it is *less* able to penetrate walls. That explains why ghosts are usually unhappy, and the increases in mass also accounts for most poltergeist phenomena. A massive high-speed ghost could easily knock over a vase."

Haggle squatted down beside Barney, his face twitching in scientific fervour. "Now do you see why I brought you up to the roof to die? You yourself worked out that the pressure of the solar wind would be enough to sweep a ghost, or maryon, away into interstellar space. That's why the world isn't crowded with ghosts; that's why vampires are so careful to avoid sunlight. And that's why, young Seacombe, you won't be able to try coming between Mary and me again.

"As soon as you die you'll be on a one-way excursion out of the solar system. Have a nice trip!"

Haggle rounded off his discourse by giving vent to a maniacal giggle. Barney, all other recourse denied to him, tried to spit in the little man's gloating face and discovered that the paralysis had now spread to his lips and tongue. He was unable even to swear. He had time for one searing stab of regret over having failed Mary, for having doomed her to an eternity closeted in an underground prison with a monster like Haggle . . .

Then he died.

On his way up through the stratosphere and the various radiation belts surrounding the Earth, Barney noticed quite a large number of other ghosts of many shapes and sizes, all being carried in the same direction by the inexorable pressure of the solar wind. The sun, mother of all life, was heartlessly driving away its young. Events had been proceeding at a bewildering pace, but his training in the science disciplines had not quite deserted Barney and he was quick to notice that he was travelling much slower than the rest of the ghostly multitude. They were whipping past him at accelerations he guessed would soon take them close to the speed of light, while he was progressing at a fairly moderate pace which gave him plenty of time to look around.

I'm a massive ghost, he deduced. *And if Haggle is right*, *it's because of the heartache I feel over . . .*

At that moment the cratered sphere of the moon swung into his field of vision and, aided by his spectral senses, Barney saw the satellite's conical shadow extending and tapering out into space behind it. He was approaching the moon's orbit with increasing speed, and until that moment had no idea he was capable of some independent motion, but a kind of instinct took over, he darted sideways on a vectoring course, and before he knew it had come to rest in the calm and pressure-free volume of space which was the shadow of the moon.

With the brilliant disc of the sun screened from his view, Barney found he could see with great clarity, and the first thing he noticed was that his immediate vicinity was quite thickly populated with other ghosts. He rotated himself into the attitude they had all adopted – feet towards the moon – and examined his neighbours with some interest. There were myriads of spirits in a variety of costumes which spanned ages and cultures. Many of them were congregated in large groups, but some were flitting about in restless isolation. Very much aware that he had been very lucky to escape being blown away into the reaches of interstellar space, Barney paused for a moment to collect his thoughts and then approached a chubby, benign-looking man – clad in Victorian tails, a stand-up collar and top hat – who was regarding him from the fringes of a nearby group.

"Allow me to welcome you to the afterlife and to congratulate you on your quick thinking," the portly gentleman said. "My name is Joshua Simms."

"Quick thinking?" Barney began to feel he had lost the power of thought altogether. "I'm sorry, but I . . ."

Simms smiled approvingly. "Oh, yes – you were very quick. Most fledgling souls get swept away into infinity before they know what is happening to them, but you were perspicacious enough to realise that the shadow of the moon is a sanctuary, and you got into it just in time. Physicist, are you?"

"Yes. How did you guess?"

"We get two main classes of people in here, apart from those who are lucky enough to be carried in by accident," Simms said, waving expansively at the surrounding ghost population. "Astronomers and physicists – people whose professional training enables them to appreciate the advantages of this select volume of space. We think of ourselves as a kind of elite, although in recent years there has been an unfortunate influx of spirits whose only qualification is that when they were corporate they read that fantastic rubbish scribbled by Bertie Wells and his followers." Simms lowered his voice to a confidential level. "Naturally, nobody bothers with them."

"Naturally." Barney struggled to assimilate the flow of new data. "So it's all true – a ghost is akin to a large-volume particle."

"Of course! Though we're not elementary particles, needless to say. We have highly complex structures."

"But if space is full of ghosts why haven't astronomers detected them?"

"They have, but they don't realise it," Simms said scornfully. "The very low mass of a ghost leads to a very large shift in any radiation which strikes its surface and is scattered by it. All short-wave radiation, such as light and infra-red, is scattered at radio frequencies – so ghosts are a major source of cosmic radio noise."

"This is all too much for me," Barney said feebly as radical new ideas about the nature of reality swarmed in his mind.

Simms nodded sympathetically. "It's obvious that you have been ill-used by fate, my friend. You are very massive for a ghost, which means you are burdened with regrets. Did you, by any chance, commit suicide?"

"No, I was murdered – and the rat who did it has got my girl."

"How distressing for you!" Simms patted Barney on the shoulder. "But take my advice, my young friend – put all thought of your mortal existence out of your head, and, above all, don't contemplate going back to Earth to haunt your murderer. If you join one of our debating societies or discussion groups you will have the inestimable privilege of conversing with Galileo, exchanging scientific ideas with the two great Isaacs, Newton and . . ."

"What did you say?" Barney cut in. "What was that about going back to Earth?"

"Some misguided souls do it," Simms said, shaking his head in disapproval. "They never achieve anything, of course. All that happens is that they eventually get swept away into infinity. It doesn't bear thinking about."

"How could anybody possibly return to Earth?" Barney said casually, disguising his intense interest in what he had heard.

"It can only be done safely during a lunar eclipse, when the Earth's shadow forms a corridor linking it to the moon. Some poor tormented souls cannot wait that long, however . . ." Simms indicated the distraught-looking individual ghosts who were restlessly keeping themselves apart from the groups. ". . . and they try to get back during an ordinary full moon, when the tip of the Earth's shadow comes near us. It means crossing a stretch of open space, which is a hazardous enterprise, but I daresay some of them must manage, otherwise the full moon would not be so prominent in the history of superstition."

"That's right," Barney said, a desperate resolve forming itself in his mind. He still felt a powerful yearning to be with Mary, a fact which was slightly puzzling, considering that neither he nor she had any physical presence to speak of; he would never rest until he got her out of Haggle's clutches; and, in the name of both justice and revenge, he craved the chance to punish the little man for all his evil ways. And if the achievement of those goals necessitated crossing the brink of hell itself – so be it.

It occurred to Barney, as he quietly slipped away from Simms, that he had grown up a lot since setting out on his bicycle from the Daisyford employment exchange only two hours earlier.

After waiting three days for the time of the full moon, Barney traversed some thousands of kilometres of open space and reached the shadow of Earth with comparative ease. He did not deceive himself that the crossing had been without risk, however – he had seen other ghosts, presumably less massive than himself, being swept away by the unrelenting pressure of the solar wind. Their cries of despair faded quickly as they were accelerated off into some unknown and remote part of the galaxy.

Barney tried not to think about their ultimate fate as he arrowed down the cone of dark stillness, identified the continent of Europe with his spectral vision, and homed in on southern England which was settling into a night of peaceful slumber. Picking out familiar landmarks, he flitted over Daisyford, and briefly considered dropping in to see his mother – before deciding that the ensuing complications would be too much for him to cope with on top of his other problems. In any case, she was likely to be busy with her boy friend.

He descended on the roof of Gibley Castle, passing through the glass of the conservatory with ease, and came to rest with a jolt on the ancient fabric of the building proper. Haggle had been right, he realised – a particle with the wave functions peculiar to a ghost was unable to pass through thick stonework. Barney glanced around and was relieved to see that his mortal remains had been tidied away. He went to the small shed-like structure of recent origin which capped the elevator shaft, and found he was able to penetrate the thin sheeting of its door with very little difficulty. He sped down the shaft, coming out at successive floors to explore the castle, and eventually was drawn by the bright lighting of a small apartment on the ground floor.

On entering the room Barney saw that it was furnished as a kitchen. The black-suited figure of Haggle was sitting at a table, poring over a book and sipping a cup of chocolate. During his three days of waiting behind the moon Barney had nurtured a plan to lurk around near the laboratory door until Haggle opened it, and then to slip inside without being seen, but at the sight of his enemy his self-control snapped. Haggle was seated under a shelf which was laden with heavy porcelain jars, and before he had considered the consequences Barney – driven by ungovernable fury – was whirling around the room at an ever-increasing rate, like a particle in a cyclotron, trying to dislodge the jars. As his speed built up his mass increased accordingly, as dictated by the laws of physics, and the ceramic containers began to vibrate and stir under the multiple impacts of his ghostly form.

Haggle looked up from his book, his eyes widening in alarm. He turned his gaze towards the overhead shelf, saw one of the jars toppling down on him, and threw himself clear an instant before it shattered on his chair.

Barney came to an abrupt halt, his disappointment giving way to relief as he belatedly realised the position he would have been in had Haggle met a well-deserved end. With the little man dead there would have been no physical agency for opening the laboratory door and Mary would have continued languishing in captivity. Barney, knowing he was invisible because of the brightness in the kitchen, paused beside Haggle and was concerned to see that he was clutching his chest with one hand and holding on to the table for support with the other. Perspiration beaded out on the white dome of his head. He emitted a strangulated gasp, staggered out of the kitchen and lurched along a passageway to the elevator.

Barney stayed close behind him the whole way down to the dungeon level, hovering solicitously as Haggle clawed the remote control box out of his pocket and opened the laboratory door. Steeling himself to endure the unpleasant intimacy of partially occupying the same space as Haggle's body, he went through the narrow aperture with the little man. The heavily shielded door swung shut behind him and, his whole body suffused with tender longing, he cast about him in the hope of espying Mary and once again hearing her voice. She was not to be seen.

"There's no point in your hiding, my proud beauty," Haggle croaked hobbling towards his bed. "I have a feeling I'm soon to be released from this physical shell, and when that happens . . . you and I . . . you and I . . ." The excitement of visualising what he would do when he finally came to grips with Mary apparently placed too great a strain on Haggle's system. He gave a quavering moan and collapsed unconscious on the bed. Barney gazed at him anxiously, half-expecting to see an astral body arise from the mortal clay, but rapid shallow movements of the chest told him that Haggle was still in the land of the living.

"Mary! Where are you, Mary?" Barney kept his voice low. "It's me – Barney. I've come back to rescue you."

"Oh, Barney!" There was a flicker of soft radiance in one of the darkest niches of the room, and Mary came into view and glided towards him.

At the sight of her Barney felt a pang of desire which almost frightened him with its intensity. He was impelled towards her, but stopped short of actual contact, partly because he was afraid of offending her innate modesty, partly because of the startled expression on her face.

"Mr. Haggle *did* poison you," she gasped. "I had hoped that part was untrue, that he was only taunting me."

"It was true, all right," Barney said. "The little swine gave me a lethal dose of something. I don't care about that, though – it didn't stop me coming back for you."

"But you are a ghost – just as I am."

"I know." Barney got an impression that Mary was not as

pleased to see him as she ought to have been. "What difference does that make?"

"What difference? You were not able to open that door when you were alive," Mary said, a note of asperity creeping into her voice. "How do you propose to do it now that you are dead?"

"I . . . Well . . ." Barney gave the door a look of baffled resentment.

"If Mr. Haggle dies now the three of us are going to be cooped up in here for ever. Have you thought of that?"

"No, I haven't," Barney said hotly. "All I've been able to think about was seeing you again. I've crossed the depths of space to be with you, because I loved you, hoping that you loved me in return – but I realise now that I was wrong. I'm sorry if all I succeeded in doing was to anger you, and in future I'll try to stay out of sight to spare you further annoyance."

Barney made to turn away, but during his impassioned speech a misty expression had appeared in Mary's eyes and she reached out to take his hand. The contact gave Barney a pleasurable thrill.

"Do you really love me?" she said softly.

"You know I do. You must know."

"And I have similar feelings for you, though we have scarcely met," Mary said wonderingly. "I don't know why that should be, because I'm a spirit now and I haven't been troubled by such desires since I quit my mortal body."

"I can't understand it, either." Barney took Mary's other hand in his, completing a circuit which intensified his feeling of delight. "There's nothing in the rules of particle physics to account for it, unless . . . unless . . ."

"Don't question it," Mary whispered urgently, moving close to him. "Hold me, Barney, hold me."

"Darling!" Barney took her in his arms, and in the instant their bodies met a pang of orgasmic rapture fountained through him with an intensity he could never have imagined, obliterating his senses, filling him with the joyous realisation that his whole life had merely been a prelude to this divine moment. He clung to Mary, and she to him, and time itself seemed to cease.

"My love," Barney said eventually, surfacing through a golden haze of pleasure, "do you know what has happened to us?"

Mary laid her head on his shoulder. "Yes – our souls have united in heavenly bliss."

"That's one way of putting it," Barney replied. "But I think I understand everything now. You were once a woman and I was a man, and a trace of sexual difference is carried over into our present state, a difference represented by the antisymmetric wave-functions characteristic of particles which obey Fermi-Dirac statistics. You have half integral spin in one direction, and I have it in the opposite direction, and when we paired up together we fully occupied the available energy state. That's what gives us this feeling of bliss and . . ."

"Don't try to analyse it," Mary said. "Just tell me we will always be together like this."

Barney smiled at her. "Of course, we will. Just the two of us."

"That's what you think!" The voice of Haggle, loaded with gloating malice, interrupted the lovers' communion, and when they turned towards the bed they saw his ghost-figure spring up from congruency with a lifeless body. He came towards them, face contorted, limbs quivering with pent-up emotion.

Mary shrank away, hiding in Barney's embrace. "Mr. Haggle has died! Oh, Barney – what are we going to do?"

"It looks as though you've already done it, you shameless wanton," Haggle hissed. "You betrayed me with this young jackass the minute my back was turned, but I'll have my revenge. You'll see! The three of us are going to be in here for a long time, and I'm . . ."

"Correction," Barney put in, sounding relaxed and unconcerned. "*You* are going to be in here for a long time – but Mary and I are leaving almost immediately."

Haggle looked alarmed for a moment, then a sneer tilted his walrus moustache. "And how do you propose to get out?"

"Through the walls, of course." Barney was aware of Mary looking up at him with an expression of surprise, but he continued to stare Haggle straight in the eye.

Haggle gave a derisive laugh. "You young fool! You've learned absolutely nothing."

"I've learned how to do this." Barney put out his right hand and thrust it into the stone wall beside him. His hand and arm slid into the ancient masonry with no trace of resistance. Mary gave a cry of wonderment.

"But that's imposs . . ." Haggled darted at the wall, bounced off it and stood glaring at Barney with impotent fury.

"There's no point in your trying it," Barney told him. "You see, it's hard enough for an ordinary ghost to penetrate a thick wall, and for a ghost like you – bursting with anger and hate – it's quite impossible. You'll be trapped in here until the building crumbles."

"So will she," Haggle snarled, pointing at Mary. "She was in here for three centuries without being able to escape."

"Ah, but that was before Mary and I were bonded." Barney gave Mary a reassuring squeeze. "The probability density distributions of our wave-functions are now finite beyond the boundaries of this room, which means that we can tunnel through the walls and exist outside. I'm using the word 'tunnel' as it is employed in quantum mechanics, of course, to account for the passage of an electron through a potential barrier in a . . ."

"I don't believe all this theoretical twaddle," Haggle snapped. "You can't leave me here alone."

"We can," Barney said sternly. "In fact, we have very little choice in the matter. If you consider this room as a quantised space, then the three of us can't continue to exist inside it without violating the Pauli Exclusion Principle."

"Balls to the Pauli Exclusion Principle." Haggle's voice thickened with venom. "There's one thing you've forgotten – the solar wind! If you go outside this castle you'll be blown away into the depths of space."

"I would have dreaded that at one time," Barney admitted "but not any more. Now that I'm pair-bonded with Mary I can see that it's our natural destiny to journey across the universe together, exploring all the wonders of creation hand-in-hand, meeting and welcoming cosmic travellers from other worlds. I'm not daunted by that prospect, and I don't think Mary is." Barney glanced down at his partner and gave her a fond smile. "Are you, sweetheart?"

"Not as long as we're together," Mary said. "Eternity seems as friendly and homely to me as a rose-covered cottage in which the love you and I have for each other will flourish and blossom, and will continue to do so long after the stars have grown cold and the galaxies have returned from their lonely flights and new cycles of . . ." Her words faded away as, still exchanging looks of mutual adoration, she and Barney faded into the stonework and were lost to view.

"Pompous bores," Haggle muttered to himself. "If that's what pair-bonding does for you, they can keep it – I think I had a lucky escape." He squatted on the floor, produced an insubstantial pack of playing cards and settled down to the first of many, many games of solitaire.

Ice two

A LOVE STORY FOR ANNA KAVAN AND BRIAN ALDISS

DANIEL WALTHER

The rivers.

You were talking about the rivers – the darkened mine-shafts buried among the high square mountains – you would say: there's nothing like the long and lazy rivers (sorry, you would apologise, sorry it's such a dull image!) – you would tell me about the rivers, the mountains so full of silence – often, your eyes would sparkle – and now, it's like a roar, my desire for you is like a scream: so fuck me, take me, love me, no! don't love me: fuck me/don't love me, be brutal with me, I'm just saying anything.

You became the mountain, you became the rivers, you became the high desolate windows imprisoning time within their dull reflections. You were the rising wheat, germinating in silence – the mountain full of convulsions, exploding, on fire, changing into resin.

BE BRUTAL WITH ME!

NO, DON'T BE BRUTAL WITH ME – NOT YET! TAKE ME SLOWLY.

LATER, WE SHALL SEE!

It was WINTER. No, not the dreary winter full of mist I had known back on Earth. It was a flamboyant winter, a sword of frozen crystal stuck into the flesh of the planet.

The planet: no larger than Mars but swept by crackling winds. The rivers flowed all too slowly under the opaque window of the solid ice. The mountains were like white beasts often reflecting unbearable shades of blue. You were sleeping, like an animal waiting for its winter hibernation, a very soft animal enclosed in dreams of warmth and luminous mist. When you awoke, I would give you some green liqueur to drink or I would make love to you, whatever you preferred, because how could I refuse you anything?

In the sky, but were those hieratic greyish curves still part of the sky? In, as I was saying, what I thought was the sky, the sun was no more than a blurred sphere of ever-changing shades, a captive balloon in a mass of caustic wadding.

"One day, I'm telling you, we shall awake and the sun will have melted away into the clouds . . ."

Tired, you would answer:

"It's not important."

Winter had closed in on us, freezing us within its solitude. But this solitude was what we had been seeking when we had taken refuge in the waste lands, beyond Tchermiansk, the border city.

The officer supervising the exit from the town had warned us, as the regulations required him to, of the dangers our decision implied:

"Beyond this limit," he had said, indicating a high wooden rotting fence with his gloved finger, "you are no longer under the protection of the dominion's agents. Your liberty will be absolute but, should you need us, we shan't be able to help you."

He then asked us to sign an exoneration form which he countersigned with an official seal of the Governor's armorial bearings. I remember him well, my love: he was a young sub-lieutenant with feverish eyes and thin lips. For a moment, I resented him when his famished gaze descended upon you. Because of the spark I saw in his pupils. That man literally stripped you with his eyes. I soon took you outside, into the brittle cold, which felt hard as woven glass. It was so difficult to walk, it was as if our bones were about to be crushed at any second. "I love you," I said, "I love you . . ." But you shivered and trembled and seemed to be flying, thousands of kilometres, thousands and thousands of versts away from me.

The electrically-operated sleigh took us on our way. In the driving-mirror, I could see the young officer's silhouette shrink as if in a dream or a film or something unreal.

"You don't regret anything?" I asked.

"Nothing."

Your voice was barely a whisper, a thin stream of speech

in the cotton oblivion through which we were rushing.

Do you remember the trees huddling together in the landscape, like hands stretching out dead phalanxes, attempting monotonous and glum prayers? As if they were alive, these trees huddled together in the landscape, with a sort of life suspended in the breath of the wind. Do you remember? When the desert closed in on us. On you and me.

Maybe you also remember (if you still want to give it a try, of course!) our short journey through the ice plains. There had never been winters such as this in the countries we came from, you and I. But you, oh love, you passionately enjoyed this earth covered with frost, you adored these silent territories in which you could rest from the anxious rhythm of the cities where your morbid fantasies had flowered so fully.

The inside of our sleigh was a warm cockpit where we felt perfectly protected from the murderous cold of the outside. While the skates kept on carving two parallel scars in the hardened snow, you had closed your eyes. A strange radiance shone over the high icy turrets, bluish organs erected under the glum luminosity of a dying sun, indefinable concretions taking on more or less phallic shapes, evanescent silhouettes, maybe mirages of the winter desert.

Although you were by my side, I was beginning to regret this foolish escapade. We had been told, time and time again, not to leave the planet's urban agglomerations. We knew nothing of the dangers of the waste lands.

We passed strange animals, oblong masses of dark and shimmering fur, leaping out of corrugated snow lairs. They were fleeing, afraid of the passage of this monster steaming out of the kaleidoscope of the snow, the wind and the smoke. The agility of these beasts was truly amazing as they ran on by and I asked you if you recognised any of them, but your answer was evasive and, dare I say it, cool.

Your hand was on my knee as I drove the sleigh through the foaming of the drab whiteness. It was like a continuing but delicious form of burning. I allowed myself to surrender to it, blissful, gently unaware of reality, in a way like being in the womb before birth.

I remember driving the sleigh only half-conscious, some forgotten form of instinct guiding me through the white phantasmagoria.

Buried in my dark and velvety cocoon, I thought, I remember thinking: this hand against me is the only living thing that keeps me alive; were it to depart, were it to slip into the night and suddenly disappear, I would die, melt into the icy wind, become an imperfect structure of fragile glass that some galloping beast would shatter into a hundred pieces under its hurried feet. I listened for the sound of your breath, but could only hear my own, the noise of my heart beating. Searching for something to say, to help me domesticate this incredible silence, I literally lost my voice.

No, not the rivers, you said, nor the mountains, or the mineshafts buried among the mountains, the high square mountains, or even the high desolate windows where the glass eats away at time, but the snow, the frost, the icy frozen cliffs. The refuge, the anonymity of the whiteness and its blue reflections. By this you meant the silence, a return to the original silence: to become part of the great silence at the Beginning . . .

MENTAL LANDSCAPE AND COSMOGONY

In the beginning of all things, you would say, there was silence, and the silence was god, and the silence was the greyish space between the worlds still unborn . . . Your cosmogony amazed me, but I accepted it with all my soul, my conscious mind never objected to its very lack of logic.

The refuge, the anonymity of the WHITENESS, you would say . . .

The house surprised me. I was expecting some sort of large isba, or at any rate a vast chalet. At least something more familiar, amidst this territory under the continuous assault of highly rigorous winters, then this angled building, with its silly-looking bell-turrets and enormous windows sheltered from the wind by greenish metal shutters. The first time I set eyes on this absurd conglomerate of stone, glass and metal I felt like a shock. It just towered over me. When I walked out of the sleigh, I was staggering. It was as if as I had become part of some bizarre dream, had become detached from objective reality, swept away by a flick of destiny, confronted by the unknown. Then, you leaned towards me, grazing my face with your breath, speaking to me, talking to me at last, saying: "This shall be our house."

THE HOUSE

To make love in a new environment is a bit like entering the mouth of a storm. You had barely crossed the threshold of the incongruity, of the stone ellipse that was to shelter the winter of our uncertainty, when the reality of your body soon made itself aware to you again. In the cold hall, you came to me and huddled closer while, the door closed against the shrieking of the wind, seeking desperately to share my warmth (to steal it?). Your hands were slipping against my body like cotton insects, wadding homunculi. My head was thrown back, almost at breaking point, and my eyes could explore the darkness surrounding us. Despite the hold of your hands (both expert and precise, accustomed to me) causing my blood to swell and the roots of my hair to shiver, my eyes roamed around the shifting shadows crowded up there in the heights of the house.

Although we were isolated from the cold by the clever architecture of the house, it felt to me as if threads of ice were sliding behind my skin and I slowly pushed you away, no longer drunk, awoken at last by the gloomy shadows creeping out of the ceiling, falling away from the walls like asexual ectoplasms, morbid angels with empty eyes. All the Demons of the Cold . . .

It was only later, once we had somewhat tidied up the house, that I made love to you. In a room on the upper floor. And even then, we only took each other with our mouths, thrown into the depths of a mysterious oval bed: your lips over my stomach were a bit cold, as if contaminated by the storms outside, your vulva sheltering within a sweet and pulsing animal warmth.

THE LIBRARY

LITERATURES

The house wasn't that disquietening, and I soon found it much less sinister. Full of surprises and possible discoveries. It was, for instance, pleasant to keep a watch for the tempests, to observe the blizzards approaching, through the tall windows of the library. These windows were made of a stronger and more resistant material than glass, although it was quite as transparent.

I found a great many interesting books in the library. Most had been written in one of the spoken languages of the planet, and I could only manage to decipher a sentence here and there, but there were also many other volumes in German, French and English worth looking up: Joyce, Tolkien, Sallis, Robert Walser, Vonnegut, Jeury, Sacher-Masoch, Perutz, Graves, Charles Duits, Anna Kavan, Conrad, Kerouac, Gene Wolfe, Trakl, Bonnefoy, Hölderlin, Drode . . .

A bizarre, eclectic, fascinating selection.

I grew accustomed to spending a couple of hours every day in the library while you drafted a few more pages of your new book. Sometimes, when you lacked inspiration, you would come and join me and sit by my side. When words eluded you, you could not turn to the words of others and found it intolerable to see me immersed in the work of those you would call your "rivals". If I tried to read you some lines or two or three verses I was particularly fond of, you would hide behind a wall of scornful silence, full of unformulated reproaches. When you found my attempts too unbearable, you would try the eternal ploy of sex. Your strategic talents allowed you to overcome me with insulting ease. At times like this, your solipsism was perfect and the reason for your anger, soon forgotten, quickly fell to the ground, its pages wide open, as we met each other on the carpet and your open legs took hold of me with a ferocious sort of possessiveness. But very soon I would discover your sweetness again and sink deep into the silt of your naked thighs, half-buried by the thick carpet, allowing myself to float away down your corridors of flame.

Slow burning of your arched body: you quietly brought me towards a welcoming final explosion.

When I came back to my senses, you were oh so proud of your victory. "What were you reading?" you would ask.

I seldom left the house and most times you would avoid accompanying me on my short walks. But these brief wanderings into the frozen mist soon became more and more indispensable. It was like a game with solitude, anguish and fear. A challenge, no doubt, to the glacial entities presiding over the waste lands. In spite of my curiosity, I would never venture too far from our odd building and always took care to scatter signs along my path, so as not to lose my direction home. As the snow plain was haunted by packs of wild "dogs", I never walked out without my automatic rifle, a weapon some experts revered. In fact, it was an instrument of death brought to utter perfection by designers all too full of love and passion.

I had been advised not to leave the civilised territories without a weapon and a well-intentioned friend had sold me, for a good price, this small marvel of ingenuity and precision.

"You might almost think it aims and fires of its own volition. It's almost impossible to miss . . ."

During my short ventures into the white ocean, I seldom used my rifle. And even then, it was only to scare away some furtive apparitions, indefinable images of peril, rather than with intent to kill.

THE DEMONS OF THE COLD

It's difficult to say, even after months of prolonged thinking, what really attracted me outside while at the same time all my energy was drawn towards you, my love. I can find no logical explanation for my behaviour. Maybe I was secretly jealous of you, your talent, the success you had had with your last two books, the respect you had earned from the master-thinkers of a society I desperately hated? Strange: while I prowled around in the cold, protected from the wind by a heated outfit and an elegant synthetic fur, you were inside writing a novel whose characters were physically and mentally losing themselves within the fantasies of a new ice age. Was there some sort of disturbing coincidence at play, here? Or just fate?

Sometimes, when I ventured thus in the labyrinths of the cold, I would feel fear descend upon me. It would begin with a feeling of unease, a sudden temptation to look over my shoulder to check whether I was being followed. Because, at times like this, I felt like I was being observed, watched, weighed by hostile presences. I would hasten on, sliding on as best I could with my rackets, fleeing the translucent Demons haunting the glass forests. I would convince myself they were about to lose me in the fog, causing me to venture even further into the solitudes, gloating over my forthcoming agony, my cries for help, my worthless entreaties. And when I would find the house again, its stupid bell-turrets, the greenish and absurd shutters protecting it from the onslaught of the blizzard, it would take some time before I could grow totally reassured. I went on thinking invisible observers were laying siege to us, watching every one of our gestures.

And I would come across you again in one of the rooms of the large building, half-asleep, a glass of liqueur at your feet. And your presence would chase away all the Demons of the Cold.

Is this what you wanted?
To live in a house that is haunted
By the ghost of you and me? (Leonard Cohen)

Sometimes I would also say to myself: the sun will not rise again. It will never be strong enough again to melt this snow, this ice. It will not find the strength to dislocate such a tenacious frost. The wind will blow with such power that the sun will be thrown back into the depths of darkness. Winter will settle once and for all over these wretched lands and we shall die of cold, you and I, in this angular house where even time crumbles away to dust between the absurd cogwheels of the whiteness. In those days, I still thought that, if I had the time and the patience, I could methodically explore every room in the house and possibly discover some strange relics. But something, always, prevented me from roaming down the badly lit corridors and opening the enigmatic doors, to bring light to the padded crypts where degenerate noblemen of old had hidden their disillusions.

"I have frozen halfway through a chapter," you told me one day, as the afternoon was drawing to an end.

I had just returned from one of my solitary strolls and had been obliged to kill a wild dog that had approached me, snarling, yellow fangs on view. I had discovered you in the library, but you had exchanged your glass of liqueur for a Lé cigarette.

". . . yes, over. Short of inspiration. The tap of words and sentences is closed . . ."

". . . . ."

". . . . of course! Do you think it's any consolation?"

"Naturally."

Miles of frozen snow were spread between us and I could feel the ghosts of the house look down upon me.

Why did the face of the young sub-lieutenant suddenly spring to my mind? Was it because I was trying to justify the jealousy eating away at my guts? To personalise it somehow. Because I was offended by your solitude, your habit of hiding behind the heavy curtains of a parallel world or a secret life.

Tchermiansk was only a village, although some pretentious sods preferred to call it a border city. I could see its low houses, huddling in the mist, again, within the indelible cotton-wool feeling of winter. The pale young officer was leaning towards us and his lips were moving slowly, his words were finding it hard to emerge. He was looking at you like a hungry wolf, a thin animal consumed from the inside by some unknown illness. I tried to remember whether you had smiled back at him, after that strange look he had given you just as we were getting into the sleigh again, a perverse sort of smile . . . He must have been bored to death in this lone posting and dreams were evidently gaining the upper hand in his personal labyrinth of obsessions and sexual fantasies.

Balancing on one elbow, you had lifted yourself up, five beautiful hand-painted claws resting on my forearm.

"It's awful," you had whispered. "Absolutely awful . . ."

"What is awful?" I had asked, my mind elsewhere.

"You haven't been listening to me!"

"No . . . I was daydreaming . . ."

The heavy breath of the wind surrounded the house and I walked out of the library to ensure that the shutters were securely fastened into their metal sockets. Pale shadows followed me around as I wandered through the corridors of the old dwelling, speaking to me, wrapping me inside an invisible shroud, attempting to draw me towards the many traps of the house. For one moment, shivering with fear, I stopped, leaning against the wall, short of breath – as if I had been running – my head full of wails and cries.

It was only after some long seconds of anguish and steady resistance that I managed to break the spell of the place. I walked on, determined to complete my work, now confident there was no reason to fear the battering of the blizzard, and returned to the library where you were reading a novel by Tarjei Vesaas. Sitting myself by you, I noticed your lips were drawn tightly together in a gesture of defiance. There was a pervading mood of bitter obstinacy in your features, carved deep like a permanent mask over your face.

"I hate this writer," you suddenly exclaimed. "I hate him

because 'The Ice Palace' is just the sort of book I would have liked to have written."

And you collapsed to the ground, like a statue crushed by storms of discomfiture, closing your eyes, half-buried within the swamp-deep carpet.

"I hate everything but the cold outside!"

Like a large silent heart preserved within the frozen guts of the world, you had said. Just an image, only an image. An idea. An approximation: a metaphor. But, wherever I go, I lose myself, and the flares of physical love extinguish themselves in the sea of time.

ECSTASY
ECSTASY!

Why are you looking at me in this way? As if you no longer recognise me! Have I become a stranger, one of the ghosts haunting the dwelling, an abstraction. Put your hands on me! There! Am I as cold as ice? Frozen like a snake surprised by winter? Or do you recognise me now because of the heat, the liquid embers, the fire flowing from my stomach? Don't all these symptoms convince you once and for all of the sincerity of my desire, the magnitude of my love?

– My hands on you, in you, are they really intercepting your heat? Flowing between my fingers all of a sudden, is it not a frozen stream? And why do my words refuse to cross my lips and surround you with a breath warm enough to melt the icebergs of my imagination? My fingers are eagerly searching the hottest, deepest zones of your body, looking for bespattered faults, melting crevices, mountains drifting on tides of lava, moors full of the smell of musk, labyrinths criss-crossed by sudden typhoons, my fingers are scouts for my hardened penis, a spear crossing the flames, my fingers only encounter a void full of snow, frost, efflorescent, my very own fingers feel as if I have just soaked them in a vat of liquid phenol!

– Why are your gestures slowing down? Why has your ardour so suddenly cooled? Look at me, listen to me: I am on fire, devoured by the flames, eaten from within by the embers of my stomach. My desire for you is like a roar, so fuck me, take me, love me. Love and fuck me! No! don't love me. All you have to do is fuck me: be brutal with me (I'm just saying anything).

I see you glide away into your mad soliloquy, into the white night adorned with the festoons of the blizzard, I see you moving away over the slope of a fantastic glacier whose caverns are full of translucent spectres. While I thrust my frozen flesh into you, while I sink, panting slowly, in your black crystal vagina, your frozen darkness.

Soon, it will all shatter. An unavoidable explosion. Two contrary, fatally intermingled forms of ecstasy: one is ice, the other is fire. Our two embracing, imbricated, locked, embedded, grafted bodies: like two corpses.

I ask you: was my sperm not like an arrow of frost?

When I look at you now, it is through a window overlaid with frost. Your lips are silent, witnessing the tiredness that follows the slow collapse of desire. Your right hand is on your stomach, the nail from one finger brushing past the last curls of your sex. A thin mist begins to rise over your features, masking the buds of your breasts. Silent ghosts brush my loins with their breath of snow, and I try to think of the days when we lived beyond the walls of this winter domain.

Snow, you are turning to snow in this cold.

Here, he was an absolute master, and, for that very reason, all other forms of life were absent. The wind of winter blew between his metal claws, always ready to seize.

This bird, cutting up the field, was none other than death.
(Tarjei Vesaas)

Winter will just not end.

It has settled down here for ever. As if to confirm my superstitious thoughts, the ceiling of the clouds steadfastly refuses to open up and allow the sun in and the radio, over the last few days, only broadcasts crackling noises. I do not dare pick up the telephone. I fear the line may have gone dead.

Winter is like a giant's hand thrown over the landscape.

Sometimes, I leave the house, but I seldom move more than a few steps away. I now hate all this whiteness, this uncertain desert. I am afraid of losing myself in the depths of this overpowering gauze sewer.

When I ask you to cut our stay here short, you do not answer.

You are moving away from me.

Winter is tenacious. It just won't die. It has frozen the sun inside the depths of immensity.

And I for one am losing myself in the circling paths that surround you.

Standing at a window, I try to see where the sleigh is, half-buried under the snow. Soon, it will be completely covered over, deep-frozen under a dome of ice full of blue reflections. Frost will devour it, cutting us off for ever from the world of the living, from Tchermiansk, for instance, from that officer so thirsty for love who wanted us to sign a form as we were about to cross the border.

Am I about to lose my sense of time and reality, in spite of all the beating clocks with their hearts of metal sunk deep down within the house?

Somewhere, in one of the rooms of this vast dwelling, you must be sleeping. Maybe you have come to understand many of the things that will remain forever incomprehensible to me, maybe you are already initiated in the seasonal rites of this world in which I shall never belong. It's even likely you will soon forget my very presence,
FROST thanks to the subtle game of the powers of frost.
You will forget my desire for you. You will end up by falling into a deeper sleep than usual and will drift in the ice currents regulating the cold realities of this world. Or is my jealousy too strong that I can no longer cure it? I am obsessed by the fear of your lengthening silence – your dying.

So, here I stand by the high window, taking advantage of a lull in the storm, my gaze lost in the mist bordering the trees, far from the mocking hillock still indicating the presence of the sleigh which is right now being methodically digested by the snow.

I am aware my hands are trembling with desire as much as fear. My desire for you and my fear of losing you.

THE COLD: I feel the cold insinuating itself under my skin, slowly penetrating my flesh, like an ivory sting polished by the frozen wind from outside, moving all the time nearer to my heart like a merciless stalagmite. I wonder if I will ever gather up sufficient courage to leave this room and go looking for you. "Have you written anything today?" "Has your inspiration returned?" These are the questions I shall certainly ask you if I find you awake.

But I am afraid.

Of the silence.
Of the house.
Because, if I do gather up all my courage and go searching for you, if I push all the doors open, if my patience is rewarded, WHAT AM I LIKELY TO FIND?

Translated by Maxim Jakubowski
Original title: *Ice Two*

The brass monkey

JOHN SLADEK

Pavel Roskan stood before the large window in Director's anteroom, trying to see his own reflection. He could not; not a ghost of his white hair and expensive tailoring moved among the shadows of pigeons flapping up in alarm or sailing down to settle on the ledge and grunt at one another. Pigeons disgusted Roskan. It was hard to believe that the late Dr. Skinner had based so much of his work on the study of these filthy, grunting creatures. And of course these Westerners had practically canonised Dr. Skinner, whose name, if Roskan translated it correctly, meant "he who flays". Still, one had to admire results. Roskan was only here, in fact, to admire some quite remarkable results.

He looked finally beyond the ledge down into the park, into a railed area where a few "soap-box" orators were trying to enrage a crowd. Almost no one seemed to be stopping or listening at all – no one except the "clowns". Odd way to handle a mob, he thought. The clowns did nothing, merely stood lounging here and there along the railing. But Roskan noticed how their painted faces scanned the crowd. As head of the police in his own country, he recognised them for men on duty. Very odd.

"Mr. Roskan? Sorry to have kept you waiting."

He turned from the window. Director, a younger man than he'd expected, did not shake hands. "I was watching your plainclothesmen At the, er, Freedom Rally. But aren't their disguises – ?"

Director flashed his boyish grin. "Not disguises, Mr. Roskan. Those are the official uniforms of our crowd-control men. Everyone down there knows perfectly well who they are. Open government, you might say – though of course that's only part of the story."

He guided Roskan into his small, informal office. "You must think they look ridiculous, and of course that's the idea. Sherry?"

"But they – no thank you, alcohol I don't – but they *are* ridiculous. How can people have respect for policeman with silly face? With nose like red pong-ping ball?" As usual, getting rattled made Roskan's English slip.

Director grinned again. "We want them to respect the law, not some bully in a uniform. After all, Hitler and his cronies took uniform-respect about as far as anyone could, didn't they? And with limited success. No, our aims are quite different, as you'll see. We hope ultimately to do away with policemen altogether. Let everyone be his own policeman."

Roskan tried not to show his contempt. "You surely do not believe you can stop people committing crimes?"

"Why not? You'll be surprised to find out how far we've gone along that road already." He pointed to a wall chart, a maze of coloured lines, each strand twisting its way from the upper left corner to the lower right. "The red line is murders. Decline of seventy-three per cent. Rapes are yellow, down ninety-two per cent. And so on, every crime from treason to traffic violations has fallen. And notice the blue line? Strength of our force, cut by more than half. That's what twenty years of Ethical Guidance can do. With twenty more years – who knows?"

Roskan suppressed a smile. "Utopia? Forgive me, but I see other possible outcomes. Even in my own small country, we find that such long-range plans do not always work out. A change of administration, suddenly your department is penniless . . ."

"Our plan is a bit more comprehensive than you imagine. For one thing, we're not just here to teach good citizenship. We teach loyalty. To the administration, I mean. No, I think it's safe to say, every year of E.G. makes another year more likely; our system is virtually self-perpetuating. Anyway, what politician of any party wants to give up law and order – and stability?"

"You seem to have answered all my questions," said Roskan, "even before I ask them. But of course I took it on faith that your system worked, it's why I'm here. My country wants 'Utopia' too, eh? But I must confess, the practical difficulties still puzzle me. Your E.G., your Ethical Guidance, is it not simply conditioning?"

"Yes."

"Very well then, how is it possible to round up millions of people and give them painful electrical shocks – or have I misunderstood again?"

The boyish grin reappeared. What a vapid young man Director was turning out to be. "Yes. Perhaps I'd better outline our entire programme. First, we need no coercion to get our subjects for the treatment. We simply advertise. Like this." He slid a newspaper cutting across the desk.

FREE PERSONALITY TEST
*Absolutely confidential – no need to give your name or thumbprint
*Government approved
*Takes only fifteen minutes
*No strings attached
*ABSOLUTELY FREE – and you could win a W50 bonus!!!

"Our testing stations are everywhere," Director went on. "The initial test is simply for I.Q., and everyone who's not an imbecile gets the bonus. The real purpose is to persuade him to take more 'tests' or 'training'. We might point out how interesting his personality is. Couldn't he be doing more with himself? Would he like medical advice? A government loan? Marriage guidance? Help with sex problems? Retraining for a really challenging job? One way or another, we get him signed up for ethical guidance."

"What if someone does not take the free personality test?"

"We generally catch him by some other means. Criminals we meet through the prison system, ditto troublesome political types. Lunatics are sent to us from the hospitals. Others come though our comprehensive welfare system."

"Then begins the rehabilitation?"

"Wrong again, I'm afraid. Let me explain some of our terms, I realise they're confusing to outsiders. We have three basic approaches to treatment: rehabilitation, temporary therapy, and ethical guidance. *Rehabilitation* means simply psychosurgery. We resort to it in only a handful of cases – really intractable antisocial types. *Temporary therapy* means that the subject is simply locked up for life, and usually kept sedated. Again, this applies to very few cases.

"*Ethical guidance*, however, is our most widely-used treatment. Also our most positive, I might add. First, it takes place at one of our luxury holiday camps. It's pleasant for most – even fun. Here, let me show you a few slides."

Roskan sat through the entire show, and though his mind digested fact after fact, his heart refused to accept the greatest fact of all – that this shambles of a system really worked. Individuals and whole families were shown arriving at the camp, putting on the festive *leis* that contained their individual monitors, and sitting down to a splendid banquet. Camp officials, wearing red plastic noses, showed them how to take care of their dormitories, make their beds, etc. Then came days of seemingly boring exercises: People sat in little cubicles before video screens and pressed buttons, and were rewarded with gaily-coloured poker chips. The poker chips appeared elsewhere, too: they were awarded for positive social behaviour at every level, from making one's own bed, to naming a mock criminal in a mock identity parade. The chips bought privileges (staying up late) or little luxuries (cigarettes, sweets).

"But I still do not see how all this relates fundamentally to the outside world," he said. "Where poker chips are once more only poker chips."

"That you'll have to see for yourself, over the next month. You see, our camp teaching machines are linked to one master ethical guidance computer. It takes careful note of each camper, his behaviour minute by minute. It tailors his personal programme for him. Believe me, almost anyone can be made to behave like a responsible social human being, given that kind of information system."

"Almost? That sounds like a challenge."

Director said nothing for a moment. "Yes, there is always that residue we cannot reach. Brass monkeys, we like to call them."

"Brass – eh?"

"Because they insist on staying out in the cold, refusing to join the human race, the social order. We generally run them through ethical guidance, but of course it does no good at all – finally we have to swallow our pride, admit our failure – and send them for alternative treatment, as I explained."

"But this brass – "

"Idiomatic expression, I suppose it doesn't translate well."

"Ah," said Roskan. He touched the knot of his tie, brushed lint from his lapel. No one in this Western country seemed to be wearing a suit, very puzzling. It made him feel odd, as though he were playing a part: the old-fashioned foreigner. And no one shook hands, ever. He had much to learn, here; a month would hardly suffice. "Brass monkey, yes."

Director summoned him into the anteroom again, and pointed at the mob in the park. "I thought I'd arrange a really challenging test. You see the men haranguing the crowd down there. The reason they're angry is, we haven't reached them yet."

"And the reason no one else is listening, is because you *have* reached *them*?"

"Exactly. Now I'd like you to pick out one of these soap-box men, any one of them, and watch us put him through Ethical Guidance. Go ahead, your choice."

Why did the word sound mocking? A dangerous man, this Director. Roskan looked at the orators, pointed at random. "The red-haired one looks brass enough, eh?"

"Yes, that's Alec – something – let me run him on the computer for you." Director turned to the console and played a silent arpeggio on its buttons. The screen began to roll up lines of information: Alec O'Smith, age 35, unemployed, no fixed address, a list of minor brushes with the law . . . score on the Raeburn-Hope Antisocial Hostility Scale, .874 . . . education . . .

"I'll have him brought up to us," said Director, playing another arpeggio. "Takes a few minutes, so let's make ourselves comfortable back in my office."

Alec knew some of the other speakers by sight: the old man who insisted that true salvation lay in becoming "at one" with one's reflection in a mirror; the muscular old woman who preached against eating meat; the bespectacled young black man who called for a new world language, Interlingo. The crowd paid little attention to them, or to Alec, or to anyone except the man in the pink ice-cream wagon on the corner. Robots, he thought. Eating ice-cream to prove to themselves they're alive.

"Money!" he shouted, and held up a crisp new ten-wek note. A few passers-by turned to look. "Money! Where would we be without it? The stuff that makes the world go round, right? *Their* world!"

When five or six people had actually stopped licking their ice-cream to stare at Money, he brought out his lighter and set fire to it. A kind of shudder passed through his little audience; he could almost feel their shock.

"All money is counterfeit. Money is bureaucratic love. Money is what they give you in exchange for your *souls*." He dropped the little smouldering piece of black rag, and, after watching it hit the ground, they turned away.

A moment later, he was arrested.

"Shouldn't be long," said Director. "They'll be giving him a drug before we see him."

"A drug? What kind of drug?"

"Nothing much, just a babbler. Want you to get a good look inside his mind before we start his E.G. After we've finished, in about a month, we'll give him the same drug again, so you can see the difference for yourself."

"Open government again?" said Roskan. Director did not respond with his boyish grin.

A few minutes later he was grinning, however, and rubbing his hands, as a man in white wheeled in Alec O'Smith on a hospital trolley. The brass monkey seemed to be asleep.

"Strapped down?" said Roskan. "I should have thought you disapproved of restraints."

"Normally, yes. But babblers – this one is pethetetra-something, very strong – well, they can make people violent.'

"Just coming round, sir," said the attendant.

Director bent close to the sleeping man's ear. "Alec! Can you hear me? ALEC!"

". . . what . . ."

"Alec, wake up. I'm the Director of Ethical Guidance, and I'd like to ask you a few questions."

The red eyebrows raised, gradually drawing open the eyelids. "But you've got . . ."

"What was that?"

"I said, you've got feet. I didn't expect that. Always thought you bureaucrats hid yourselves behind desks to disguise the lack of feet. Nothing but machinery from the waist down, I thought." He struggled to sit up, looked at the straps, and lay back. "And who's the old boy in the suit?"

Roskan said, "Allow me to introduce myself. I am Pavel Roskan, Chief of State Security Police in the – '

"In some bloody puppet people's republic," said Alec. "A cop, I should have known. Only damned way the East and West ever co-operated, police co-operation against the people. Oops, I mustn't say 'people', forgot you've made that a dirty word. Police co-operation against the puppets, then, how's that?"

Director said, "Shall we have a little talk, Alec?"

"I am talking. I am bloody talking. I'm talking about, about . . . let's talk about Czechoslovakia."

Roskan raised a slender hand in protest. "No, I am from – "

"Czechoslovakia I'm talking about. Police against the *robota*, an old story there. John Hus, back in whatever it was, fifteenth century, know what happened to him? He claimed the pope was a fornicator and a murderer, so they tricked Hus into coming to Rome for peace talks, only when he got there they burned him."

"What is this you're trying to say?" Roskan asked.

"Funny thing is, Hus was right, the pope was deposed for fornication and murder, John XXIII, they had to re-number the Johns after that, had to re-number the . . ." His voice trailed off.

"We'd rather talk about you," said Director. "I understand you have some grievance against society. Want to talk about it?"

"I am talking about it. Always meant to sit down and write a poem about it, a Czechoslovakiad, say . . . Start with Hus and maybe go on to Rabbi Low of Prague, trying to protect the Prague ghetto with his golem, robots again, by God. You know the story? The golem was a clay man, Rabbi Low wrote the name of God on a slip of paper and put it into the golem's mouth, it came to life. The secret name of God, that was the programme, the software. See, the golem could go and spy among the Gentiles, planning their programme – pogrom, I mean – and report back to Rabbi Low. Of course no one would spot that it was just a clay man, a robot, hell they were all just robots, right?

"No wonder, no wonder Capek wrote 'Rossum's Universal Robots', the fucking Czechoslovaks knew all about slavery, they knew what it's like to be a slave machine, right? Right, three hundred years under the Austrians, government by the puppets and for the puppets and over the puppets. They no sooner got rid of them than the Nazis sent in their tanks, after the Nazis, Russia. What happened in 1939 happened again in 1968, and the robots, the poor robots still didn't understand it."

Alec closed his eyes. Director nodded, and the attendant gave him another injection.

". . . because it's about control, control, I saw an old movie the other night on TV, 'Tale of Two Cities', Ronald Colman climbing the scaffold and droning on about a far, far better thing he was doing than he had ever done, everybody else running around calling each other Jacques, Jacques One and Jacques Two and – any number of 'em, one of 'em was Fritz Leiber, you know? He was the one who ran around with his knife, put a hole in the wicked Marquis, started me thinking about science fiction. I mean, the real revolution was going on behind the scenes, all the time, right?"

Roskan whispered to Director, "I'm not making much of this, are you?" Director shrugged.

"I mean, the real revolution was the Jaquard loom. Original programmed machine, used punched cards. Cards full of holes as a wicked Marquis, I mean you have to laugh. I mean you have to laugh, all those yokels watching Dr. Guillotine's wonderful machine finish off Ronald Colman, and *it's the wrong machine*. The real loom of history isn't there at all, it's backstage, offscreen, clicking away quietly like Madame Defarge at her knitting. The old Jaquard loom, waiting for history to catch up with it, for men to give it a voice and hands and thoughts, prepare it to make the leap from slave to master. Christ, how else can you read the history of the past two hundred years, Mary Shelley worrying about Frankenstein, Hoffman worrying about women who were really wooden puppets, Hawthorne dreaming of mechanical butterflies, what the hell do you think they were so worried about. I mean – what?"

Roskan said it again. "I disagree. I must disagree with

you, Mr. Alec, this is ridiculous! You can't hope to compare the rise of proletarian class consciousness with the invention of machines – what is the expression? – data processing machinery! This I cannot allow! In the first instance – "

The man on the table raised his head to look at Roskan. "Okay, fine, just answer me this: Who do *you* work for? Who really runs your little puppet people's republic, anyway? Or the government here? Or anywhere?"

"Our central committee, I can assure you, is composed entirely of flesh-and-blood men like myself. As for this country, you surely know that the cabinet – "

"Take their orders from machines who tell them what is 'optimal' or 'feasible' or whatever the latest expression is. And it works, I'm not denying it works. No wars for thirty years, no major wars for what, sixty years now, Christ, not even a civil disturbance for the past ten, oh, it works – the machines couldn't allow anything that might spoil their predictions. Right?"

"This is preposterous!" Roskan stepped forward and seemed about to slap his face when Director said quietly:

"Don't argue with him, Roskan. He's not fully conscious, you know."

Alec struggled in his straps. "Who's not fully – you bastard, let me up, I'll show you who's fully conscious, what do you think I am, one of your robotomised – let me up." He sank back after a moment, and said, "Your world and welcome to it, Director. If you are the Director himself, and not some Disneyland creation with a cable running down out of your trouser leg and off to some central data bank."

Director grinned. "You feel that all authority figures are machines, do you? Why is that?"

"Why is what? Why do I feel anything? Hard to explain feelings, really, especially to the insentient. How do you explain anything to robots, audio-animatrons, automatons, androids, cyborgs, information processing systems, puppets, dolls, golems, you got that processed yet? And that? And that? And . . ." He drifted into a mumbling trembling reverie, while the attendant looked from his watch to Director.

"Almost run out, Director. You want another jab?"

"No, no. Alec, can you hear me? What did you want to say about your feelings?"

"My . . . I feel . . . Jesus, how am I supposed to feel? How do you feel? What am I . . . I wonder how Rabbi Low felt when his golem started disobeying orders. Because you masters can't understand that, you think you want robots, but even robots get out of hand, they want freedom just like everybody else. Maybe machines feel, you ever think of that? And maybe they feel like taking over, just like in the old horror science-fiction stories, just like the movies, Fritz Leiber I mean Lang, living inside a state machine when he made it, all it needed was a Hitler to punch in the programme. Funny thing there, just about the time Fritz Lang was fleeing Germany, Thomas B. Watson, the father of IBM, he was going to Germany to get a medal. Feelings? How do you think Watson felt when Hitler pinned a medal on him personally? Feelings, but IBM never put up any signs telling anyone to feel anything, just *Think!* Sound of a guillotine there, *Think!* Kind of a contradiction when you hear that and they're cutting off your thinker at the same time. Why you brought me here, right? To cut me off, to stop me feeling and thinking, to cut me off? But just tell me first, am I the robot or are you? Who's cutting off whom? Whom's cutting off who? I've said that. I've said all that. And I've said all that. And I've . . ."

Director nodded and Alec was wheeled away. The last Roskan saw of him was the soles of his shoes at the end of the trolley. One did not have a hole in it. Or one did. Take your choice.

"A brass monkey, after all, eh?" Roskan enjoyed using the foreign expression, rolling it off his tongue. He now wore Western clothes, and did not offer to shake hands so much. "A copper-bottomed one, we might say."

"Afraid so," said Director. Over the past month, he had ceased to look quite so boyish, become simply another face Roskan saw daily. Likewise the clown detectives no longer seemed ridiculous, nor the holiday camp officials with their red noses of authority. Of all faces, only the pathetic freckled mask of Alec O'Smith remained unchanged, unchangeable, hard as brass.

"We've done our best," said Director. "Yet we've failed him, somehow. A failure of communication."

Roskan accepted a glass of sherry. "I had great hopes of him, you know. He seemed to be doing so well, collecting thousands of chips, hoarding them away – salting them, is that the expression? – he seemed the best subject, the best of subjects."

"I know, I know. Could hardly believe it myself, when I heard what he was up to. Trying to make a big bonfire of poker chips and burn himself to death – imagine!"

"But the computer guessed it, all along."

"Ah, the computer! Yes, out-thinks them all." Director seemed about to raise his glass in a toast, but did not. "No failure there. A perfect record. The computer has never lost a patient yet."

"And never will, Director. So in a way, we can't call this a failure at all."

"Not at all, Roskan. O'Smith is alive and well, working in the North somewhere, selling shoes. I call that a modest success."

Roskan felt restless. He carried his drink into the anteroom and stood once more before the big window. At night, like this, he could see his own reflection clearly, even the gleam of his sleek black hair. Outside, not a pigeon in sight, nothing but the lights of the city.

"Pity about his poetry, though," he called out.

"What was that?" Director came to stand beside him. Their reflections looked alike, though perhaps it was only a trick of the glass.

"I said, pity about his poetry. I believe the man – undisciplined as he was – might have made a poet out of himself, you know. Before we had to rehabilitate him, of course. Think of his 'Czechoslovakiad', eh?"

"What made you think of that? The lights?"

"No, the absence of pigeons. They remind me of a little poem I dashed out myself, the other day."

The younger man cleared his throat, as though the idea of a poetic policeman irritated him. "Really?"

"It's only doggerel, but I call it 'Skinnerian Scene'. It goes like this:

From the ledges of a tall building
Pigeons fly up to other ledges where
They were just now sitting deciding
Whether to fly up to other ledges where
They were just now sitting,
Deciding."

He was aware of Director looking at him, but then he was aware only of the city lights. It was precisely 11.30 p.m., official bed-time.

All but a very few of the lights were going out.

The alabaster garden

TERESA INGLÉS

. . . but us lonesome travellers know only too well how vain mankind is to think the universe has been conquered.

We have established a wavering path of foam between two ports, and we claim to be masters of the oceans.

We have joined two coastlines together with a double track of metal and we think we own continents.

We have unfolded a thin asphalt furrow through the dark skin of the Amazon and we pretend to have mastered the virgin forest.

But all we can do is move, like spiders, along prefabricated lines: lines of asphalt, lines of metal, lines of ink across sea and air travel charts. Neural lines traced by boredom through our brain. Poor diagrams that belittle the fullness, the immensity of our landscape reducing it to the level of a roughly sketched and repetitive play written by some bureaucrat.

Now has come the time to draw the space charts; a meagre one hundred straight lines on the one-dimensional maps of the Solar System, and nineteen solitary dotted lines on a three-dimensional model representing the small area of the Galaxy we have already explored.

And beyond those lines, like in the old parchment maps, lies an invisible void full of the horrors of the unknown. Here there be tygers. Hic sunt tigres.

Nineteen solitary lines; one day, there will be twenty . . .

Having reached this point in the manuscript, I raised my eyes and took a close look at the man sitting in front of me: Oram Duma, about forty, tall, thin, angular features, well-known biochemist and archaeologist, and most of all, a close friend of the dead Rigel Olse.

"What does this all mean, nineteen lines and soon twenty?" I asked him.

"Exactly what it says," he answered with a wry smile. "There is a twentieth hyperspace route which isn't indicated on the navigation charts."

"Do you know anything more about this route? Would you tell . . ."

"Would I tell you," he interrupted politely, "whether I have any firm evidence and this is no wild tale dreamt up by a crazy old man. Isn't that what you wanted to ask?"

"You know my admiration for Olse," I protested. "In fact, isn't that why you selected me . . ."

"Only one of the reasons. The other is that you have an excellent reputation as a pilot."

"Thanks. But, with all due respect to your and Olse's mental equilibrium, I would like to see some more concrete form of evidence."

"Do you know the poem called 'The Alabaster Garden'?" he asked me, seemingly changing the subject.

"Every lover of good poetry knows it," I answered. And I recited the famous first stanza:

Your kingdom is the time
Within the hours of the dreams,
The suspended garden
Where the roses grow . . .

"Very good," said Duma. "The last time I saw Olse, a few days before his death, we were talking of 'The Alabaster Garden', and when I asked him about the symbolic significance of the poem and the metaphors it uses, he answered: 'They are not metaphors, Oram. The alabaster garden really exists. I have been there, and the poem is no more than a poor description of it'."

"I am sorry, I don't want to appear sceptical, but Olse was a visionary genius, and his poetical meanderings cannot be considered as irrefutable evidence; he was old, he was about to die . . ."

"Just what occurred to me, my friend," Duma interrupted, all of a sudden truly excited. "Which is why I didn't attach any particular importance to what he said. But when Olse died, having designated me as his testamentary executor, I often came across references to the 'suspended garden' or 'the alabaster garden' amongst his notes. And, most important of all, I discovered the data pertaining to the hyperspace route used by Olse to get there."

If he was trying to impress me, he had now succeeded.

"But it doesn't make sense!" I protested. "If Olse had been *somewhere*, why didn't he communicate the relevant data to the Astronautical Department? You certainly are aware that five of the existing hyperspace routes, as well as many of the interplanetary ones, were discovered and charted by independent operators, and that the Department has always taken a very close interest in our activities and endeavours."

"Of course," he answered disdainfully. "Fools can prove useful, but if you will forgive my saying: the madmen who take all the risks and try out hyperspace jumps are only ruled by their own enthusiasm and a thin veneer of dubious astronomical knowledge, two contradictory assets, to say the least. So, from time to time, a madman achieves his goal and the official science of astronautics gains a new route. What about it?"

"OK, OK. There's no need to convince *me* of the Department's opportunistic policy. But the fact remains that every time a lone navigator or a group of independent operators have overreached a target by more than a light year, the Department, in all its proverbial stinginess, has not reimbursed the expenses. From what you are telling me, Olse *landed* on a planet. But, if that is the case, how come the Department has no maps? Why did Olse maintain it a secret until his death? And, assuming that, what motivated his strange behaviour?"

"He did not keep it a secret. I have here a copy of his report to the Department," answered Duma, indicating the shiny portfolio he was clutching between his knees, from which he had earlier taken the manuscript I now held in my hands.

"But then . . ."

"Then, following the routine procedure laid out for such cases, the Department investigated the astral co-ordinates Olse provided for the planet and discovered they corresponded to a point in space where there was absolutely *nothing*. According to the Department, all Olse had discovered was a great area of void, and the ensuing disappointment had caused him to fantasise a series of compensating visions, heavily influenced by his poetic temperament. They say he dreamed he had discovered a beautiful world and supplied them with non-existent co-ordinates, those of his dream."

"I must admit," I said cautiously, "that it's not such an extravagant hypothesis. He wouldn't have been the first to hallucinate out in space. Men with much less imagination have reported seeing half-naked witches out there dancing on the wings of elephants . . ."

"I agree," Duma said. "I would not deny the possibility of an hallucination. But I knew Olse well, and I must confess that my faith in his sanity is such that I am willing to repeat the experience myself."

"But if the calculations say there is nothing in the centre of Olse's bearings for . . ."

"No body capable of being detected by our instrumentation at a distance of forty light-years, which is the distance that separates us from the planet in question. Which, as far as the blockheads in the Department are concerned, is the equivalent of a cosmic abyss. But, not for me and, I hope, you."

"So you think we might be talking of an invisible star system?"

"Absolutely. If you don't mind reading through the notes you are holding in your hands, as well as the rest of the documents I have here, you will see that Olse's planet orbits around a major sun, just a touch colder than our own. A red star . . ."

"But that's not possible!" I exclaimed. "There can be no such star forty light-years away that our instrumentation could not detect."

"Doesn't that fact make the whole venture even more intriguing?" he answered, with a slight, encouraging shrug of the shoulders. "If there is such a sun, and it both confirms Olse's version and eludes detection, wouldn't it be interesting to find out why, don't you think?"

Rigel Olse, one of the greatest poets of his time, also one of its most famous lone navigators.

The astronaut poet, the youthful idol of a generation of dreamers, and in particular, of a bunchful of madmen like myself, who had dedicated our fates and our lives to the exploration of space inside small, frail spaceships.

But Olse was not only a poet and an astronaut, he was also

a cryptologist and archaeologist like his friend Oram Duma, an untiring detective who had explored archives and libraries with the same enthusiasm as the depths of the galaxy.

And, by the looks of it, Olse had not embarked at random on his last journey of exploration, having been guided along by a series of mysterious references he had come across in particularly old documents. It had not proved possible for Duma to reconstruct in their entirety Olse's investigations or pin down his sources, but there was little doubt that the choice of the route had been as much the work of the archaeologist as that of the astronaut.

The implications of this were stunning. Hyperspace travel was still in its infancy and clouded with theoretical unknowns. When making a jump, you could only be certain of arriving at a predetermined point if you followed instructions laid down by whoever had survived and, thus, often accidentally charted the route. It had only been through experimentation of this sort that a minimally trustworthy network of hyperspace routes had been set up. A tenuous line of points where each dot represented a brief flight through the normal universe and each gap an incredible jump through the unknown. That Olse might have stumbled over references in antique documents enabling him to draw a new hyperspace route was more than amazing, it was awesome and frightening.

But more than the origins of Olse's investigation, however exciting that may prove, what interested us most was his ultimate goal, if there really was one. Which is why, barely a few months after our first encounter, Duma and I, already good friends, embarked on my creaking spaceship the *Tinker Bell*, ready to make the first hyperspace jump in accordance with Olse's instructions.

"At least," I said, "we don't run the risk of hurtling ourselves into a nova. The worst that could happen to us is that we find a hole in space as big as the one in our pockets!"

"Which would assuredly be a revolutionary discovery," Duma said, smiling. "As you know, there is no such thing in nature as a complete form of void . . ."

There was only one jump left and already there was nothing more around us any lighter than a first-magnitude star.

In heavy silence, we went through all the routine checks and retreated to our couches in readiness for the final jump.

"Do you have your sunshield, ready, Oram?" I asked, before pulling the switches.

"They won't prove necessary. Don't forget it's only a red star," he answered, attempting a feeble smile; but his voice did not belie his open nervousness. I was no calmer myself.

"Here we go," I said.

When the almost subliminal humming that usually accompanied hyperspace transit ceased, indicating that we were once more within normal space, we jumped out of our couches like slices of bread from an automatic toaster.

"As empty as our pockets," I said, with an edge to my voice. "Well, I suppose the kids in the Department must be right sometimes."

Duma did not appear to be particularly troubled, which surprised me. Anticipating my question, he said:

"We're not defeated yet, Len. If there is something preventing a large red star from being detected forty light-years away, it makes sense that the same would apply, even more so, at a few hundred million kilometres' distance. And you should know better than I that it's impossible to negotiate a hyperspace route without a margin of error approaching one light-hour . . . If Olse's star exists, and I'm still not convinced of the contrary, there must be some sort of barrier around it, restraining all its radiations . . ."

"But, being so close to the star," I objected, "it would have to be a sort of barrier capable of enclosing all the system, a sort of . . . shell surrounding it . . ."

"And why not? A big cosmic egg, where the red star stands for the yolk."

The possibility made me shiver. We had speculated earlier that what prevented Olse's star from being detected from the Solar System might be an immense cloud of cosmic dust or some sort of natural obstacle of a similar kind sited between the two systems. But a barrier like the one Duma suggested, was more like an obstacle put there by *someone* for a purpose, and the possibility of a being capable of such things was rather intimidating."

"Know what?" I said. "I'd almost prefer if we found it to be as empty as it appears."

"In any case, we shall soon know," he said. "The likely dimensions of the barrier must be very big if they extend to here. If it were situated between the Solar System and us, which I am about to investigate, we would not be able to see Sol. If, on the other hand, our ship is standing between the barrier and Sol, we would not see most of the stars which are according to our maps in this sector of space, this would prove that the barrier occupies a specific zone of the celestial sphere and obscures them from us. Now, if the imaginary line drawn between Sol and *Tinker Bell* doesn't cut across the barrier, that is to say, if our line is not situated *above* or *under* (taking Sol as our nadir) but *on the side* . . . we'll have to feed the work into the computer, get it to determine the stellar distribution we should be able to recognise from here and indicate any possible discrepancy with what we are actually seeing. If any star we should theoretically detect is missing in our panorama, we shall then know where to go."

"Thank you for the astronomy lesson," I said. "But I thought I was supposed to be the astronaut on this expedition."

There was no "above" or "under" us. But the computer, after a lengthy session of squeaks and grunts, discovered a discrepancy between the theoretical stellar distribution pattern and the visible one.

"We must keep one thing in mind," said a tense Oram, making a noticeable effort to contain his excitement. "We cannot discard the possibility that Olse landed straight from hyperspace inside the barrier. If that was the case, he had no need to cross it, as we do. For all we know, this barrier seems to stop electro-magnetic radiations from seeping out. It could well be the traffic might also travel the other way and the barrier is transparent . . . in which case there is no way of knowing whether solid objects can get through, either."

"We could send a survey probe ahead," I suggested.

"Yes, of course; but it wouldn't really prove anything . . . unless it doesn't succeed in penetrating the star's shield, in which case we know we can't get through either. If the probe penetrates the barrier, we should be able to monitor its signals so that we shall know if anything happens to it. We may need to programme the probe, and also . . ."

"One moment!" I interrupted him. "There are two possibilities: either Olse, on his final jump, reappeared outside the barrier as we have done, in which case he was obliged to make his way through it and it is therefore harmless, or he emerged on the inside, which would indicate the barrier is opaque – if it were not so, how could he have noted the star bearings which he transcribed in his papers. So, if the barrier allows electro-magnetic waves to move between the outside and the inside, we should also be able to receive signals back."

"Thanks for the lesson in elementary logic." It was his turn to be sarcastic. "But I thought I was the scientist on this expedition. What you have said is quite right and, I suppose, we shall soon have some solid evidence; however, it doesn't cover every possibility. Suppose the probe doesn't return. Who do we blame? The barrier or something else?"

The probe crossed through the barrier . . . or at any rate disappeared from our view. But it didn't return.

"Good, at least we shan't blow ourselves to bits," I said "That's a relief."

Duma kept on staring at me. He seemed nervous. At last, he said:

"You're the pilot, Len. I can't force you to do it, I can't put any pressure . . ."

"Every time I've ventured out into space in this old piece of junk," I interrupted him, "I've risked my life, and I've done that for many less interesting things than what we have here. *You* might be satisfied, but I ain't going back without finding out what's on the other side of *that*."

There was a star as red as Sol at dawn, and a solitary planet circling it on a lazy orbit. The planet had a breathable atmosphere and a gravity somewhat lower than that of Earth, although it was lacking in rotatory movement. Its seemingly slow rotation was in fact due to its strange orbit around the sun, the position of which in the sky of the planet varied greatly: the day and the year of this world lasted the same length of time – in fact they were the one and same thing – and were the equivalent of ten Earth years.

"Olse was here some five years ago," said Duma, looking all around him, although there was little to see in this desert of red sand, "and, in all his notes, he situates the alabaster garden within a zone of twilight."

"According to him," I observed, "we should soon come

across the garden . . . if it really exists."

"Indeed."

"So shall we begin our exploration of the twilight zone?" I asked. "I'm fed up with all this sand."

It was a cruel paradox that a world so similar to Earth did not at first sight appear to be anything more than a vast lifeless desert without even a trace of wind, clouds or water . . . Only motionless sand under a motionless red sky under a motionless sun.

We felt its presence before we truly saw it, a small obstacle in the absolute monotony of the desert landscape: an oasis of shapes in the amorphous world of the sand.

And when we finally arrived there, we soon understood why Rigel Olse, one of the greatest poets of his age, had been so overcome by his last journey into space . . . And why people had thought he had gone mad.

It really *was* an alabaster garden. And, undoubtedly, although quite alien, it was also a human kind of garden. Gravity of 0.8g., breathable atmosphere, average temperature 20° Centigrade . . . these coincidences were so improbable, but they could just have been mere coincidences. But not this garden.

It was a rose garden. A marvellous petrified rose garden, where motionless alabaster corollae sought refuge in the light of a motionless dawn.

As we entered the garden, a strange drowsiness invaded me, as well as an intense feeling of melancholy . . . and peace of mind. I had never been very aggressive, but at that precise moment I would have been quite incapable, say, of even brushing away a bee poised to sting me.

But there were no bees about, tasting the roses of the alabaster garden.

Only once, during our somnambulistic stroll, did I even brush against a flower to assure myself of its physical presence. Seeing them from afar, I had logically assumed we would be able to pick some samples for analysis. But once inside the garden, I felt quite incapable of perturbing the natural order of this beautiful creation.

I suppose that under normal circumstances, I would have screamed with fear. But when I discovered the statue, possessed by this strange and soothing drowsiness, I just stood there gazing at it in wonderment, as if the prisoner of a spell. I could not even speak to Duma, although he was at my side, as incredulous as I, watching the incredible vision.

The sculpture, as exquisitely built as the garden that housed it, represented a bald and naked woman, standing with her legs crossed on a white pedestal, next to a pool of motionless waters (it was the first time we had seen water on the planet). Her eyes were closed and her arms were held slightly away from her body, the palms of her hands turned towards the sun.

Your kingdom is the time
Within the hours of the dreams,
The suspended garden
Where the roses grow . . .

We didn't touch her or even dare approach her. Fascinated, we kept on admiring her for an uncertain amount of time, both quite breathless. At last, we walked away in silence, and we found ourselves once more on board the ship before we even said anything to each other.

"I don't think I should go and leave you here alone."

"Be reasonable, Len, it's the only thing we can do. There is some unknown force at work here, capable of controlling our will . . . What else can we do? Until now, it has only prevented us from touching anything in the garden . . . If we stay here, it might destroy us next time along. We can't both run that risk. If you go now and return within a reasonable time, you might discover something back home that could be a clue to all this."

"In which case, the least we can do is draw lots to see who stays on."

"Len, you're the pilot on this expedition and I'm the scientist. Let the pilot deal with the ship and the scientist keep busy with the laboratory we're going to set up here . . . Isn't that more logical?"

It *was* more logical, so I left Duma with his organic synthethiser and all the necessary scientific instrumentation housed under an inflatable dome, some thirty metres away from the alabaster garden, and returned to Earth.

I installed myself in Duma's house and busied myself with a thorough examination of Olse's notes, searching for something there that might enable me to determine the relationship between that mysterious planet, all of forty light-years away, and mankind's past.

But Olse's files were far from complete; they seemed to have been deliberately mutilated to prevent anyone from accurately reconstructing the archaeological investigation that had led to his fantastic discovery.

I was consumed by impatience and worried about Oram. Had the strange force annihilated him? Or had it driven him mad, incessantly pursued by an inner voice urging him to flee?

Oram had asked me to stay away for a year, maintaining that any shorter period of time would not prove sufficient for his experiments; however, when I had immediately refused to stay away for such a long time, we had soon settled on six months. Anyway, it would take me that long to gather sufficient funds for a second journey, as we had decided to dispense with the Department inasmuch as possible (on the other hand, it was also unlikely they would have listened to me).

Those were the longest six months of my life.

The alabaster garden, which we had discovered first time around within the twilight zone, was now fully lit by the red sun. For a day that lasted ten years, six months represented less than an hour, enough time, no doubt, for dawn in the garden to have turned to morning.

Oram was not in the dome, nor did I find any messages in the laboratory, as we had agreed upon. A bad start. No two ways about it.

Nor had he answered the signals I had been transmitting since crossing the barrier. So I was filled with apprehension when I made my way towards the garden. I wasn't particularly worried about my own safety, partly because I was too busy thinking of Duma, partly because if he had been killed, it had not been soon after my departure. There were clear signs of lengthy activity inside the laboratory.

But although I entered the garden fearlessly, I wasn't at all prepared for what I saw.

There was no longer one statue, but two. Next to the one of the woman there was the statue of a man, frozen in the attitude of writing something on the pedestal. It was Oram. Not a sculpture representing him, but a petrified Oram. I could recognise his wrist-watch and the ragged clothes.

I had to make a superhuman effort to overcome my fear of the place; but I finally managed to move closer to the statue of what had once been my friend Oram Duma and, with clouded eyes, gazed over his shoulder at the notebook he was holding against the statue's pedestal.

He had begun to write something on a new page and there were only four words: *Len, I am alright.*

The pencil was still resting against the sheet of paper, immobilised just as the final letter had been drawn. The paralysis had seemingly caught him by surprise, at the very moment when, by an ironical twist of fate, he was leaving me a comforting message.

It was then I fully understood the significance of this beautiful but horrendous place. Some evil and powerful being had fashioned itself an abominable playground in this corner of the universe or, at any rate, some sort of laboratory. The statue of the woman was probably a girl it had kidnapped back on Earth, many centuries ago, and whom it had changed into a statue for its monstrous garden. This must have been part of the clue Olse had discovered in his search through the antique documents relating the possible visit of the builder (or builders?) of the garden to our home planet.

Why he had not captured Duma and me immediately, whether his motives were scientific or merely crazy, did not bother me too much now, given the circumstances. Maybe it was all some complicated ritual, which involved trapping his victims this particular way, just as an expert fisherman will use a rod and not a suction pump. I was now fully alert. All I was concerned with at present was the fact that my best friend had been changed into an alabaster statue.

The strange force controlling this place was about to try and calm me down and suggest I move away, but I was ready to face it, full of savage anger. Screaming like a man possessed in the midst of this temple of silence, I hurled myself towards the magnificent rose bushes and began destroying the exquisite flowers at random when earlier I had not even dared rub against them. The rigid petals fell to the ground all around me, tintinnabulating wildly, shining like the scales of a salmon in the red light of the motionless morning.

But the mental force soon smothered my anger and vanquished me. Strengthened by the feeling of guilt in me caused by the fact I had allowed Oram to remain here on his own in this beautiful version of hell (and also in fear of succumbing to a similar fate), I now felt an uncontrollable urge to flee or face going insane.

When I recovered my senses and again became conscious of what I was doing, I was once more in space.

Four years have gone by since I fled the alabaster garden. Four years exclusively spent trying to overcome that horrendous experience.

I went in person to inform the Astronautics Department, but when I was about to relate the whole story I suffered a violent attack and they had to intern me for a few days. The Department's technicians came to the conclusion that somewhere along Olse's route there might be radiation belts affecting the brain. So the possibility of gaining any official form of help is now more remote than ever.

I've wanted to go back there a number of times, but until now it has not proved possible. Sometimes, it wasn't just fear but a real phobia; at other times, it was something much more subtle, like a lasting fear planted in my brain by the builders of the garden or some mental Cerberus: the same force that prevented Olse from repeating his journey and made him expurgate his notes. A man with his fame could have relied on public opinion and easily have found some rich patron willing to finance a fully-equipped expedition; but, after an incoherent and very partial report to the Department, he had given up on this project. And it was only through the power of poetry that he was allowed to talk about the alabaster garden, which he kept on referring to as something real until the day he died.

But, whatever it was that was holding me back, I somehow managed to overcome it.

I did not have to cross the barrier, like on the two previous occasions: after the last jump, I found myself in normal space inside the vast shell that surrounded Olse's planet.

On the planet, not a speck of sand in the desert seemed to have changed in the last four years. But, today, the alabaster garden stood in the crepuscular zone, where Olse had discovered it the first time around.

When I saw the inflatable dome, I caught my breath; over its silvery surface there was a message drawn in large red letters: WELCOME, LEN.

I entered. What else could I do? If this was some clever trap devised by the masters of the garden, what the hell? They had me at their mercy, anyway.

But it was no trap.

On Oram's desk, I found his notebook, the same he had been clutching when petrified. I recognised the first words; those he had already written, back then: "Len, I am alright", but this time the message continued.

My legs were shaking. I sat myself down on the chair and read:

"Len, I am alright.

"Dear Len, you have just departed and I didn't have enough time to write down a satisfactory explanation for you. All you saw was the first line, and I know it won't be much help. But I know you will return and I am now writing this with peace in my heart.

"The woman is alive, Len. She is not a statue. She appears to us that way because her temporal rhythm is much slower than ours. I have calculated it after monitoring her respiratory and cardiac rhythms. It wasn't an easy task, as I had to fight off the mental resistance of the garden all along. The nature of this power is still very much unknown to me.

"It took me some time to determine that the woman's vital rhythms were 4,000 times slower than our own. That is to say that for us (or rather you) a subjective hour is no more than one of her seconds.

"When we arrived here and encountered her, she was sunk in deep meditation (or maybe it's her way of sleeping). When you returned after six months, only an hour had gone by for her, and she was still in the same state of sleep or meditation. But I was confident she would awaken. And when she would open her eyes, she would find me at her side, now accustomed to her temporal rhythm.

"Of course, I was hoping to write out a complete report for you, but the mental force generated by the garden, or possibly the woman herself, made me forget it completely.

"The fact is that, as a biologist, I had in the past specifically researched metabolic time and the alteration of vital rhythms (which must be why Olse, who had known or guessed the truth, was so interested in my experiments and we became very good friends); and, over the last months, I have developed a treatment capable of aligning my own biological and subjective time alongside that of the woman in the garden. I wasn't sure whether it would work (I was the only guinea-pig available here to try it on), but I thought it was worth taking the risk and might well prove successful.

"When you arrived, I had spent almost one month with my vital rhythms slowed down (although for me it had felt no more than a few minutes). When I saw your ship (by a sheer stroke of luck, because your descent was for me just like the instantaneous fall of a meteorite), I realised I had left you no message. Forgive me, Len. I can just imagine how awful an experience it must have been to see me changed into a statue. But the inhibiting force of the garden was holding me captive. It is not an invincible force, Len, as you must have noticed yourself (I saw the petals you pulled out) and I think its strength is diminishing all the time; but when I tried to do something, spurred on by the brief vision of your ship, it was already too late. My vital rhythm was 4,000 times slower than yours, I only had time to take my notebook out and write four words before you arrived, checked the laboratory and later found me.

"Now you have gone, and I can write all this down calmly as I don't expect you to return for some months still.

"I hope that by the time you come again, the woman will have awoken and I will have managed to initiate some form of communication with her. And I hope that one day we shall understand what the significance of this garden and this world is, and what the connection with our Earth's past might be.

"And if the woman is held here against her will, I trust that I shall find a way of freeing her from the time-cage that surrounds her. I have good reasons to believe this is not her normal habitat and these are not the biological rhythms she was born with. The woman's subjective time seems to correspond to the length of the days and nights of the planet, but doesn't tally, for example, with this world's gravity. I could give you many logical scientific explanations that bear my theory out, but will spare you the boring details.

"Basically, we cannot judge such an extraordinary situation by our own standards. It could well be this woman is truly happy here, and it's conceivable that the force surrounding the garden and the barrier shielding the system are obstacles she has set up to protect her privacy. But, on the other hand, there are too many Earth-like connotations here that I can't rule out as coincidences. What if the woman does come from Earth? And if this closed system and the woman's temporal rhythm are none other than a prison or a punishment of sorts, a terrible spell devised with the help of a highly advanced form of technology?

"Anyway, we shall only find out if I succeed in communicating with her, and, in order to do this, I must suspend the time barrier that separates us.

"I don't know when you will come, Len, but I'm convinced you will. I hope these lines reassure you and prove of some help to you should I fail . . ."

I had nervously reached the first rose bushes, but to my surprise, the force no longer seemed to prey on me. In fact, the alabaster roses, wildly lit by the fire of the twilight, seemed to welcome me.

I walked slowly into the garden, afraid to disturb the holy quietness of the place with my clumsy movements.

On the white pedestal, next to the motionless pool, sat two alabaster statues. They were holding hands and smiling.

Translated by Maxim Jakubowski
Original title: *El Jardin de Alabastro*

Idiosyncrasies

MAXIM JAKUBOWSKI

Some people collect stamps, marbles, beer mats or cans, matchboxes, butterflies, books, records or even women. I even know a very amiable fellow, an export representative in the food flavourings, essential oil and natural spices business, who preciously hoards in his Hampstead Garden Suburb flat an incomparable set of hotel DO NOT DISTURB signs, stolen each and every one from high-class establishments he has visited throughout the world. Like a true collector, he only retains one of each and seldom visits the same hotel twice, not for fear of reprisals – it's highly unlikely that the local chambermaids ever notice his subtle thieving activities – but because every further night spent away from home in a new air-conditioned room is likely to reap a particularly rare or innovative sign. They come in all shapes, sizes and materials. Square, oval, circular, rectangular, almost always with some sort of hole enabling them to be hung on the outside doorknob. They are made of thin paper, thick paper, rough cardboard, plastic, usually red or green sometimes white with blue lettering. DO NOT DISTURB, they all say in a weird assortment of languages. NE PAS DERANGER. NON DISTURBARE. NIE PRZESZKADZAĆ. НЕ БЕСРОКОИТЬ. The last I heard of our flavours specialist, he was on his way to Pointe-Noire in the Congo to acquire a new piece for his collection at the recently-built Holiday Inn, using as a pretext for the call a visit to a major local factory set up by a large French brewery group where a rather poor Orangeade (with 5% juice) was presently being manufactured.

But I digress.

Ever since my earliest childhood spent under the tall and towering pine trees of the Newski Prospect, I have been an impenitent collector. You see, for me, collecting in the true sense of the word is not just a hobby, it is an art, a way of life which has been carefully nurtured, an expression of faith in one's sense of humanity and reality, the one true vocation.

My father, a sombre remote figure whose features I now find it difficult to recall, encouraged my involvement from an early age onwards. I remember with warmth and pleasure the many evenings we would enjoy together examining my more recent acquisitions, sitting by the sea shore at X., while my mother looked on silently, that unmistakable spark of kindness gleaming in her eyes.

At first, I collected insects. Later, I graduated to live domestic (and less domestic) animals.

Now, with pride and dedication, I collect people.

Not anyone, do understand that clearly. They are only valuable to me if they possess a touch of madness, some individuality that distinguishes them from the common herd. I am proud of my collection. In all modesty, I think it is quite without compare.

There stands David Orf. He studies the Kabbalah night and day, seeking out the true meaning of the Word with unflagging faith and energy. The world he lives in, perched between the Aleph and the Omega, stands precariously 'twixt the ever-shifting masses of light and darkness. His lamp glows in the wilderness. His brown-eyed Jewish wife sings a sad song of woe while in the garden outside their tree-house his three teenage daughters carelessly dance away the light fantastic and David Orf's eyes dig deeper into the sacred and profane texts, deciphering the most holy recesses of Talmudic law and tradition, drilling ever closer through the abysses of Knowledge and the caverns of despondency. He will never complete his task; that, I do know. It is written. But Orf, whose once curly hair is now growing thin on the top and who grew a drooping mandarin moustache on the occasion of his thirty-sixth birthday, keeps on seeking the meaning of the word within the word within the word, a delicately embedded structure that may or may not be the key to all the answers, mortal and divine. Secret garden of Kabbalic delights, where the paths are forked and the bushes are full of alchemical gold. Orf's folly.

"You're a poet," I tell him. "You're wasting your life

away in this vain pursuit of the Word. Give it all up, I implore you. Become a chiseller of rhymes and melodic love songs again. Unleash the old mood of fierce moral tracts."

"I am secure in the knowledge that what I am doing is right," he answers, looks down, away from me, puts his reading glasses on again and renews acquaintance with the sacred lines of the Kabbalah.

A fine specimen.

And, over here, is my science-fiction writer.

His alien universes are full of sound and fury, abysses of time where double suns never set and dark holes impact with shattering sounds of silence. Flamboyant cathedrals of neo-gothic design lie mysteriously buried under the layers of ice of enigmatic planets.

His reality is deformed. When one woman or another leaves him yet again because he didn't do this, because he didn't say that, he retreats headlong into his own alternate reality, into novellas where all the women look the same, be they virginal star princesses with alabaster breasts or earthy whores in the brothels of the Black Rigel souks.

My science-fiction writer is obsessed by time and death and has been promising publishers and agents alike for some years now that one day he will create the ultimate novel (preferably to be serialised in *ANALOG* or *AMAZING*) about the taboo territory that lies on the other side of death.

"Maybe you will."

"Of course I will," he says. "It's just a question of finding the time."

And goes on writing his thinly disguised autobiography yet again, where the space boy always loses the space girl, people die like flies and the inner landscapes look just like Paris when he was young, when he was happy (or thought he was).

I chuckle softly.

In another section of the collection, they call them worlds, I just call them rooms, lives the vivisectionist. He enjoys cutting cats up with a finely sharpened scalpel. See him cut. See him smile as he slices adroitly through layers of fur and skin, bares the inner membranes of the animal, saws with awesome precision across the bone, severs the muscles with unreserved delight.

He started early, this one. Poisoned his aunt's overweight

cat by mixing turpentine from his Painting-By-Numbers set with its milk when he was only eight. Kicked his first Siamese to death at twelve.

"I know what I like," he says.

The vivisectionist is a very popular man with the ladies. They find him so polite and attractive, a brooding, intense young man, extremely lovable in an odd sort of way.

Shall we continue? Follow me through this guided tour of my collection. You don't have to. But if it's the type of thing you enjoy . . . I've never been too keen on visiting museums, myself, but this is different, isn't it?

D. J. Barnes is a personal favourite. He's a pornographer.

"I write erotic stories," he says, correcting me.

"Slip of the tongue, sorry . . ."

There's more to sex than life in his spurious achievements. Thrill to the slurping sound of the erect cock hastily burying itself with spasmodic jerks into the puckered arsehole of the strangled, dead girl, whose body is already rotting away in the moist heat of the Caracas terraces. Open your eyes wide with amazement as the ex-*Penthouse* model positions herself, standing spreadeagled over the double bed and the two Dutch extras painfully try to place their impossibly well-endowed and rigid members into her rear aperture while a swarthy Puerto Rican inserts his bunched fist into her lubricated cunt and a young, rather pretty, brunette nibbles at her tits with mechanical ardour. Admire the perfect set of white teeth delicately grazing, sliding over the pulpy pink/pale brown/purplish penis and the humid tongue lingers expertly over the crown of the cock, explores the folds of the wilting foreskin, licks clean the pulsating balls in their wrinkled sack. See the warmth of the young girl's pale white body as she lovingly moves nearer, inch by inch, towards the expectant arms of her shy lover whose sad eyes wonder in the darkness of the room how in hell this can all be happening to him, after the months of anguish and loneliness, the telephone that just wouldn't ring, the letters all unanswered; and she says, "Come nearer, my love. Touch me, feel me, do to me whatever you want."

"First and foremost, I'm a realist," says D. J. Barnes, fingering the scar across his belly where some anonymous New York spade knifed him for no apparent reason in the 1960s on the Lower East Side as he was leaving a literary cocktail party to celebrate the publication of "Down Here".

Meanwhile, in the bright corner I have allocated to him, my perfumer creates new fragrances. In his white, spotlessly polished laboratory, he blends and he mixes at his console, combining science and artistry in one full swoop. He evaluates aromatic chemicals, precious aldehydes, natural raw materials of sometimes dubious origin, essential oils of spices, fruit and plants. The perfumer in the laboratory sees himself as the saviour of womankind, a magician whose craft provides untold pleasure to the poorer sex (he's also a mysogynist), adorns the female body with green auras of flowery sweetness, masking the unworthy odours of sweat, sundry secretions and excrement.

With painstaking precision, he weighs the musk ambrette on his electronic scale, pours the exotic ylang ylang oil into the test tube and dilutes the cloying coumarin powder in iso-propyl alcohol with one hand while simultaneously sucking 2.5 cc of veratraldehyde into his elongated pipette. His nose is a finely tuned instrument, capable of recognising up to a couple of thousand ingredients by smell alone. He is proud of his talent. He is fatuous.

Let us leave him for now, as he excitedly chases that fresh jasmin hay note required to round off his latest creation.

Follow me.

Come on, don't be lazy.

That's better.

Over here, is one of the finest pieces in my collection: Pierre Ménard.

I had to exchange him for a visionary mystic and an out-of-fashion rock star, but I still believe the deal was worth while.

Pierre Ménard thinks he is Tolstoy.

He has grown a long bushy beard and, every morning when he awakes, inspects his features closely in the mirror, searching for new white hairs that might improve his appearance further to resemble old Count Leo. He drinks bowls of hot milk at breakfast, although he hates the stuff and it makes him sick for hours.

Once upon a time, he had been a brilliant academic, a specialist in comparative literature whose master thesis on "Aspects of Despair in the Novels and Short Stories of F.

Scott Fitzgerald, Pierre Drieu la Rochelle and Cesare Pavese" is still the recognised authority on the subject, arcane though it may be. Until one day he realised, much to his dismay, that he had totally overlooked the complete body of Russian literature. Pierre Ménard instantly reconverted himself. The first sign of madness occurred when he published under the pseudonym of Erik Satie an apocryphal biography of the imaginary Russian dissident novelist Samuel Joseph Maximov (1944-2001). Shortly after the avalanche of adverse reviews, his mind cracked and I obtained him.

Ten years later, Ménard is now busy writing "War and Peace" in the original Russian all over again. The going is slow, but he is a very patient man. He has faith, despite an earlier botched attempt at a modernised version of "Anna Karenina" set in the Gulag twilight world. Time is on his side and nothing can now discourage him. Ménard is aware of the difficulties that face him. One must genuinely admire his courage; a writer of lesser talent might have chosen the easy way out and rewritten Don Quixote, for instance. "War and Peace" sure is a different kettle of fish!

Pierre Ménard even calls his dog Sonya.

A great man in the making.

I have many other fine people in my collection, but I do not wish to bore you. Collectors are very often that way inclined; they fail to notice how their passion can conceivably leave their guests indifferent.

Of course, I would have liked to show you my compulsive masturbator, the wide-eyed kid with the long, dark lashes or my lady-editors, tall and thin and shy, in their natural habitat. Another time, maybe?

Look at them all, sitting tightly in their cosy, warm boxes. Soon, it will be feeding time.

See them smile.

See them cry.

See them laugh, when I wink or pull my outsize tongue at them in jest.

Take me down the river

SAM J. LUNDWALL

A man was preparing to go over the edge of the world when the others came down the road from the hotel. He worked doggedly with some detail on his contraption, a dull metal cylinder resembling an oversized beer barrel richly adorned with projecting boltheads and spidery rods, stolidly refusing to meet the eyes of the few spectators who stood around him and his vehicle, offering him and themselves joking advice and wisdom. The man, an elderly, surly fellow with small piercing eyes and a thin, disapproving mouth, finished tightening a series of bolts, crept with amazing agility into his contraption and banged the lid shut with a loud crash. The sound of more bolts being tightened from the inside could be heard for a while, then everything was quiet again. An expectant hush fell over the dozen or so spectators around the metal barrel. The incessant roar from the wide river falling over the edge and into space seemed to swell and engulf the group on the riverside.

"He is inside, now," said one of the bystanders, a woman in her sixties with unmemorable features but a piercing voice, one of those eternal summer resort people always drawn to scenes of madness and death.

"So he is," said her companion, a sombrely dressed man who for the past few minutes had been staring at the new couple like a lonesome dog looking at possible new and kinder owners.

"Someone ought to help him over the edge," declared the woman. "He can't stay here all day."

"He should have thought about that before he got himself into that thing," said another bystander. "*We* didn't ask him to do it."

"He could suffocate in there!" said the woman in sudden

alarm. "He might die!"

"He *will* die when he falls over the edge," said an unseemly cheerful young man in garish clothes and very shiny hair. "He can't wait. If it was *me* in there, I could wait for ever, I tell you that." He turned to the newcomers, a middle-aged man in a sports jacket and a much younger girl. A mistress, thought the garish young man who had never had a mistress but had always longed to. Or a daughter. He smiled at her. "What do you think?"

The man shrugged his shoulders. The girl smiled shyly and looked away.

"Someone ought to *do* something!" said the woman, appealing for moral support.

The barrel lay motionless on the riverside, only a few feet from the rushing water, its various projecting rods and pins sticking out like the legs of an overturned beetle. Several hundred yards away, the river, at this point almost a mile wide, had eaten its way down through the hard rock at the sharp edge of the world and went in a gently curving slope down to a point some fifty yards below the plain until it fell over the edge, down into an abyss that literally had no end. Standing at the outmost edge of the cliff, one could see the face of the cliff drop straight down into nothingness, and far away distant stars, even in the middle of the day. No one was near the edge now. It was off-season, no fruit vendors, no souvenir hawkers, only a dozen people staring with varying degrees of interest and boredom at the unmoving barrel.

"He should have done it last month," said a wise old man, underlining his words with energetic nods. "A lot of people come here during the season, a damn waste to do it like this, if you ask me. No one here who can appreciate it, no . . ."

The barrel started rocking back and forth, like an overturned beetle trying to right itself. The surly man inside threw himself forward, then backwards, shifting his weight in impatient, jerky movements. The bystanders ooh'ed and aah'ed as the barrel turned slightly, rocked back again, then fell over towards the frothing waters. One projecting rod caught in the muddy ground, bent a little but wrenched itself free when the barrel slowly rolled down to the edge of the river. The surly man inside banged furiously at the metal with hands and feet, anxious for the indescribable, vertiginous moment when the barrel would start its unending fall through space. The man in the sports jacket nudged the girl (*Mistress*? wondered the garish young man. *Daughter*?) with his elbow and made a gesture towards the outmost cliff. They moved away, unnoticed except by the young man who gazed wistfully after them, dreaming of forbidden carnal love, or any sort of love at all.

"Some summers they come by the thousands," said the wise old man, blissfully unaware that no one was listening. "They do it in barrels and boats and riding on logs or just swimming, but all go over the edge and no one ever sees them again. Only foreigners do it, though. None of us who live here. They come from all parts of the world and just fall over . . ."

The barrel finally fell into the churning waters of the river and was swept away. A boy ran alongside it on the bank, shouting joyously. The rest of the bystanders just stood looking after the glint of metal bobbing on the waves.

"I really don't understand them," confessed the wise old man. "I really don't."

The man and the girl had just reached the outmost edge of the world when the barrel flew out into space. It shot straight out for almost a hundred yards before it started falling; the midday sun gleamed on polished metal and glass. The crafty old devil inside must have started working as soon as the barrel left the world; the projecting rods turned into wide metal wings; a large parachute suddenly burst out like an enormous flower over the gleaming cylinder. It checked the fall somewhat, but could not halt the descent. The barrel slowly sank down into the eternal night.

Behind them, the little group of bystanders had scattered for tea and slow, meandering conversations. They sat at the edge of the world, with their feet dangling over eternity. Faint stars gleamed down there, far beyond the cliff which fell down into the gathering darkness. The world ended abruptly at the edge. Inside it was still autumn, off-season, the sleeping hotel at the edge of the world, old people noisily drinking tea on the worn lawn where summer's croquet wickets still stuck out above the grass. Outside was an unending, cold, black space. A hundred yards to their left the river fell roaring out in the gulf, waterdrops flashing like precious jewels in the sunlight until darkness swallowed everything a few hundred yards down.

"I wonder what there is down there," she said, leaning dangerously far out over the edge. Her thin forearms bent sharply outwards from the elbows, long fingers digging into the soil at the edge of the world.

"Nothing," he said curtly, and immediately regretted it. "I don't know," he said. "Something . . ."

"Something different," she said, looking down into space.

"Perhaps."

She was shivering in her light dress. It was winter outside the world. She was thin, almost scrawny, very freckled, very blonde. The light eyebrows stood out in startling white against her skin. She seemed very young.

"I have never seen the river before," she said shyly, as if revealing a shameful secret. "I had heard so much about it, but never seen it."

"No one sees it twice," he said.

"Except those who live here," she said, practically.

"Except those who couldn't go on," he said. "They don't count."

She looked down the slope at her left where the mile-wide river fell down into space. A big red-brown bird dived into the churning water only a few yards from the fall, re-appeared with something glittering in its beak and ponderously flew back towards the world.

"I wonder where that man is now," she said. "The one with the barrel, I mean."

He shrugged.

"Falling," she said. "Still falling. He'll never stop falling. What do you think?"

"That parachute won't help him much, that's for sure," he said.

"No."

"Or that barrel." He smiled. "A crackpot. Going over the edge in a barrel!"

"Yes."

"A *barrel*!" he repeated incredulously. "The world is full of nutcases," he told her. "And most of them come here sooner or later, dragging their barrels and diving suits and one-man submarines and God knows what else, and then they go over the edge, thousands of them every year, and that's that . . ." His voice trailed away. He looked at the river which fell out into endless space in the most graceful and natural of curves. A faint rainbow hung above the rushing water, the scene was painfully beautiful.

"I wonder what he can see now," she said.

He shrugged and, without thinking, put his arm around her shoulders. She leaned against him, still looking out over the fall.

"Yes," he said slowly. "Yes, I wonder."

Dinner was being served when they got back to the hotel. The talkative woman with the piercing voice sat at a window table, talking to her sombrely dressed husband.

"It's a shame," she told him in a voice that would not accept any contradictions, "to allow that poor man to suffocate inside that . . . *thing*. And no one cares. No one! What is the world coming to?" she wanted to know, "when a man can die like that right in front of so-called respectable people?" She observed the man and the girl sitting down at a nearby table and turned to them. "Is that," she asked, "right?"

The girl smiled at her. The woman turned back to her husband, obviously pleased.

"He was mad," said the husband, at a loss for words, looking around for some support but finding none. "Crazy. And in the off-season, too. Going over in a barrel like that . . ." He threw out his hands. "What could *I* do?"

The woman turned to the girl again, hanging over the back of her chair like a huge, trapped animal reaching for an unreachable prey. The girl smiled mechanically at her, not really seeing her. "The problem with me," she told the girl, "is that I am too kind. I care too much for other people. I can't let a poor madman die like that, in a barrel, without any air, trapped like an animal. But some people," she continued, turning back to her husband, "some people couldn't care less. Now, a nice secure boat," she said, suddenly shifting track, "*that* I could understand. A boat like ours, a decent little thing, nothing ostentatious. I could understand *that*. But a *barrel*!"

The man and the girl ate slowly, saying almost nothing, while the woman at the other table kept on her interminable monologue. The hotel stood on a small hill right by the edge of the world. On the other side of the narrow veranda the bottomless gulf yawned at them, immensely enticing and terrifying. The depth tugged at them, whispering, persuasive. They ate slowly, without looking out through the window, and then went up to their room, grateful to get away from the persistent, nagging voice of the woman.

The garish young man would have been gratified to learn that they were neither lovers, nor relatives. In fact, they hardly knew each other. There was a mutual feeling of trust, maybe of sympathy, but that was all. They had met two days earlier, on a train speeding across the immense fertile plains that ended at the edge of the world, and decided to go together to the hotel at world's end. One hotel room is cheaper than two, and both were almost out of money after having travelled across the world to reach this place. Fellow travellers with a common goal, they went the last bit of the long journey together, ending up in a cheap room in the last hotel, off-season, paying for the room in advance each day, spending the unchanging autumn days walking by the fabled river. They were both kite flyers; indeed, this was what had first brought them together on the train, both recognising the familiar package the other carried. Now they waited for the wind, the beautiful, strong wind at world's end which would carry them along and away. That night, they sat at the window in the hotel room, looking out at the changeless plains. Nothing moved.

Long after the girl had fallen asleep, he lay awake and stared up at the ceiling. She lay fully dressed close to him, with her right arm across his chest and her right knee shyly drawn up a bit over his legs, seeking a comfortable position but not quite daring. The gesture was very intimate and very trusting, much more so than the simple lovemaking of two strangers. He held his arms around her, rocking her gently, thinking of the wind. The ever present sound of the river falling over the edge of the world was clearly audible and he remembered a song she had recited to him on the train:

> Take me down the river
> To evergreen and fragrant meadows
> Where blindfolded maidens praise
> The subtle light of dawn . . .

The deep tugged at him, whispered soothingly, promising peace and bliss beyond the understanding of man. He clasped the girl's thin body like a drowning man reaching for safety. She sighed in her sleep, settling down with her right knee at last drawn up over his legs. He lay still on his back, holding her thin body close, listening to the slowly swelling sound of the river as it triumphantly fell into eternity.

The wind came during the night. The garish young man saw them coming out from the hotel at dawn, carrying their strange packages, opening them, unfolding majestic and wonderful kites. His was shaped like an enormous black bird, with a wing-span of almost eight yards. Cold, painted eyes gazed at him as he snapped together rods, tightened paper-thin canvas, readied lines and handgrips. The wide, black wings flapped in the wind, trying to soar up and away from the ground. He worked quickly and methodically, assembling his kite with a skill that spoke of long practice. The girl's kite was a mess. A many-coloured butterfly, much larger than his bird of prey, delicate and beautiful, but ripped and torn from the long journey. The sparkling gossamer wings were bent, rods and edgings hung dead in her hands, strips of wood jutted out like broken ribs. As he finished assembling his magnificent, proud bird, she sat listlessly, staring down at her dead butterfly.

The wind rose. He sat for a long time, looking back and forth between the girl and his bird. On the veranda of the hotel, a few hundred yards away, a small group of residents watched them with disapproving eyes, talking among themselves. They saw the man and the girl (Daughter? Wife? Mistress?) talk, with many imploring gestures, like all foreigners do, over their childish playthings. This went on for quite some time. Then they rose, and the man strapped the big ugly bird to the girl's back. She ran up against the wind, spreading out the great black wings, and suddenly took off from the ground. She soared up towards the overcast sky, clumsily at first, then with growing skill as she used the wind and the thermals to gain height. She made a pass around the man, dipped her wings and then steered out over the wide river. The talkative woman on the veranda followed her flight with disbelieving eyes.

"Madmen!" she said breathlessly as the slim white form under the black bird climbed up towards the sky, leaving the lone man standing silent and still on the ground far below. "How could you let her do it? Why didn't anyone stop her? Why doesn't anyone *care* any more?"

That night, the man in the sports jacket ate alone in the

dining hall, under the hostile gaze of the talkative woman. She spoke incessantly to her husband and the garish young man, who kept on thinking of the slim white figure dwindling in the distance, borne away by the black bird. The man in the sports jacket pretended not to hear; he ate slowly and methodically, talking to no one, and then went up to his room. That night, and the next day, and the day after that, he worked with infinite patience on the girl's broken butterfly. He worked slowly, repairing strips of wood and torn gossamer gauze, glued and bound and strapped. The dazzling wings grew and strengthened until he had to move outdoors with his work. He slept alone at night with one forearm over his eyes, as if to protect himself from unknown and unseen dangers. He went out in the first grey light of dawn the third day, carrying the wonderful butterfly in his arms like a loved one. The wind was rising over the immense plains; he strapped on the exquisite butterfly and lifted gracefully, almost without effort, from the ground. No one saw him when he soared up over the frothing river, circled around a certain spot once, like the girl had done, and then steered out over the edge of the world where thundering water crashed down into the total darkness and emptiness of space. The wonderful butterfly carried him far out, shimmering like a precious jewel in the dark. As the world dropped away beneath and behind him he smiled, for the first time since the girl had flown away over the edge. Then, when the frail gossamer wings gracefully folded and broke, his lips moved soundlessly. He fell into the endless darkness, following the girl, whispering as she had done, as she perhaps still whispered somewhere in the darkness where there was no beginning and no end and no distance, where the surly man's metal barrel still tumbled clumsily down and the wide, strong wings of the black bird carried the girl down, down, down:

> Take me down the river
> To evergreen and fragrant meadows
> Where blindfolded maidens praise
> The subtle light of dawn.
> I'll dream you as the shadow
> On the softly singing grasslands
> In a never-never dreamland you can't pawn.

I'm walking down the alleys
Of my memory, don't disturb me.
I might smile at you and whisper: "Please
  be kind."
But there's really nothing to it,
I'm far away, a-strolling
In the self-contained universe
And the wastelands of my mind.

The white death

STANISLAW LEM

Aragena was a planet built up on the inside, because its ruler, Metameric – who in the equatorial plane extended three hundred and sixty degrees and thereby encircled his kingdom, being not only its lord but also its shield – wishing to protect his devoted subjects, the Enterites, against cosmic invasion, forbade the moving of anything whatever, even of the smallest pebble, upon the surface of the globe. Therefore the continents of Aragena lay wild and barren, and only the axe-blows of lightning hewed its flint mountain ridges, while meteors carved the land with craters. But ten miles beneath the surface unfolded a region of exuberant industry; the Enterites, hollowing out their mother planet, filled its interior with crystal gardens and cities of silver and gold; they raised up, inside-out, houses in the shape of dodecahedrons and icosahedrons, and also hyperboloid palaces, in whose shining cupolas you could see yourself magnified twenty thousand times, as in a hall of giants – for the Enterites were fond of splendour and geometry, and were topnotch builders besides. With a system of pipes they pumped light into the heart of the planet, filtering it now through emeralds, now diamonds, and now rubies, and thanks to this they had their choice of dawn, or noon, or rosy dusk; and so enamoured were they of their own forms, that their whole world served them as a mirror. They had vehicles of crystal, set in motion by the breath of heated gases, windowless, since entirely transparent, and while they travelled they beheld themselves reflected in the walls of palaces and temples as marvellously multiple projections, gliding, touching, iridescent. They even had their own sky, where in webs of molybdenum and vanadium flashed spinels and rock crystal, which they cultivated in fire.

The hereditary and at the same time perpetual ruler was Metameric, for he possessed a cold, beautiful and many-membered frame, and in the first of his members resided the mind; when that grew old, after thousands of years, when the crystal networks had been worn away from much administrative thinking, its authority was taken over by the next member, and thus it went, for of these he had ten billion. Metameric himself descended from the Aurigens, whom he had never seen, and all he knew of them was that when they were faced with doom at the hands of certain dreadful beings – beings that engaged in cosmonautics and for it had abandoned their native suns – the Aurigens locked all their knowledge and hunger for existence into microscopic atom seeds, and with them fertilised the rocky soil of Aragena. They gave it that name, a name like their own, but never set armoured foot upon its rocks, so as not to put their cruel pursuers on the scent; they perished, every last one, having this consolation only, that their enemies – called the pale race – did not even suspect that the Aurigens had not been totally wiped out. The Enterites, who sprang from Metameric, did not share his knowledge of their own uncommon origin: the history of the terrible demise of the Aurigens, as well as that of the rise of the Enterites, was recorded in a black vesuvian protocrystal hidden at the very core of the planet. So much the better was this history known and remembered by their ruler.

Out of the stony and magnetic ground that the resourceful builders cut away in expanding their subterranean kingdom, Metameric ordered made a row of reefs, which were cast into space. These orbited the planet in infernal circles, closing off all access to it. Cosmic mariners therefore avoided that region, known as the Black Rattler, for there enormous chunks of flying basalt and porphyry collided continually, giving rise to whole swarms of meteors, and the place was the breeding ground for all the comet heads, all the bolides and rock asteroids that today clutter the entire system of the Scorpion.

The meteors also pounded in waves of stone the ground of Aragena, bombarded it, furrowed and ploughed it; with fountains of fire-spouting impacts they turned night into day, and day – with thick clouds of dust – into night. But not the least vibration reached the realm of the Enterites.

Anyone who dared approach their planet would have seen, if first he did not dash his ship against the vortices of stone, a craggy globe, rather like a skull all crater-eaten. Even the gate that led to the underground levels was given by the Enterites the appearance of a sundered stone.

For thousands of years no one visited the planet, still Metameric did not relax his injunction of strict vigilance for an instant.

It happened however that one day a group of Enterites, who went up on the surface, came across what seemed to be a giant goblet, its stem embedded in a pile of boulders and its concave cup, which faced the sky, crushed and punctured in a dozen places. Immediately the polysage-astromariners were sent for, and they announced that what they had before them was the wreck of some foreign starcraft from unknown parts. The vessel was quite large. Only up close could one see that it had the shape of a slender cylinder, nose buried in the rock, that it was covered by a thick layer of soot and cinder; the construction of the rear, goblet-like section brought to mind the sweeping vaults of their vast subterranean palaces. Up from the depths crawled pincered machines, which with extreme care lifted the mysterious ship from where it lay and carried it back down to the interior. Afterwards a group of Enterites smoothed over the hole created by the nose of the vessel, in order that there be no trace of foreign presence on the planet's surface, and the basalt gate was closed with a hollow boom.

In the main research laboratory, sumptuous and full of lustre, rested the black hulk, looking much like some charred log, but the scientists, familiar with this sort of thing, trained upon it the polished surfaces of their most radient crystals, and with diamond bits they opened the first outer shell. Beneath it was another, of amazing whiteness, which disconcerted them somewhat, and when that shell too was pierced by carborundum drills, there appeared a third, impenetrable, and – set in it hermetically – a door, but they were unable to open it.

The eldest scientist, Afinor, carefully examined the closing mechanism on the door; it turned out that for the lock to be released, one had to activate it with a spoken word. They did not know the word, they had no way of knowing it. For a long time they tried different ones, like

"Universe", "Stars", "Eternal Flight", but the door never moved.

"Methinks we do wrong, attempting to open the vessel without the knowledge of King Metameric," said Afinor at last. "As a child I heard a legend telling of white creatures who throughout the Universe hunt down all life born of metal, and annihilate it for the sake of vengeance, which . . ."

Here he broke off and with the others stared in horror at the side of the ship, large as a wall, for at his last words the door, till now inert, suddenly stirred and rolled aside. The word that had opened it was "Vengeance".

The scientists cried for military assistance and, soon having it at hand, when the sparkthrowers were held in readiness, entered the still and stuffy darkness of the ship, lighting their way with crystals blue and white.

The machinery was to a great extent shattered. For hours they wandered among its ruins, seeking a crew, but no crew did they find, nor any sign of one. They considered whether the ship itself might not be a thinking being, for such oftentimes were very large: in size their king exceeded the unknown vessel many thousandfold, yet *he* was an entity. However the junctures of electrical thought which they uncovered were all quite small and loosely connected; the foreign ship therefore could be nothing but a flying machine, and without a crew would be as dead as stone.

In one of the corners of the deck, against the very armour-plated wall, the scientists came upon a puddle, a ruddy sort of spatter that coloured their silver fingers when they drew near; from this puddle they extricated shreds of an unknown garment, wet and red, and in addition a few slivers of something not very hard, fairly chalky. They knew not why, but a feeling of dread came over them as they stood there in the dark, in the prickling light of their crystals. But now the king had learned of this event; his messengers arrived at once, with the strictest orders to destroy the foreign vessel including everything that was upon it, and in particular the king commanded that the foreign travellers be committed to atomic fire.

The scientists replied that there was no one at all on board, only darkness and broken fragments, metal entrails and some dust speckled with tiny stains of red. The royal messenger started and immediately ordered the atomic piles to be ignited.

"In the name of the King!" he said. "The red that you have found is the harbinger of doom! It carries the white death, which knows nothing but to wreak vengeance upon those whose only crime is their existence . . ."

"If that was the white death, it can threaten us no longer, for the vessel is without life and whoever sailed it has perished in the ring of fortified reefs," they answered.

"Infinite is the power of those pallid beings, that if they die, they are reborn anew countless times, far from the mighty suns! Carry out your orders, O atomisers!"

The wise ones and the scientists were greatly troubled when they heard these words. Still, they did not believe the prophecy of doom, for its likelihood seemed to them remote. Nevertheless they lifted the entire ship from its resting place, smashed it on anvils of platinum and, when it fell apart, immersed the pieces in heavy radiation, so that it was reduced to a myriad of flying atoms, which keep eternal silence, for atoms have no history, all are equal to each other, whether they come from the strongest of stars or from dead planets, or intelligent beings, both good and evil, because matter is the same throughout the Universe and no one need have fear of it.

However they took even these atoms and froze them down into a single lump, and shot that lump out towards the stars, and only then did they say to themselves with relief: "We are saved. Nothing can happen now."

But while the platinum hammers had been striking the ship and as it crumbled, from a scrap of cloth besmeared with blood, from a torn-out seam there dropped an invisible spore, a spore so small that even a hundred like it could have been covered by a single grain of sand. And from this spore there hatched – at night, in the dust and ashes among the stones of the cavern – a white bud. From it sprang a second, a third, a hundredth, and in a gust of air they gave off oxygen and moisture, wherewith rust attacked the flagstones of the mirror cities, and imperceptible threads wound and wove about, incubating in the cool bowels of the Enterites, so that by the time they rose, they carried with them their own deaths. And a year did not pass, and they were stricken down. In the caves machines stood still, the crystal fires went out, a brownish leprosy ate at the sparkling domes, and when the last atomic heat had leaked away, darkness fell, and in that darkness there grew, penetrating the brittle skeletons, invading the rusted skulls, filling the extinguished sockets – a downy, damp, white mould.

Translated by Michael Kandel
Original title: *Biala Smierc*

Crossing into Cambodia

AN INCIDENT IN THE GREAT WORLD WAR

MICHAEL MOORCOCK

I approached and Savitsky, Commander of the Sixth Division, got up. As usual I was impressed by his gigantic, perfect body. Yet he seemed unconscious either of his power or of his elegance. Although not obliged to do so, I almost saluted him. He stretched an arm towards me. I put the papers into his gloved hand. "These were the last messages we received," I said. The loose sleeve of his Cossack cherkesska slipped back to reveal a battle-strengthened forearm, brown and glowing. I compared his skin to my own. For all that I had ridden with the Sixth for five months, I was still pale; still possessed, I thought, of an intellectual's hands. Evening light fell through the jungle foliage and a few parrots shrieked their last goodnight. Mosquitoes were gathering in the shadows, whirling in tight-woven patterns, like a frightened mob. The jungle smelled of rot. Yakovlev, somewhere, began to play a sad accordion tune.

The Vietnamese spy we had caught spoke calmly from the other side of Savitsky's camp table. "I think I should like to be away from here before nightfall. Will you keep your word, sir, if I tell you what I know!"

Savitsky looked back and I saw the prisoner for the first time (though his presence was of course well known to the camp). His wrists and ankles were pinned to the ground with bayonets but he was otherwise unhurt.

Savitsky drew in his breath and continued to study the documents I had brought him. Our radio was now useless. "He seems to be confirming what these say." He tapped the second sheet. "An attack tonight."

The temple on the other side of the clearing came to life within. Pale light rippled on greenish, half-ruined stonework. Some of our men must have lit a fire there. I heard noises of delight and some complaints from two of the women who had been with the spy. One began to shout in that peculiar, irritating high-pitched half-wail they all use when they are trying to appeal to us. For a moment Savitsky and I had a bond in our disgust. I felt flattered. Savitsky made an impatient gesture, as if of embarrassment. He turned his handsome face and looked gravely down at the peasant. "Does it matter to you? You've lost a great deal of blood."

"I do not think I am dying."

Savitsky nodded. He was economical in everything, even his cruelties. He had been prepared to tear the man apart with horses, but he knew that he would tire two already over-worked beasts. He picked up his cap from the camp table and put it thoughtfully on his head. From the deserted huts came the smell of our horses as the wind reversed its direction. I drew my borrowed burka about me. I was the only one in our unit to bother to wear it, for I felt the cold as soon as the sun was down.

"Will you show me on the map where they intend to ambush us?"

"Yes," said the peasant. "Then you can send a man to spy on their camp. He will confirm what I say."

I stood to one side while these two professionals conducted their business. Savitsky strode over to the spy and very quickly, like a man plucking a hen, drew the bayonets out and threw them on the ground. With some gentleness, he helped the peasant to his feet and sat him down in the leather campaign chair he had carried with him on our long ride from Danang, where we had disembarked off the troop-ship which had brought us from Vladivostok.

"I'll get some rags to stop him bleeding," I said.

"Good idea," confirmed Savitsky. "We don't want the stuff all over the maps. You'd better be in on this, anyway."

As the liaison officer, it was my duty to know what was happening. That is why I am able to tell this story. My whole inclination was to return to my billet where two miserable ancients cowered and sang at me whenever I entered or left but where at least I had a small barrier between me and the casual day-to-day terrors of the campaign. But, illiterate and obtuse though these horsemen were, they had accurate instincts and could tell immediately if I betrayed any sign of fear. Perhaps, I thought, it is because they are all so used to disguising their own fears. Yet bravery was a habit with them and I yearned to catch it. I had ridden with them in more than a dozen encounters, helping to drive the Cambodians back into their own country. Each time I had seen men and horses blown to pieces, torn apart, burned alive. I had come to exist on the smell of blood and gunpowder as if it were a substitute for air and food – I identified it with the smell of Life itself – yet I had still failed to achieve that strangely passive sense of inner calm my comrades all, to a greater or lesser degree, displayed. Only in action did they seem possessed in any way by the outer world, although they still worked with efficient ferocity, killing as quickly as possible with lance, sabre or carbine and, with ghastly humanity, never leaving a wounded man of their own or the enemy's without his throat cut or a bullet in his brain. I was thankful that these, my traditional foes, were now allies for I could not have resisted them had they turned against me.

I bound the peasant's slender wrists and ankles. He was like a child. He said: "I knew there were no arteries cut." I nodded at him. "You're the political officer, aren't you?" He spoke almost sympathetically.

"Liaison," I said.

He was satisfied by my reply, as if I had confirmed his opinion. He added: "I suppose it's the leather coat. Almost a uniform."

I smiled. "A sign of class difference, you think?"

His eyes were suddenly drowned with pain and he staggered, but recovered to finish what he had evidently planned to say: "You Russians are natural bourgeoisie. It's not your fault. It's your turn."

Savitsky was too tired to respond with anything more than a small smile. I felt that he agreed with the peasant and that these two excluded me, felt superior to me. I knew anger, then. Tightening the last rag on his left wrist, I made the spy wince. Satisfied that my honour was avenged I cast an eye over the map. "Here we are," I said. We were on the very edge of Cambodia. A small river, easily forded, formed the border here. We had heard it just before we had entered this village. Scouts confirmed that it lay no more than half a verst to the west. The stream on the far side of the village, behind the temple, was a tributary.

"You give your word you won't kill me," said the Vietnamese.

"Yes," said Savitsky. He was beyond joking. We all were. It had been ages since any of us had been anything but direct with one another, save for the conventional jests which were merely part of the general noise of the squadron, like the jangling of harness. And he was beyond lying, except where it was absolutely necessary. His threats were as unqualified as his promises.

"They are here." The spy indicated a town. He began to shiver. He was wearing only torn shorts. "And some of them are here, because they think you might use the bridge rather than the ford."

"And the attacking force for tonight?"

"Based here." A point on our side of the river.

Savitsky shouted. "Pavlichenko."

From the Division Commander's own tent, young Pavlichenko, capless, with ruffled fair hair and a look of restrained disappointment, emerged. "Comrade?"

"Get a horse and ride with this man for half-an-hour the way we came today. Ride as fast as you can, then leave him and return to camp."

Pavlichenko ran towards the huts where the horses were stabled. Savitsky had believed the spy and was not bothering to check his information. "We can't attack them," he murmured. "We'll have to wait until they come to us. It's better." The flap of Savitsky's tent was now open. I glanced through and to my surprise saw a Eurasian girl of about fourteen. She had her feet in a bucket of water. She smiled at me. I looked away.

Savitsky said: "He's washing her for me. Pavlichenko's an expert."

"My wife and daughters?" said the spy.

"They'll have to remain now. What can I do?" Savitsky shrugged in the direction of the temple. "You should have spoken earlier."

The Vietnamese accepted this and, when Pavlichenko returned with the horse, leading it and running as if he wished to get the job over with in the fastest possible time, he allowed the young Cossack to lift him onto the saddle.

"Take your rifle," Savitsky told Pavlichenko. "We're expecting an attack."

Pavlichenko dashed for his own tent, the small one close to Savitsky's. The horse, as thoroughly trained as the men who rode him, stood awkwardly but quietly beneath his nervous load. The spy clutched the saddle pommel, the mane, his bare feet angled towards the mount's neck. He stared ahead of him into the night. His wife and daughter had stopped their appalling wailing but I thought I could hear the occasional feminine grunt from the temple. The flames had become more animated. His other daughter, her feet still in the bucket, held her arms tightly under her chest and her curious eyes looked without rancour at her father, then at the Division Commander, then, finally, at me. Savitsky spoke. "You're the intellectual. She doesn't know Russian. Tell her that her father will be safe. She can join him tomorrow."

"My Vietnamese might not be up to that."

"Use English or French, then." He began to tidy his maps, calling over Kreshenko, who was in charge of the guard.

I entered the tent and was shocked by her little smile. She had a peculiar smell to her – like old tea and cooked rice. I knew my Vietnamese was too limited so I asked her if she spoke French. She was of the wrong generation. "Amerikanski," she told me. I relayed Savitsky's message. She said: "So I am the price of the old bastard's freedom."

"Not at all." I reassured her. "He told us what we wanted. It was just bad luck for you that he used you three for cover."

She laughed. "Nuts! It was me got him to do it. With my sister. Tao's boyfriend works for the Cambodians." She added: "They seemed to be winning at the time."

Savitsky entered the tent and zipped it up from the bottom. He used a single, graceful movement. For all that he was bone-weary, he moved with the unconscious fluidity of an acrobat. He lit one of his foul-smelling papyrossi and sat heavily on the camp bed beside the girl.

"She speaks English," I said. "She's a half-caste. Look."

He loosened his collar. "Could you ask her if she's clean, comrade?"

"I doubt it," I said. I repeated what she had told me.

He nodded. "Well, ask her if she'll be a good girl and use

her mouth. I just want to get on with it. I expect she does, too."

I relayed the D.C.'s message.

"I'll bite his cock off if I get the chance," said the girl.

Outside in the night the horse began to move away. I explained what she had said.

"I wonder, comrade," Savitsky said, "if you would oblige me by holding the lady's head." He began to undo the belt of his trousers, pulling up his elaborately embroidered shirt.

The girl's feet became noisy in the water and the bucket overturned. In my leather jacket, my burka, with my automatic pistol at her right ear, I restrained the girl until Savitsky had finished with her. He began to take off his boots. "Would you care for her, yourself?"

I shook my head and escorted the girl from the tent. She was walking in that familiar stiff way women have after they have been raped. I asked her if she was hungry. She agreed that she was. I took her to my billet. The old couple found some more rice and I watched her eat it.

Later that night she moved towards me from where she had been lying more or less at my feet. I thought I was being attacked and shot her in the stomach. Knowing what my comrades would think of me if I tried to keep her alive (it would be a matter of hours) I shot her in the head to put her out of her misery. As luck would have it, these shots woke the camp and when the Khmer soldiers attacked a few moments later we were ready for them and killed a great many before the rest ran back into the jungle. Most of these soldiers were younger than the girl.

In the morning, to save any embarrassment, the remaining women were chased out of the camp in the direction taken by the patriarch. The old couple had disappeared and I assumed that they would not return or, if they did, that they would bury the girl, so I left her where I had shot her. A silver ring she wore would compensate them for their trouble. There was very little food remaining in the village, but what there was we ate for our breakfast or packed into our saddle-bags. Then, mounting up, we followed the almost preternaturally handsome Savitsky back into the jungle, heading for the river.

II

When our scout did not return after we had heard a long burst of machine-gun fire, we guessed that he had found at least part of the enemy ambush and that the spy had not lied to us, so we decided to cross the river at a less convenient spot where, with luck, no enemy would be waiting.

The river was swift but had none of the force of Russian rivers, and Pavlichenko was sent across with a rope which he tied to a tree-trunk. Then we entered the water and began to swim our horses across. Those who had lost the canvas covers for their carbines held them high in the air, holding the rope with one hand and guiding their horses with legs and with reins which they gripped in their teeth. I was more or less in the middle, with half the division behind me and half beginning to assemble on dry land on the other side, when Cambodian aircraft sighted us and began an attack dive. The aircraft were in poor repair, borrowed from half-a-dozen other countries, and their guns, aiming equipment and, I suspect, their pilots, were in worse condition, but they killed seven of our men as we let go of the ropes, slipped out of our saddles, and began to swim beside our horses, making for the far bank, while those still on dry land behind us went to cover where they could. A couple of machine-gun carts were turned on the attacking planes, but these were of little use. The peculiar assortment of weapons used against us – tracers, two rockets, a few napalm canisters which struck the water and sank (only one opened and burned but the mixture was quickly carried off by the current) and then they were flying back to base somewhere in Cambodia's interior – indicated that they had very little conventional armament left. This was true of most of the participants at this stage, which is why our cavalry had proved so effective. But they had bought some time for their ground-troops who were now coming in.

In virtual silence, any shouts drowned by the rushing of the river, we crossed to the enemy bank and set up a defensive position, using the machine-gun carts which were last to come across on ropes. The Cambodians hit us from two sides – moving in from their original ambush positions – but we were able to return their fire effectively, even using the anti-tank weapons and the mortar which, hitherto, we had tended to consider useless weight. They used arrows, blow-darts, automatic rifles, pistols and a flamethrower which only worked for a few seconds and did us no harm. The Cossacks were not happy with this sort of warfare and as soon as there was a lull we had mounted up, packed the gear in the carts, and with sabres drawn were howling into the Khmer Stalinists (as we had been instructed to term them). Leaving them scattered and useless, we found a bit of concrete road along which we could gallop for a while. We slowed to a trot and then to a walk, as the pavement was pot-holed and only slightly less dangerous than the jungle floor. The jungle was behind us now and seemed to have been a screen hiding the devastation ahead. The landscape was virtually flat, as if it had been bombed clean of contours, with a few broken buildings, the occasional blackened tree, and ash drifted across the road, coming sometimes up to our horses' knees. The ash was stirred by a light wind. We had witnessed scenes like it before, but never on such a scale. The almost colourless nature of the landscape was emphasised by the unrelieved brilliance of the blue sky overhead. The sun had become very hot.

Once we saw two tanks on the horizon, but they did not challenge us. We continued until early afternoon when we came to the remains of some sort of modern power installation and we made camp in the shelter of its walls. The ash got into our food and we drank more of our water than was sensible. We were all covered in the grey stuff by this time.

"We're like corpses," said Savitsky. He resembled an heroic statue of the sort which used to be found in almost every public square in the Soviet Union. "Where are we going to find anything to eat in this?"

"It's like the end of the world," I said.

"Have you tried the radio again?"

I shook my head. "It isn't worth it. Napalm eats through wiring faster than it eats through you."

He accepted this and with a naked finger began to clean off the inner rims of the goggles he (like most of us) wore as protection against sun, rain and dust. "I could do with some orders," he said.

"We were instructed to move into the enemy's territory. That's what we're doing."

"Where, we were told, we would link up with American and Australian mounted units. Those fools can't ride. I don't know why they ever thought of putting them on horses. Cowboys!"

I saw no point in repeating an already stale argument. It was true, however, that the Western cavalry divisions found it hard to match our efficient savagery. I had been amused, too, when they had married us briefly with a couple of Mongolian squadrons. The Mongols had not ridden to war in decades and had become something of a laughing-stock with their ancient enemies, the Cossacks. Savitsky believed that we were the last great horsemen. Actually, he did not include me, for I was a very poor rider and not a Cossack, anyway. He thought it was our destiny to survive the War and begin a new and braver civilisation: "Free from the influence of women and Jews". He recalled the great days of the Zaporozhian Sech, from which women had been forbidden. Even amongst the Sixth he was regarded as something of a conservative. He continued to be admired more than his opinions.

When the men had watered our horses and replaced the water bags in the carts, Savitsky and I spread the map on a piece of concrete and found our position with the help of the compass and sextant (there were no signs or landmarks). "I wonder what has happened to Angkor," I said. It was where we were supposed to meet other units, including the Canadians to whom, in the months to come, I was to be attached (I was to discover later that they had been in our rear all along).

"You think it's like this?" Savitsky gestured. His noble eyes began to frown. "I mean, comrade, would you say it was worth our while making for Angkor now?"

"We have our orders," I said. "We've no choice. We're expected."

Savitsky blew dust from his mouth and scratched his head. "There's about half our division left. We could do with reinforcements. Mind you, I'm glad we can see a bit of sky at last." We had all felt claustrophobic in the jungle.

"What is it, anyway, this Angkor? Their capital?" he asked me.

"Their Stalingrad, maybe."

Savitsky understood. "Oh, it has an importance to their morale. It's not strategic?"

"I haven't been told about its strategic value."

Savitsky, as usual, withdrew into his diplomatic silence,

indicating that he did not believe me and thought that I had been instructed to secrecy. "We'd best push on," he said. "We've a long way to go, eh?"

After we had mounted up, Savitsky and I rode side by side for a while, along the remains of the concrete road. We were some way ahead of the long column, with its riders, its baggage-waggons, and its Makhno-style machine-gun carts. We were sitting targets for any planes and, because there was no cover, Savitsky and his men casually ignored the danger. I had learned not to show my nervousness but I was not at that moment sure how well hidden it was.

"We are the only vital force in Cambodia," said the Division Commander with a beatific smile. "Everything else is dead. How these yellow bastards must hate one another." He was impressed, perhaps admiring.

"Who's to say?" I ventured. "We don't know who else has been fighting. There isn't a nation now that's not in the War."

"And not one that's not on its last legs. Even Switzerland." Savitsky gave a superior snort. "But what an inheritance for us!"

I became convinced that, quietly, he was going insane.

III

We came across an armoured car in a hollow, just off the road. One of our scouts had heard the crew's moans. As Savitsky and I rode up, the scout was covering the uniformed Khmers with his carbine, but they were too far gone to offer us any harm.

"What's wrong with 'em," Savitsky asked the scout.

The scout did not know. "Disease," he said. "Or starvation. They're not wounded."

We got off our horses and slid down into the crater. The car was undamaged. It appeared to have rolled gently into the dust and become stuck. I slipped into the driving seat and tried to start the engine, but it was dead. Savitsky had kicked one of the wriggling Khmers in the genitals but the man did not seem to notice the pain much, though he clutched himself, almost as if he entered into the spirit of a ritual. Savitsky was saying "Soldiers. Soldiers" over and over again. It was one of the few Vietnamese words he knew. He pointed in different directions, looking with disgust on the worn-out men. "You'd better question them," he said to me.

They understood my English, but refused to speak it. I tried them in French. "What happened to your machine?"

The man Savitsky had kicked continued to lie on his face, his arms stretched along the ashy ground towards us. I felt he wanted to touch us: to steal our vitality. I felt sick as I put the heel of my boot on his hand. One of his comrades said: "There's no secret to it. We ran out of essence." He pointed to the armoured car. "We ran out of essence."

"You're a long way from your base."

"Our base is gone. There's no essence anywhere."

I believed him and told Savitsky who was only too ready to accept this simple explanation.

As usual, I was expected to dispatch the prisoners. I reached for my holster, but Savitsky, with rare sympathy, stopped my movement. "Go and see what's in that can," he said, pointing. As I waded towards the punctured metal, three shots came from the Division Commander's revolver. I wondered at his mercy. Continuing with this small farce, I looked at the can, held it up, shook it, and threw it back into the dust. "Empty," I said.

Savitsky was climbing the crater towards his horse. As I scrambled behind him he said: "It's the Devil's world. Do you think we should give ourselves up to Him?"

I was astonished by this unusual cynicism.

He got into his saddle. Unconsciously, he assumed the pose, often seen in films and pictures, of the noble revolutionary horseman – his head lifted, his palm shielding his eyes as he peered towards the West.

"We seem to have wound up killing Tatars again," he said with a smile as I got clumsily onto my horse. "Do you believe in all this History, comrade?"

"I've always considered the theory of precedent absolutely infantile," I said.

"What's that?"

I began to explain, but he was already spurring forward, shouting to his men.

IV

On the third day we had passed through the ash-desert and our horses could at last crop at some grass on the crest of a line of low hills which looked down on glinting, misty paddy-fields. Savitsky, his field-glasses to his eyes, was relieved. "A village," he said. "Thank god. We'll be able to get some provisions."

"And some exercise," said Pavlichenko behind him. The boy laughed, pushing his cap back on his head and wiping grimy sweat from his brow. "Shall I go down there, comrade?"

Savitsky agreed, telling Pavlichenko to take two others with him. We watched the Cossacks ride down the hill and begin cautiously to wade their horses through the young rice. The sky possessed a greenish tinge here, as if it reflected the fields. It looked like the Black Sea lagoons at midsummer. A smell of foliage, almost shocking in its unfamiliarity, floated up to us. Savitsky was intent on watching the movements of his men, who had unslung their carbines and dismounted as they reached the village. With reins looped on their arms they moved slowly in, firing a few experimental rounds at the huts. One of them took a dummy grenade from his saddle-bag and threw it into a nearby doorway. Peasants, already starving to the point of death it seemed, ran out. The young Cossacks ignored them, looking for soldiers. When they were satisfied that the village was clear of traps, they waved us in. The peasants began to gather together at the centre of the village. Evidently they were used to this sort of operation.

While our men made their thorough search I was again called upon to perform my duty and question the inhabitants. These, it emerged, were almost all intellectuals, part of one of the Khmer Rouge re-education programmes (virtually a sentence of death by forced labour). It was easier to speak to them but harder to understand their complicated answers. In the end I gave up and, made impatient by the whining appeals of the wretches, ignored them. They knew nothing of use to us. Our men were disappointed in their expectations. There were only old people in the village. In the end they took the least aged of the women off and had them in what had once been some sort of administration hut. I wondered at their energy. It occurred to me that this was something they expected of one another and that they would lose face if they did not perform the necessary actions. Eventually, when we had eaten what we could find, I returned to questioning two of the old men. They were at least antagonistic to the Cambodian troops and were glad to tell us anything they could. However, it seemed there had been no large movements in the area. The occasional plane or helicopter had gone over a few days earlier. These were probably part of the flight which had attacked us at the river. I asked if they had any news of Angkor, but there was no radio here and they expected us to know more than they did. I pointed towards the purple hills on the other side of the valley. "What's over there?"

They told me that as far as they knew it was another valley, similar to this but larger. The hills looked steeper and were wooded. It would be a difficult climb for us unless there was a road. I got out the map. There was a road indicated. I pointed to it. One of the old men nodded. Yes, he thought that road was still there, for it led, eventually, to this village. He showed me where the path was. It was rutted where, some time earlier, heavy vehicles had been driven along it. It disappeared into dark green, twittering jungle. All the jungle meant to me now was mosquitoes and a certain amount of cover from attacking planes.

Careless of leeches and insects, the best part of the division was taking the chance of a bath in the stream which fed the paddy-fields. I could not bring myself to strip in the company of these healthy men. I decided to remain dirty until I had the chance of some sort of privacy.

"I want the men to rest," said Savitsky, "Have you any objection to our camping here for the rest of today and tonight?"

"It's a good idea," I said. I sought out a hut, evicted the occupants, and went almost immediately to sleep.

In the morning I was awakened by a trooper who brought me a metal mug full of the most delicately scented tea. I was astonished and accepted it with some amusement. "There's loads of it here," he said. "It's all they've got!"

I sipped the tea. I was still in my uniform, with the burka on the ground beneath me and my leather jacket folded for a pillow. The hut was completely bare. I was used to seeing a few personal possessions and began to wonder if they had hidden their stuff when they had seen us coming. Then I remembered that they were from the towns and had been brought here forcibly. Perhaps now, I thought, the war would pass them by and they would know peace, even happiness, for a bit. I was scratching my ear and stretching when Savitsky came in, looking grim. "We've found a damned burial ground," he said. "Hundreds of bodies in a pit. I think they must be the original inhabitants. And one or two soldiers – at least, they were in uniform."

"You want me to ask what they are?"

"No! I just want to get away. God knows what they've been doing to one another. They're a filthy race. All grovelling and secret killing. They've no guts."

"No soldiers, either," I said. "Not really. They've been preyed on by bandits for centuries. Bandits are pretty nearly the only sort of soldiers they've ever known. So the ones who want to be soldiers emulate them. Those who don't want to be soldiers treat the ones who do as they've always treated bandits. They are conciliatory until they get a chance to turn the tables."

He was impressed by this. He rubbed at a freshly-shaven chin. He looked years younger, though he still had the monumental appearance of a god. "Thieves, you mean. They have the mentality of thieves, their soldiers?"

"Aren't the Cossacks thieves?"

"That's foraging." He was not angry. Very little I said could ever anger him because he had no respect for my opinions. I was the necessary political officer, his only link with the higher, distant authority of the Kremlin, but he did not have to respect my ideas any more than he respected those which came to him from Moscow. What he respected there was the power and the fact that in some way Russia was mystically represented in our leaders. "We leave in ten minutes," he said.

I noticed that Pavlichenko had polished his boots for him.

By that afternoon, after we had crossed the entire valley on an excellent dirt road through the jungle and had reached the top of the next range of hills, I had a pain in my stomach. Savitsky noticed me holding my hands against my groin and said laconically, "I wish the doctor hadn't been killed. Do you think it's typhus?" Naturally, it was what I had suspected.

"I think it's just the tea and the rice and the other stuff.

Maybe mixing with all the dust we've swallowed." He looked paler than usual. "I've got it, too. So have half the others. Oh, shit!"

It was hard to tell, in that jungle at that time of day, if you had a fever. I decided to put the problem out of my mind as much as possible until sunset when it would become cooler.

The road began to show signs of damage and by the time we were over the hill and looking down on the other side we were confronting scenery if anything more desolate than that which we had passed through on the previous three days. It was a grey desert, scarred by the broken road and bomb-craters. Beyond this and coming towards us was a wall of dark dust; unmistakably an army on the move. Savitsky automatically relaxed in his saddle and turned back to see our men moving slowly up the wooded hill. "I think they must be heading this way." Savitsky cocked his head to one side. "What's that?"

It was a distant shriek. Then a whole squadron of planes was coming in low. We could see their crudely-painted Khmer Rouge markings, their battered fuselages. There were half-a-dozen different types of jet in the squadron. The men began to scatter off the road, but the planes ignored us. They zoomed by, seeming to be fleeing rather than attacking. I looked at the sky, but nothing followed them.

We took our field-glasses from their cases and adjusted them. In the dust I saw a mass of barefoot infantry bearing rifles with fixed bayonets. There were also trucks, a few tanks, some private cars, bicycles, motor-bikes, ox-carts, hand-carts, civilians with bundles. It was an army of defeated soldiers and refugees.

"I think we've missed the action." Savitsky was furious. "We were beaten to it, eh? And by Australians, probably!"

My impulse to shrug was checked. "Damn!" I said, a little weakly.

This caused Savitsky to laugh at me. "You're relieved. Admit it!"

I knew that I dare not share his laughter, lest it become hysterical and turn to tears, so I missed a moment of possible comradeship. "What shall we do?" I asked. "Go round them?"

"It would be easy enough to go through them. Finish them off. It would stop them destroying this valley, at least.'

He did not, by his tone, much care.

The men were assembling behind us. Savitsky informed them of the nature of the rabble ahead of us. He put his field-glasses to his eyes again and said to me: "Infantry, too. Quite a lot. Coming on faster."

I looked. The barefoot soldiers were apparently pushing their way through the refugees to get ahead of them.

"Maybe the planes radioed back," said Savitsky. "Well, it's something to fight."

"I think we should go round," I said. "We should save our strength. We don't know what's waiting for us at Angkor."

"It's miles away yet."

"Our instructions were to avoid any conflict we could," I reminded him.

He sighed. "This is Satan's own country." He was about to give the order which would comply with my suggestion when, from the direction of Angkor Wat, the sky burst into white fire. The horses reared and whinnied. Some of our men yelled and flung their arms over their eyes. We were all temporarily blinded. Then the dust below seemed to grow denser and denser. We watched in fascination as the dark wall became taller, rushing upon us and howling like a million dying voices. We were struck by the ash and forced onto our knees, then onto our bellies, yanking our frightened horses down with us as best we could. The stuff stung my face and hands and even those parts of my body protected by heavy clothing. Larger pieces of stone rattled against my goggles.

When the wind had passed and we began to stand erect, the sky was still very bright. I was astonished that my field-glasses were intact. I put them up to my burning eyes and peered through swirling ash at the Cambodians. The army was running along the road towards us, as terrified animals flee a forest fire. I knew now what the planes had been escaping. Our Cossacks were in some confusion, but were already regrouping, shouting amongst themselves. A number of our horses were still shying and whickering but by and large we were all calm again.

"Well, comrade," said Savitsky with a sort of mad satisfaction, "what do we do now? Wasn't that Angkor Wat, where we're supposed to meet our allies?"

I was silent. The mushroom cloud on the horizon was growing. It had the hazy outlines of a gigantic, spreading cedar tree, as if all at once that wasteland of ash had become promiscuously fertile. An aura of bloody red seemed to surround it, like a silhouette in the sunset.

The strong, artificial wind was still blowing in our direction. I wiped dust from my goggles and lowered them back over my eyes. Savitsky gave the order for our men to mount. "Those bastards down there are in our way," he said. "We're going to charge them."

"What?" I could not believe him.

"When in doubt," he told me, "attack."

"You're not scared of the enemy," I said, "but there's the radiation."

"I don't know anything about radiation." He turned in his saddle to watch his men. When they were ready he drew his sabre. They imitated him. I had no sabre to draw.

I was horrified. I pulled my horse away from the road. "Division Commander Savitsky, we're duty-bound to conserve . . ."

"We're duty-bound to make for Angkor," he said. "And that's what we're doing." His perfect body poised itself in the saddle. He raised his sabre.

"It's not like ordinary dying," I began. But he gave the order and began to trot forward. The men followed. There was a rictus of terrifying glee on each mouth. The light from the sky was reflected in every eye.

I moved with them. I had become used to the security of numbers and I could not face their disapproval. But gradually they went ahead of me until I was in the rear. By this time we were almost at the bottom of the hill and trotting towards the mushroom cloud which was now shot through with all kinds of dark, swirling colours. It had become like a threatening hand, while the wind-borne ash stung our bodies and drew blood on the flanks of our mounts.

Yakovlev, just ahead of me, unstrapped his accordion and began to play some familiar Cossack battle-song. Soon they were all singing. Their pace gradually increased. The noise of the accordion died but their song was so loud now that it seemed to fill the whole world. They reached full gallop, charging upon that appalling outline, the quintessential symbol of our doom, as their ancestors might have charged the very gates of Hell. They were swift, dark shapes in the dust. The song became a savage, defiant roar.

My first impulse was to charge with them. But then I had turned my horse and was trotting back towards the valley and the border, praying that, if I ever got to safety, I would not be too badly contaminated.

In homage to Isaac Babel, 1894-1941?